Small-town PI and part-time assassin Bonnie Parker may have thought the hit on Alec Dante was pretty routine—but Alec's uncle, mob underboss Frank Lazzaro, has other ideas. He's sworn to avenge Alec's death, and he's willing to wade through an ocean of blood to do it.

But Bonnie's troubles don't end there. A street gang is gunning for her. A local police chief thinks he has the evidence to put her away. And a hurricane named Sandy is about to make landfall ...

It all adds up to a superstorm of murder, conspiracy, and betrayal. In a desperate fight, Bonnie will need all her skills to save herself as the storm waters rise.

BLOOD
IN THE
WATER

ALSO BY MICHAEL PRESCOTT

Manstopper

Kane

Shiver

Shudder

Shatter

Deadly Pursuit

Blind Pursuit

Mortal Pursuit

Comes the Dark

Stealing Faces

The Shadow Hunter

Last Breath

Next Victim

In Dark Places

Dangerous Games

Mortal Faults

Final Sins

Riptide

Grave of Angels

Cold Around the Heart

Steel Trap and Other Stories

Chasing Omega

BLOOD
IN THE
WATER

MICHAEL PRESCOTT

The road was so dimly lighted.
There were no highway signs to guide.
    But she made up her mind
    If all roads were blind
She wouldn't give up 'til she died.

—Bonnie Parker, "The Trail's End" (1933)

1

BONNIE PARKER DROVE through torrents of slashing rain, into the teeth of a hurricane, in pursuit of a dead man.

Well, okay, he wasn't dead yet. But that was a technicality. He'd been as good as dead for the past two weeks, and today, with any luck, she would make it official.

A line of traffic blurred past her as she gunned the Jeep across Cohawkin Bridge onto the beckoning finger of land called Devil's Hook. Everybody with any sense was leaving the island. Naturally, she was headed in the opposite direction. In her line of work, a little thing like the storm of the century wasn't a deterrent. How did the postal thing go? Neither snow nor rain nor heat nor gloom of night ...

She was kind of like a postman, in a way. You know, if your average mail carrier toted an unregistered Smith .38 with the serial number filed off, and killed people for money.

The bridge dumped her onto a two-lane stretch of Route 35, known in this vicinity as Lamplight Road. She went south. Traffic wasn't an issue; all the other vehicles were in the northbound lane, clearing out. A lot of them were cop cars. The island was thick with local law enforcement, assisting in the evacuation. Happily, the authorities here, unlike the ones in Brighton Cove, didn't know her.

Under other circumstances she liked coming to Devil's Hook Island. This place had more of a shore-like feel than her part of Millstone County. Boats, marinas, marine supplies and repairs, bait-and-tackle shops. Sand and gravel instead of lawns. Water was everywhere, hemming her in on both sides; the island was only a half mile wide at its widest point, narrowing at times to a few hundred yards.

Today there was more water than usual. Parts of the road were already flooded. She navigated around ditches swollen with rainwater, past scattered traffic cones and the occasional tree branch. To her left, beyond the eroding beach, the gray Atlantic seethed. To her right, visible through breaks in the rows of buildings, the waters of Shipbreak Bay roiled and chopped.

She liked the names around here. Shipbreak Bay—from the Dutch word for shipwreck, because the bay's sandy shoals had run many vessels aground. Devil's Hook—meaning devil's corner, because the island's southern end took a wicked jag that had foundered still more ships.

There had always been a lot of death in Jersey. The hurricane would only add to the toll.

And soon, with any luck, so would she.

Not that she was looking forward to it or anything. She wasn't some kind of sicko. She was just as sane as any other gal who worked as a PI and moonlighted as an assassin. Which, come to think of it, wasn't saying a whole hell of a lot.

A trashcan spun at her, turning cartwheels in the wind. She tapped the brakes and let it tumble past.

Halfway to the end of the island now. Another ten minutes.

Truth was, she must be at least a little bit crazy to go

out in this mess. Not that she'd wanted to. But duty called. In this case, literally. Thirty minutes ago her cell phone had played a special ringtone, Clint Eastwood's theme from *The Good, the Bad, and the Ugly.* She'd downloaded it herself. Hitman humor. The flurry of high, whistling notes told her that the motion sensor she'd placed in Alec Dante's cottage had been activated.

She'd been waiting two weeks for Dante to visit the cottage. Of course, it was possible that a gust of wind had blown apart a window and sent debris flying across the sensor's field. Or maybe the police had entered the house to be sure nobody was defying the evacuation order.

Only one way to know: make tracks to the southern tip of Devil's Hook Island and hope Dante was there. And if he was ...

Well, a girl had to earn a living in all kinds of weather.

It wasn't even her first job of the day. She'd gotten started early. At 8:00 AM she'd been hiding inside a store in Algonquin that sold teddy bears. Just teddy bears. Go figure.

Her presence in the store was strictly illegal; the place didn't open for business till ten, and today, given the weather, it might not open at all. She'd gained admittance through a back door and stationed herself in a rear store room, at a window overlooking an alley. Across the way was the employee entrance of Brown's Fish Market.

She smoked three Parliament Whites before the assistant manager arrived to open up the fish store. She watched, taking an occasional photo, as he carried a large cooler into the shop and emerged a couple of minutes later, the cooler visibly heavier in his arms. He deposited it in the rear of his SUV and disappeared inside with a second cooler, thoughtfully leaving the SUV's rear door open. Bonnie approached it at a brisk walk and flipped up the lid of the cooler. To her not very great surprise she found a large glassy-eyed tuna staring up at her in a nest

3

of dry ice.

"Well, it beats stealing cable," she said to herself, taking another drag on her cig.

She'd snapped a couple more photos, and then her cell phone had played the spaghetti Western theme, and suddenly she'd had other things on her mind. Before leaving, she'd taken the precaution of closing the cooler so the guy wouldn't know he'd been made. She hadn't wanted him disposing of the evidence in a panic. Not that it really mattered, since she had the pix, but it would have been a waste of some perfectly good fish.

She plowed through a flooded intersection, water fanning past her on both sides like the parting of the Red Sea. The Jeep's dashboard radio, which had been busted for most of the past six years and only recently repaired, was tuned to a news station. According to the newscasters, Hurricane Sandy wouldn't make landfall for hours, but already the tidal surge had drowned Atlantic City in waist-high floodwaters, and rising winds were taking out trees and power lines.

Bonnie drove on, half hypnotized by the drone of the radio, the steady thwack of her windshield wipers, the drumbeat of rain on the Jeep's canvas roof. She was moving fast—too fast for a road that was nearly washed out, studded with new potholes, strewn with windblown debris. But if Dante was at the cottage, she had no idea how long he might stay.

Two weeks ago she had determined that the cottage presented her best opportunity. It was lonely and isolated, a beachfront retreat walled in by scrub pine and seagrass-tufted dunes. There were no close neighbors, which meant no witnesses. In the off-season—and October was definitely the off-season for the Jersey shore—the island's population was only a fraction of what it would be in summertime.

Days of surveillance had established that Dante was

4

alone in life. No significant others, no one likely to accompany him to his island hideaway. If he went there, he would go alone.

In his day-to-day activities he was tougher to get at. Not exactly a hardened target, but a tricky one. He lived in a Jersey City high-rise with doormen stationed 24/7 at the lobby door. He ate at crowded restaurants, though always by himself. He took public transportation in the city. She could have executed the hit, but she wasn't sure she could do it without being eyeballed.

But the cottage—identified as his via an online search for properties in his name—would be ideal. She'd visited the place and easily defeated the do-it-yourself alarm system. In the foyer she'd attached a thumbnail-size motion sensor to the baseboard molding; it was hardwired into the main current and equipped with a backup battery. In a hollow behind the baseboard she'd wired up a throwaway cell phone which would dial her number and activate her special ring tone if the sensor went off.

During the two weeks since she'd installed the device, the sensor hadn't noticed a damn thing. She was beginning to think it had malfunctioned, or maybe Dante never used his cottage out of season. It might be necessary to do the job in Jersey City, after all. She'd been mulling possible scenarios for an urban hit—until her phone alert offered her a better option.

"Just be there, you asshole," she told Dante as she steered the Jeep past a twenty-foot awning that lay flapping in the street. "I really don't wanna make this trip for nothing."

The newscasters were still yakking. As of now, Sandy was expected to make landfall by 8:00 PM at close to hurricane strength. It looked like Devil's Hook—and Brighton Cove to the north—would be right in the crosshairs.

And speaking of crosshairs ...

Up ahead, the turnoff for the street to Dante's cottage came into view. Gravesend Road, it was called. Poetic irony, or poetic justice, or something poetic anyway.

She tooled down the rutted lane, the Jeep's shocks complaining with every bounce. The beach that fronted the house was shedding sand at a furious rate. A shower of grit set her windshield shivering.

As she steered past the cottage, she glanced down the driveway and saw a Porsche Boxster sitting there. Dante's ride. Good news—for her, at least.

For him, not so much.

Parking at the house was out of the question. She drove fifty yards down the road and hid the Jeep in a stand of pines. The muddy forest floor made for poor traction, and the tires shimmied alarmingly, but she managed to avoid crashing into any trees. She jerked the Jeep into park and killed the engine.

Before taking off on foot, she checked her purse. Her .38, the compact Bodyguard model, was still safely tucked away in its special compartment, loaded with five rounds that she'd handled with gloves so as to leave no prints on the shell casings. Unlike a semiautomatic, a revolver couldn't be fitted with a silencer, but that didn't matter. The whole point of doing the job out here in the boonies was that no one would be within earshot.

The rest of her junk was in there too—flashlight, cell phone, lockpicks, glass cutter, and, for some reason, a Swiss Army knife. Dan Maguire, police chief of Brighton Cove, would be very happy to get his mitts on her right now. The unlicensed gun was good enough for a conviction, and the burglary tools only sweetened the pot.

Well, Brighton Cove was miles away, and so was Danny boy. At this moment she needed to forget about him and get her head in the game. Alec Dante might not be the toughest guy she'd gone up against, but he was violent and amoral and possibly crazy, and she needed to take him seriously.

Leaving the Jeep, she plunged into the storm. Steely pellets of rain jabbed at her like needles. She jammed her hands into the pockets of her nylon windbreaker and sprinted through the forest to the beach, keeping her head down, eyes half shut against the blinding wetness.

Killing Alec Dante was the kind of thing that might have given some people pause—if not from pangs of conscience, then at least from fear. She was pretty much past fear these days, and as for conscience ... she wasn't sure she'd ever had one, or much of one, anyway. She'd been fourteen years old when she'd learned about killing, first as a witness, then as a practitioner of the art. Her philosophy was simple. Pencils needed erasers, and some people just needed to be rubbed out.

And what gave her the right to do the erasing? Well, shucks. Somebody had to do it. Anyway, she'd been playing the game by her own rules her whole life, and she hadn't lost yet. As career choices went, it might not be ideal, but it beat sacking groceries at Stop & Shop.

She was twenty-eight years old, and what with smoking Parliaments, chugging Jack 'n' Coke, shooting people, and her general lifestyle, she reckoned she faced long odds in making it to thirty. Even so, she was having a hell of a ride. And if her sideline made her feel dirty and low at times—more and more often, it seemed, in the past year or so—well, that was the price she paid for doing her job. She couldn't expect to do this kind of thing on a regular basis and not have it affect her.

Exactly how it might be affecting her was something she preferred not to think about. Not now. Not ever. Introspection wasn't her thing. Besides, there was plenty of Jack Daniel's in the world—enough to drown any doubts. Wasn't there?

At the edge of the woods she crouched in a thicket of bayberry and beach plum, glassing the cottage with binoculars from the Jeep's glove compartment. She panned the windows, saw no movement. Dante had to be inside, because no one but an idiot—you know, someone like her—would be outdoors on a day like this. But he was nowhere in sight.

She stood and approached the cottage at a walk, making no attempt at concealment. If by chance he spied her, she wanted him to think her intentions were purely benign. She could be a traveler stranded in the storm, or a policewoman checking the progress of the evacuation.

The front door was the closest entry point, and she'd defeated the lock once before. That time she'd used a technique called lock bumping—effective but noisy. This time, with stealth at a premium, she took out her pick set and inserted a pick and an L-shaped tension wrench into the mechanism. She got the door unlocked within a minute.

Before opening the door, she pulled on gloves and drew the .38 from her purse.

Entering the house was the largest risk. If he'd seen her coming or heard her scratching at the lock, he would be waiting. And this guy could be armed. He fit the profile of someone who'd be carrying.

She nudged open the door with her foot and hung back to see if he would fire. He didn't. Peeking would do no good, so she pivoted inside the doorway, sinking to her knees to make herself small.

The house was surprisingly dark for midmorning. It took her a moment to realize that the power was out. The dismal day and the absence of electric light added up to a study in gloom.

No one was there. She straightened up, listening. From somewhere in the house, she heard a faint clanging intermixed with sotto voce curses.

Irrelevantly she remembered that old Christmas movie where the dad was always beating his wrench against a balky furnace and saying things like "Flabgabbit!"

Alec Dante wasn't saying "Flabgabbit!" He was cursing like a drunken sailor, or like Bonnie herself on a bad
day. Or on any day, really.

His voice was distant enough to give her confidence.
She shut the door and followed the stream of profanities
like a bloodhound following a scent.

Having explored the cottage on her last visit, she was
familiar with the layout. It was a decent-sized one-story
place with an eat-in kitchen and a patio facing the beach.
Unlike last time, the sliding glass doors were a mess of
rain and packed sand and gluey leaves, and the patio's
wooden flooring was beginning to come apart.

From the direction of the kitchen rose Dante's voice.
Oddly, it seemed to coming from below. Either someone
had done her job for her and the schmuck was already in
hell, or the house had a basement, a feature that had es-
caped her notice last time.

She checked out the kitchen. A branch had splintered
off a maple tree and punched a hole through the window,
ramrodding the fridge sideways and jerking a plumbing
pipe out of the wall. Probably the pipe had been hooked
up to an ice maker or something. Anyway, it was broken
in two, and water was gushing out, pooling on the floor
and streaming through an open doorway.

She hadn't paid any attention to that particular door
on her first visit. Now that it stood open, she could see
that it led downstairs.

She moved through the kitchen. Her sneakers, already wet, sopped up the ankle-deep water. She wondered what would happen if the power suddenly came
back on. She could be electrocuted in the water, maybe.
Now that would be a stupid way to die.

At the basement doorway she bent low and took a
look.

Water cascaded down the stairs in a foaming Niaga-
ra. More water poured from the basement ceiling. It was

percolating through the kitchen floorboards to produce a steady indoor rain.

The pipe must have broken some time ago. The water in the basement was already knee-high. She could see the whole room clearly enough in the gray illumination from a row of casement windows along the ceiling.

In the far corner stood Alec Dante, his back to her, a wrench gripped in both hands. His voice and the wrench's clangs came back at him in slapbacks of echo from the cement walls as he struggled with a plumbing valve. "Turn, motherfucker. *Turn!*"

Bonnie was no handyman—she was, in fact, neither handy nor a man—but she had a fair idea of what was going on here. Dante had come to the cottage ahead of the storm in order to salvage some of his belongings, only to find that the place was being flooded. Now he was trying to stop the flow by closing the main shutoff valve. But the damn thing was stuck.

She could see right away that he wasn't carrying. His T-shirt was pasted to his torso, leaving no room for a concealed weapon. And he sure as hell wasn't wearing an ankle gun below the waterline.

Even so, she took care to make no sound as she removed her windbreaker, then slipped out of her sneakers and socks and rolled up her pants legs to her knees. She left all those items, along with her purse, on a kitchen table before she descended the stairway.

Had she been the philosophical sort, she might have pondered the mystery of what she was about to do. The man before her was alive and thinking, and there was blood in his veins and breath in his lungs. In another minute or two she would take all of that from him and leave him a corpse adrift in the water.

It was a fearsome and awful thing, if she stopped to think about it. Ordinarily she never would. But lately, thoughts like this had been crowding in on her, and she didn't like it. Too much thinking wasn't healthy for someone in her profession.

She even knew what lay behind it. It was the episode with Pascal in August, just two months ago. She'd nearly bought it more than once that time. There was something about coming face to face with your own mortality that made you a little more respectful of other people's lives.

And there was the whole moral component, too. She couldn't deny it. Looking at Pascal had been like seeing herself in a mirror—an older, more sophisticated, and more sadistic image of herself. She hadn't liked what she'd seen. It had frightened her. Sometimes the memory kept her up at night. She'd even thought about quitting the life. But she didn't know if she could. It was addictive—the thrill of the kill.

She felt the familiar stirrings of that thrill as she closed in on her quarry. He was a fucking clay pigeon and she had him dead in her sights.

She wanted to do the hit fast and clean, take him from behind before he knew what happened. A single slug to the head, then a couple more between the shoulder blades for insurance.

But at the last moment he turned. How he knew she was there, she couldn't say. Some people had a sixth sense about being watched. Or maybe he'd glimpsed her reflection in the water or sensed a change in the pattern of ripples around his knees.

Whatever the reason, suddenly he was confronting her, the wrench upraised like a weapon—a pitifully inadequate weapon, as they both knew.

"Did Chiu send you?" he asked, seeming a lot less surprised than he ought to be.

She faced him squarely from a yard away. "I don't know any Chiu."

He blinked, taking this in. "So what the fuck is this?"

"Ask Aaron Walling."

"Walling? The fucking *orthodontist*? Are you shitting me?"

"I am not."

"He hired a hitter?"

"Looks that way."

"Listen to me, lady." Dante took a half step forward, spirals of water unspooling around his legs. "You are about to make a very big-time mistake. I have some powerful relatives."

"I know all about your relatives."

"Then you know it's suicide, if you go through with this."

"I'll take my chances."

She steadied the gun. He knew what was coming. He made one last try at saving his life.

"Hear me, okay? Just hear me. I swear to you. I will never make trouble for the Wallings again."

"You got that right," she said, and fired twice into his center body mass.

The shots were well placed, left side of the chest. They must have stopped his heart instantly. She doubted he had time to know he'd been hit. The stupidly amazed look on his face was probably just reflex. She hoped so.

Alec Dante fell forward, knees buckling, and splashed facedown in the water, his T-shirt ballooning around him, the wrench separating from his grasp and settling on the basement floor. A maroon stain spread out around him in widening circles, diffusing with distance. Close to him it was thick and opaque, like a second skin, a caul wrapping his body. Farther away, it was only a mist of reddish purple bubbles.

She didn't like standing in a lake of blood. Bonnie made her way back to the stairs and started to climb. Though it was only her imagination, she could swear the echoes of the shots still reverberated off the cinderblock walls.

2

TAKING THE BRIDGE off the island, Bonnie slowed down just long enough to toss the murder gun out the window and into the drink. When she hit the mainland, she pulled out a burner—an untraceable flip phone she'd picked up at Rite Aid—and called Aaron Walling.

"It's done," she said. "No worries."

"You mean—"

"You know exactly what I mean." Clients tended to get stupid at times like this, and she didn't have a whole lot of patience with stupidity. "Only thing left is the balance of payment."

He'd already ponied up a retainer of $2,500, but the balloon payment—ten times that much—had yet to be delivered. The cost was $27,500 in all. Given that she routinely put her life on the line, and risked a life sentence in prison with every job, she didn't think her fee was exorbitant. Hell, a mob hit could easily cost twice that much, and then you had to deal with some Brando wannabe chopping on a cigar and mumbling about omertà.

She figured she would use some of the scratch to buy

new brake pads. The Jeep could use them. Actually the Jeep could use a lot of things. She'd purchased the puke-green Wrangler secondhand six years ago, when it was already kind of a wreck. These days it was a rattletrap mess with duct-taped seat cushions, rusty hinges, bad shocks, and a rearview mirror that was stuck on the windshield with Krazy-Glue. She could have afforded a new vehicle, but the Jeep had been there when she needed it, and she was loyal to the old gal.

"You're sure there were no complications?" Walling asked.

"None. Your wife is safe, and you're in the clear."

She heard him swallow. "We shouldn't have done this."

"It's a little late for second thoughts."

"I know."

"Hey, chill. I met the guy. The world is a better place without him."

"Probably. I mean, yes, sure. Of course it is. Only ..."

"Only what?"

"Nothing."

She knew what this was about. It made no sense, but logic didn't play a big role in situations like this. She'd done the job he'd hired her for, and now he hated her for it. It was easier than hating himself.

Putting somebody out of the way was all well and good when it was safely theoretical, but when the call came through, confirming that the hit had actually gone down ...

Then suddenly her client saw her in a different light. He saw her with blood on her hands. And let's face it, he wasn't wrong.

"The police will talk to me," Walling said in a tone of surprise, as if this had never occurred to him before. "I'm his neighbor, after all."

"We've been over this, Aaron. Yeah, they'll talk. But

it'll be strictly pro forma."

"I hope so."

"Why wouldn't it be? Nobody knows what happened to your wife. Not the real story. Right?"

"Right. Right ..."

She wondered if it had been a mistake to take the job. Walling was the nervous type. Apparently a career in orthodontics hadn't prepared him for a leading role in a murder-for-hire plot.

He'd been antsy the day he visited her office with the medical records and the police report. He'd kept saying his wife could never know. Nobody could know. As if Bonnie was in the habit of broadcasting her resume. She'd told him not to worry. Let him stick to putting braces on overbites, and she would deal with his other problem. He had seemed a lot calmer by the end of the interview. But he was going all goofy on her now.

"When do you think they'll ... find the body?" he asked. She heard cold dread in his voice.

"Probably not for a couple days. But it could be any time. You'll just have to be ready. Stay cool."

"Cool." He uttered a noise that might have been a chuckle. "Sure."

"Hey, suck it up, cupcake. They'll just ask a few standard questions—how well did you know him, did he have any enemies, that kind of thing. Just say you don't know anything. You passed him in the lobby sometimes, saw him at the mailboxes. Period. They won't pursue it. You're a respectable citizen. Nobody's gonna suspect you."

"Okay."

She changed the subject. "How are you handling the storm?"

"I'll be closing my practice early. Then Rachel and I are heading to a hotel in Philly to ride it out."

"Smart."

"You?"

"I'm staying put." It took more than a hurricane to make her run. "When the weather clears, we'll set up a time to meet. Not at my office. Someplace neutral. Bring cash."

"Of course it'll be cash. You think I'm putting this on my American Express?"

"You'd better not. I only take Visa." She thought that was kinda funny, but he didn't laugh.

"I'll have the payment," he said, the words a whisper.

She knew he would have it, and he'd be happy to get rid of it, too. Happy to pay his blood money—after which, Dr. Aaron Walling would do his best to forget he'd ever had anything to do with someone like her.

"Stay safe," he said. "And ... wish me luck."

Bonnie smiled. "Don't sweat it, Aaron. The hard part's over. It's all smooth sailing now."

3

FRANK LAZZARO WAS having a bad fucking day.

This goddamn storm was part of it. It had closed down the ports, and without the ports, the arrival of his latest inventory—two hundred kilos of Turkish heroin and Moroccan hashish—had been indefinitely delayed. Plus, it was a serious pain in the ass to deal with high winds and rain and all the shit that came with a hurricane.

And then there was Victoria, who'd been acting up lately. Sure, he could keep her in line with a modest beating or two, administered as needed, like medicine; even so, she didn't seem nearly as deferential as she used to be. Last week she'd actually had the temerity to drop the D-word—*divorce*—in his presence, a first for her. Divorce—with two newly minted babies less than a year old. What the fuck was she thinking?

It looked like she was serious. She'd even let it slip that she'd started documenting her cuts and bruises with a cell phone camera, storing the photos in "the cloud," whatever the hell that was. He thought she'd been talking to her brother again, that putz with the glasses, a lawyer in Hoboken with an Obama sticker on his Prius. Over the years Frank had given serious thought to putting a big hurt on that asshole, but he knew Victoria would pitch a fucking fit, and he'd wanted to keep peace in the household. Now he was thinking maybe he should have taught the cocksucker a lesson. And maybe he still could.

So yeah, he was pissed as he navigated the shopping cart around the A&P, past largely depleted shelves, muscling his way through knots of last-minute buyers like himself. The storm had everybody worked up, and people were snatching at canned peas and boxed granola bars like they were made of solid gold.

Frank wasn't concerned about simple survival—after Hurricane Irene, he'd installed a generator in his house, hooked up to a gas main, and he kept a subzero freezer well stocked—but according to Victoria, the household was dangerously low on toilet paper, facial tissue, diapers, and other inedible essentials.

So why wasn't his wife out shopping, instead of him? Lately she didn't want to lift the god damn finger. He didn't know what the hell had gotten into her.

Things had been okay between them for most of the five years of their marriage. She was only thirty-two, nearly two decades younger than he was, but the age difference had never been a problem. He treated her good enough. He could've gotten himself a little goombata on the side, put her up in an apartment in Hoboken, but he hadn't. He'd been faithful. Mostly, anyhow. No guy was ever completely faithful. It wasn't human nature.

Their marriage was a fair exchange. She'd given him babies, two sons, and he'd given her a twelve thousand square foot house in Saddle River—a trophy house for a trophy wife. And so what if he knocked her around a little? Every marriage needed discipline. Jesus Christ, to even think about divorce—

"Hey."

An annoyed grunt. Frank turned and saw a thin-faced little mook with a spindly pussy-tickler mustache glaring at him through rectangular lenses. On his head rode a baseball cap emblazoned with the words *Proud American.*

"You banged my cart. Watch where you're going."

Frank hadn't noticed, but he probably had banged Proud American's cart, not that he gave a crap. It was no part of his philosophy to own up to anything. Somewhere he'd picked up John Wayne's guiding maxim: Never apologize, never explain.

"Fuck yourself," Frank said, not really angry, because the motherless cooch wasn't worth it.

It might have ended there, except as Frank was turning to press forward down the aisle, he heard Proud American mutter one word: "Jerkoff."

Huh.

Jerkoff.

Frank had been called a lot of names, but he'd never developed much of a sense of humor about it. Besides the John Wayne thing, there was another philosophical lodestar he followed.

Take no shit from nobody. Ever.

Didn't matter if the shit in question came from a smart-ass ten-year-old or a drooling geezer or the president of the motherfucking United States. Disrespect could never be tolerated, and must always be answered.

He turned and gave the potty-mouthed little prick a long, thoughtful stare.

LATER, WHEN HIS cart was loaded up with twelve-packs of towels and toilet paper and diapers and assorted other shit, some of which he'd filched from other people's carts in opportune moments, he stood online in aisle eight, watching Proud American in aisle ten. The kids called it hard-looking a guy. Mad-dogging. An intimidation play.

Proud American, conscious of his gaze, first looked at him, then looked away.

Frank was enough of a student of human nature to know that by looking away, the sad little shit was signaling surrender. Without benefit of words, he was acknowledging that Frank Lazzaro was the alpha dog in this situation, and that he, Proud American, was Frank's bitch. He also was expressing a wistful hope that bygones could be bygones, past misunderstandings forgotten in a spirit of mutual goodwill and common decency.

It wasn't going to play out that way.

Frank reached the cashier before Proud American did. Sometimes he flirted with checkout girls, but not today; he didn't want anybody remembering him. Besides, the checker in this aisle was a butt-ugly sow. He spied an engagement ring on one stumpy finger. Some guy must be really fucking desperate if he wanted to suckle at that pig's udder for a lifetime.

He paid cash. There would be no credit card entry to place him at the scene.

It was easy to beat Proud American out the door. He even had time to stow his groceries in the trunk of his Mercedes—a black 550, the S-Class model—and to settle behind the wheel for a moment of reflection.

Frank buttoned his raincoat all the way up to his collarbone. He had no intention of ruining his expensive Armani suit and the silk necktie Victoria had given him for his birthday. He had done some business earlier today, and he liked to dress well for his job.

Pulling on black gloves, he reached under the driver's seat and extracted a hunting knife in a leather sheath. It had a curved six-inch blade, and the mahogany handle was scored with deep notches. The knife went into the side pocket of his coat.

Then he summoned the animal.

That was how he thought of it—the animal, the black beast, sinuous as a panther, hissing like a snake, with evil fangs and cruel talons, a composite spirit of all predators, all natural killers everywhere.

He let it come to him, enter him. The animal took over and he, Frank, stepped aside to let the black beast do its work.

When he left the car, he was not anything human any longer.

The storm spat at him as he crossed the parking lot. Though the downpour had subsided for now, the asphalt was checkered with pools of rainwater. He sloshed through them, indifferent to the fate of his shoes. His world had narrowed to a single focus—the mustached man unpacking his shopping cart by an ancient orange hatchback, the man who had shown disrespect. Shoes cost only money. Respect was beyond price. A man could endure anything, sacrifice everything, take any risk, suffer any punishment, if only he preserved his respect.

Uomini di rispettu—that was how his Sicilian forebears had been known. Men of respect.

Proud American had parked in a corner of the lot, next to a Ford pickup that screened him from the view of anyone in the store. He had just finished transferring the contents of his cart to his vehicle when Frank stepped up behind him, the knife already unsheathed.

"Hey," he said. "Jerkoff."

It felt good, using the same epithet Proud American had used on him.

Before the guy could turn, Frank slammed the knife down, gripping the handle in one hand, hammering the pommel with the other. The impact of the blow drove the blade into the gap between his victim's neck and left shoulder, drilling through veins and arteries.

The man sagged with a groan. Frank shoved him into the rear of the hatchback, where he lay facedown amid the grocery bags.

The trick was to leave the knife embedded until the heart stopped pumping. Pull it out too soon and you'd be splashed by a foaming fountain of arterial blood. That was a lesson he'd learned the hard way.

Frank crawled into the back of the car and flopped his victim onto his back. The little shitbag stared up at him, eyelids flickering, mouth working without sound. A dying man. There was nothing more fascinating, nothing in the world.

"What ..." The man's voice was a croak. "What're you doing ...?"

"I'm killing you, Proud American." Frank felt his mouth expand in a smile. "If you don't like it, you got no-body to blame but yourself. Don't try putting this on me. *You* made me do it. *You* fucked up. You pissed me off, so I had to end you. 'Cause that's the rule, *cazzo.* That's how it works."

It wasn't Frank who was speaking. It was the animal, with its inbred sense of jungle justice, its instinctual knowledge of the logic of life and death.

He leaned in closer, his mouth brushing the man's ear. "You're just lucky I got a lot on my plate right now. 'Cause otherwise, you know what I do? I get your driver's license, and I go to your house, and I kill your wife, and I kill your kids, and I kill your dog, and I burn the fucking place to the ground. I wipe out everything that's got any connection with you, so there's nothing left, and your life is a black fucking hole. Like you was never even born." Frank straightened up. "You're getting off easy, shit-for-brains. Too fucking easy."

He nodded, satisfied that he'd gotten his point across, though his last words had been addressed to a corpse. The spirit, he knew, would hover close to the body for a short time after death, before it was borne away into the next world. And in that earthbound state, the spirit could hear his words.

What the hell. It was never too late to learn.

Frank fisted his hand over the knife handle and wrenched it free. The heart had stopped, and the blood that emerged was sluggish and molasses-thick. It puddled around Proud American's head, a glossy halo.

He wiped the blade on a headrest and slipped it into its sheath, reminding himself to score a new notch in the mahogany. He checked his raincoat and found it mostly unspotted. Already the beast, having fed, was retreating into its cave, where it would hibernate, waiting with a predator's infinite patience until it was called again.

Carefully he withdrew from the SUV and surveyed the area, blinking raindrops out of his eyes. Nobody had been around. Nobody had seen a thing.

He pushed Proud American entirely into the cargo area, folding the legs to make sure the body fit, then shut the rear door. With luck, the dumb bastard would remain unnoticed until closing time.

Frank returned to his car, walking casually, unafraid of being caught. Long ago he had grasped a great truth, that anything is possible to a man without fear.

He replaced the knife under the driver's seat. These days he didn't keep it strapped to his arm. New Jersey's statutes on carrying a concealed weapon, even a fucking blade, were the toughest in the country. The authorities already had a hard-on to run him in. He wouldn't give them a reason.

Before putting the Mercedes in gear, he drew a cleansing breath, collecting himself. As he drove out of the parking lot, he called his nephew again. Still no answer.

It was getting worrisome. The last he'd heard, Alec Dante had been on his way to his cottage on Devil's Hook, and Frank hadn't been able to reach him since.

4

THE ASSISTANT MANAGER'S SUV was still parked at the back of Brown's Fish Market. Two coolers were inside, camouflaged by a blanket. Mr. Brown's Cadillac wasn't there, which meant the boss hadn't come in yet, a development that suited her purposes just fine.

Bonnie put on a hat before going inside. She felt strongly that everybody should have a thing. Her thing was hats. This one was a snappy little Panama that worked pretty well as a rain shield.

She went around to the front of the store and asked to speak with the guy in charge. She found him in a back office yakking it up with someone on the phone—a supplier, she gathered, probably one of the commercial fishermen who sailed out of the Miramar marina. The office smelled of fish. Actually, the whole establishment smelled of fish.

While waiting, she took a seat and lit a cigarette. The assistant manager might not want her smoking in here, but although he didn't know it yet, he was in no position to complain.

When he hung up, he leaned across the desk and shook her hand, making brief but sincere eye contact, just the way he'd been trained. "Walt Churchland. And you are ...?"

"Name's Bonnie Parker," she said without smiling. "I'm a private detective." She handed him a business card bearing the name of her agency, Last Resort.

He retreated into his swivel chair, visibly nervous. Guilt would do that.

"Bonnie Parker?" He handled the card with fidgety fingers, foxing the edges. "Hey, that's like Bonnie and Clyde, right?"

"Yeah." She exhaled a long feather of smoke. "I'm Fay Dunaway."

"Your folks name you after a criminal on purpose, or didn't they know?"

"My dad knew."

"And he still thought it was a good idea?"

"Why not? He was a criminal himself."

Walt made a funny face, halfway between a smile and a wince. He couldn't tell if she was joking. She wasn't.

"Well, um, what can I do for you, Miss Parker?"

"Nothing. It's more about what I can do *to* you."

"I don't understand."

"Yeah, you do, Sparky. Your boss hired me to investigate pilferage. Somebody's been filching fishies. He thought it was one of the minimum wage guys, sneaking 'em out at closing time. The Mexicans, as he put it. But I spied on the Mexicans, and I didn't see any funny business. Then it occurs to me, maybe the fishes aren't going missing when the store closes, but when it opens. So I watched you today. I took photos. Wanna see?"

She scrolled through the shots on her cell phone, ending with the glassy-eyed tuna in the cooler.

Walt was working the swivel chair like he was doing aerobics. "That doesn't mean anything. I was just taking them for safekeeping. There's a storm on the way, and we could lose power ..."

"I think that's what we call a fish story, Sparky."

"Why do you keep calling me that?"

"I dunno. You just look like a Sparky."

"What I told you about the inventory—it's true."

"Want me to confirm it with Mr. Brown?"

His downcast eyes gave her the answer.

She let him tell his story in fits and starts. It seemed he had an arrangement with the chef at the Mute Swan. Every day, several pounds of fresh fish found their way to the kitchen. The chef got the merchandise at less than cost, and Walt pocketed a steady stream of cash.

"So it works out great for everybody," Bonnie said. "Except poor Mr. Brown. He kinda gets the fuzzy end of the lollipop, huh?"

"I thought he'd never miss them."

"He did."

"There's always waste and spoilage in this business."

"Not this much. I guess you got greedy. It's the old story, Sparky. You went a fish too far."

He shut his eyes, his face going pale. "Oh shit."

"You just think of something nasty?"

"My wife."

"Well, I'm sure she'd appreciate that."

"No, what I mean is—I'll have to tell her. I'll lose my job over this, and she'll have to know why."

"So she'll find out you're a schmo. She probably already knows."

"She'll never forgive me."

"You're breaking my heart. Next you'll be telling me you only stole the goods to raise money for your kid sister's eye operation."

"No, it's for ghost hunting."

"Come again?"

"I needed a prosumer camcorder that can shoot infrared video. You know, so you can film in pitch darkness. The one I bought is a Panasonic. I got it off eBay for twelve hundred bucks. It's the same one they use on *Ghost Hunters* on SyFy."

"You bought a $1200 camera so you can shoot videos of ghosts?"

He nodded. "In my spare time. I'm hoping I can get something good and parlay it into a TV job. I don't intend to work in retail forever."

"Sounds like a plan." She sighed. "Maybe I should've gone directly to your boss about this."

"Why didn't you?" His face assumed a sly expression. "You thinking we can work out an agreement?"

"No, Sparky, I'm not thinking that. Look, you got a good job here, and apparently you've found a girl dumb enough to marry you. So how about you stop desperately seeking Casper, quit ripping off old Mr. Brown, and go back to being a good little boy?"

"And if I do?"

"Then nobody has to know. I'll tell Mr. Brown the situation's been handled. He'll want details, but I won't give him any. But if the inventory starts swimming away again, he'll only need to ring me up once. And then I think you know what'll happen."

"I'll be saying so long and thanks for all the fish?"

This was apparently a joke. She didn't get it. "You won't get a second chance, Sparky. I'm already giving you more of a break than you deserve."

She rose to leave. He stopped her with a question. "Why?"

"Huh?"

"Why are you going so easy on me?"

"Let's just say I like your face."

She left the store, taking the rear exit, and returned to her Jeep. His face, of course, had nothing to do with it. She just didn't expect a lot from people. They did stupid shit and expected to get away with it. They always thought they were smarter than they really were. Some could be scared straight. She was betting Walt was that sort.

Besides, she didn't want to see him tossed out on the street. He might never get another job, especially with the rep he'd acquire from Brown, and his marriage might fall apart, too.

All so he could hunt ghosts. Jeez.

Didn't he know it was never a good idea to disturb the dead?

5

SHE ATE LUNCH at the Main Street Diner, located in what was known optimistically as downtown Brighton Cove. There were model train sets with bigger commercial districts. Still, the four-block area was large enough to house a variety of knickknack shops and art galleries, an old-fashioned five-and-dime, too many real estate offices, and one detective agency, belonging to Bonnie herself.

According to the clock in the town square, the time was only 11:45, but she was already hungry as hell. It was kinda twisted, but she always worked up an appetite after doing a hit. Sometimes it made her a little horny too. Oh yeah, she was the picture of mental health.

The diner was crowded with people getting in a last restaurant meal before a bitch named Sandy shut everything down. Bonnie found a small table in the back and ordered clam chowder with lots of those crumbly little crackers. Oyster crackers, she thought they were called. She hoped they weren't fattening. Watching your weight wasn't easy in an area that boasted more pizza parlors and Italian delis per square mile than Sicily. Luckily she was a heavy smoker. It kept the pounds off.

The place had Wi-Fi, allowing her to spend some quality time with her phone. It was a Samsung, and its name was Sammy. Well, actually this little guy was Sammy II, son of Sammy. His dad had suffered a cracked screen during her run-in with Pascal and had to be humanely put down. Given how close she'd come to getting decommissioned herself, she couldn't complain about the loss of a piece of hardware. At least she'd salvaged the DayGlo pink case.

As she scrolled through her email inbox, she became aware that some of the other patrons were looking at her. Since developing a local reputation, she'd always gotten some stares. Lately it had gotten worse because of Dan Maguire's whisper campaign. The police chief was just jonesing to find something on her and put her away. Failing that, he could at least make her life hell.

That was the thing about small-town living. She'd settled in Brighton Cove—the first place she'd ever settled, in fact—six years ago. The spot had its charms: a two-mile stretch of boardwalk, fine Victorian homes in the wealthiest part of town, a lake where folks went ice-skating in winter. But there were drawbacks, especially for someone like her.

In a city nobody knew you. You could walk the streets and dine out and shop in glorious anonymity. Brighton Cove, population 7,000, was a different story. Here, enough people knew her, or at least knew about her, to ensure that she seldom went unrecognized in public. And since a lot of what they'd heard wasn't too complimentary, she got a lot of nervous glances, usually accompanied by whispered conversation. Like now, for instance. About ten percent of the patrons had identified her, and were breathlessly gossiping to the other ninety percent.

The waitress, Lizbeth, returned with a bowl of soup.

She was one of the few locals Bonnie counted as a friend, but she'd been strangely standoffish in recent weeks.

"Everything okay, Liz?" Bonnie asked as the soup was set down.

"Hunky-dory." But her eyes were darting.

"You seem a little antsy around me these days."

"Well, it's just ... You know how people talk."

Did she ever. "They've been talking like that for a long time."

"It's different now. Ever since that thing on the boardwalk last August. They found bullets all over the place. Must've been a real shootout."

It had been. Bonnie could attest to that personally, not that she intended to.

"What's that got to do with me?" she asked evenly.

"Nothing. But some people ..."

The words faded out into uncomfortable silence.

Bonnie mashed up some crackers and stirred them into the soup. "You know I'm no desperado, don't you, Liz?"

"Um, sure, Bonnie. Sure. I know."

She watched the waitress walk away. She'd counted two *sures* and an *I know*. That was a lot of affirmatives in response to a simple question.

If even Lizbeth had turned against her, she really was the town pariah. Well, fuck 'em. She really didn't care what other people thought of her. She only cared that they just might be right.

That was the thing. They hated her and feared her and saw her as a freak. So be it. But there were times when she hated herself. Feared herself. Saw herself as a freak. And that, she didn't like.

Maybe it was inevitable that she would end up this way. Maybe being an outcast and a lawbreaker was built into a girl's destiny when she was named after America's most notorious female outlaw. Her dad, a penny-ante

31

criminal rogue named Tom Parker, had christened her in honor of the cigar-chomping, pistol-toting twenty-something matriarch of Clyde Barrow's gang, a mere slip of a girl who'd robbed banks, shot it out with lawmen, and terrorized and titillated the whole country for a brief time during the grim Depression years. There was even a slight physical resemblance—the original Bonnie had been wiry and blond and arrestingly blue-eyed, just like the modern edition.

Sometimes she thought she just might be the first Bonnie reincarnated. Like Sammy II, she might be Bonnie 2.0. It could explain why violence and orneriness and being on the wayward side of the law came so naturally to her. Of course, genetics could have played a role—an inheritance from her ne'er-do-well pop. Or it might have had something to do with the hectic mess that was her childhood, which had been spent in constant flight, moving from motel to motel until she was fourteen, and then—well, then childhood became a luxury she couldn't afford anymore.

Any way you looked at it, she'd been fated to go off the rails, at least as far as polite society was concerned. And vigilantes were never too popular with law-abiding folks, were they? Especially in Jersey, a state so nannyish its citizens weren't even trusted to pump their own gas.

Her clients—the special ones—probably assumed she'd gotten into PI work purely as a cover for her illegal activities. Not so; she'd been a boring old bona fide PI for three years before branching out, and she still did plenty of ordinary gumshoe work, like the fish market job. She'd started using extralegal methods when she found that working within the law didn't always work. Corrupt people could use the law to their advantage, hide behind it, even wield it as a weapon. Sometimes direct action was needed. It wasn't pretty, but it had to be done.

And it wasn't like she was some kind of friggin' serial

killer. She only took jobs that satisfied her personal re-quirements—jobs where she really was, to borrow the phrase painted on her office door, the last resort. She plugged loopholes in the law, that's all. She was a fixer, and there were things in this world that needed fixing.

So if people came to her when all other options were off the table, having heard a rumor somewhere that Bon-nie Parker could make their problems go away, could anyone really blame them?

When she thought of it that way, it all seemed very clear.

But then she remembered Alec Dante floating in a widening circle of his own blood while the echoes of the gunshots splashed back at her from the cellar walls, and suddenly she wasn't so sure.

6

FRANK LAZZARO WAS a big man, six foot four, tipping the scales at 270. Much of that bulk was fat, but enough of it was muscle. He might have hit the half-century mark on his last birthday, but he hadn't gone soft. In his business a man couldn't afford to get soft.

His head was small and oval, bullet-shaped, cushioned by a pillow of fat at the back of his neck. He had his hair shaved close in a crew cut once every two weeks by a barber named Angelo who told dirty jokes and kept a stash of *Penthouse* magazines for his customers. Frank's hair had been thick and black in his youth, but as he'd gone gray, he'd cut it shorter and shorter, until now it resembled a thin spread of iron filings. Even his eyebrows were gray. They flickered over small eyes tucked away inside wrinkled folds of fat.

Those eyes were narrowed in worry now, as he drove south to Devil's Hook.

For the past few days, his nephew had been pestering him with voicemail messages, insisting he had something important to talk about, something that required a face-to-face. Frank had ignored the kid as long as possible. Alec was always getting enthused about something. Mostly he wanted to get in on the action, join the organization, an option Frank had steadfastly refused. He was a good judge of talent, and he knew his nephew didn't have the stuff for that kind of life. He would never be a player, only a wannabe.

Probably the recent spate of calls was about the same fugazy bullshit. It made his head hurt just to think about it. But he hadn't been able to dodge his nephew forever. Today he'd agreed to a sit-down after the kid got back from the cottage; they would connect by phone and work out the details of a meet.

But Alec hadn't called, hadn't answered Frank's calls, hadn't returned Frank's messages. This was troubling. There was no answer at the cottage, and according to news reports, the island had been completely evacuated. Frank was going there anyway.

Frank knew the cottage well. He'd bought it himself and given it to Alec. The transfer was not an example of his largeness of heart. It was basically a ruse. If the feds ever came after him with that RICO shit and tried to seize his assets, it wouldn't hurt to have some property tucked away in another person's name.

Cohawkin Bridge, the main causeway to the island, had been blocked off with a row of huge trash bins to prevent looters from taking advantage of the storm, but Frank found a smaller bridge obstructed only by a parked police car, currently unoccupied. He slipped the Mercedes into low gear, dug his bumper into the cruiser's side door, and bulldozed the offending vehicle out of his way. There would be some damage to his car's front end, but he had a mechanic who owed him a favor and would fix it at cost.

With the car butted aside, the way was clear—well, as clear as it could be in the midst of a fucking hurricane.

It was weird, passing through miles of desolation, a chain of ghost towns with boarded-up windows and sandbagged yards. Weirder still to know that a lot of this real estate would be gone, washed away, before Sandy was through. The bars and diners were all closed, the rows of 1950s era motels abandoned, the Army and Navy surplus stores shuttered. Over one town loomed a water tower sporting an image of two happy dolphins at play. It looked out of place, like a clown at a funeral.

The weather was rapidly deteriorating. Driving south along the main drag on Devil's Hook was like taking a trip through one of those drive-through car washes. Sheets of rain rippled across the windshield. The wind gusted with enough force to knock both sideview mirrors off kilter.

Frank didn't care. He'd been through many kinds of hell. By his standards, a hurricane hardly even registered as an inconvenience.

Half an hour after crossing over, he arrived at the cottage. Alec's Porsche was out front, a bad sign. The kid should have been gone hours ago, along with everybody else.

From a gym bag in the Mercedes' trunk Frank retrieved a Ruger .22. He kept it cocked and locked as he explored the cottage.

The front door was ajar, another cause for concern. The power was off, naturally. Every traffic light Frank had passed on the island had been dead, not that it had mattered, since nobody was on the road.

Gusts of windblown sand lashed the windows. Through the rippling glass he could see a bloom of whitecaps on the ocean. The walls trembled; pressing his palm flat against the plasterboard, he could feel the fury of the wind.

In the kitchen he discovered a flood tide of water and an open door to the cellar. Down below, the water was waist-high and still rising.

He had a feeling Alec was down there, and his feelings rarely steered him wrong. He stripped to his briefs and waded into the chilly black water. It took him five minutes of searching, guided by the beam of a big steel flashlight, but in the end he found his nephew, afloat in a corner near the plumbing's main shutoff valve.

Frank had seen a lot of death, and he wasn't troubled by the sight of a corpse. The fact that it was his nephew disturbed him in a distant way, like the first faint rumble of thunder that announced the approach of a storm. The rumble grew distinctly louder when he flipped the kid over and his flashlight pinpointed two holes in his chest.

Those holes had stopped leaking blood a few hours ago, but Frank had no difficulty identifying them as bullet holes—.38 caliber, he estimated—a pair of them, nice and neat, the work of a pro.

"Fuck," he whispered. "Fucking fuck *fuck*."

His bare foot trod on a wrench that lay on the cellar floor. Evidently Alec had been trying to close the shutoff valve. Frank didn't need a wrench. With one hand and only modest effort, he cranked the valve shut. He'd never lost an arm wrestling contest or failed at any other test of strength.

Then he muscled his nephew's body into his arms. The dead man's clothes were sodden and heavy, and the high water impeded movement, but Frank barely noticed the strain of carrying his burden across the flooded room and up the dripping stairs.

7

BONNIE WAS A BLOCK from her home when the black-and-white behind her blooped its siren and flashed its light bar.

Great. What now?

Maguire's troops had been riding her pretty hard lately. Traffic stops, bullshit citations. Harassment—that's what it was. They were treating her like a criminal. Well, okay, she was a criminal, but she still didn't like it.

At least she'd ditched the murder gun. It had gone out the window into Shipbreak Bay during her drive home. If the local constabulary were to find that piece of hardware on her, she'd have some 'splainin' to do.

Reluctantly she pulled over to the curb and cranked down the window on the driver's side. The cop was riding solo, and she was surprised to see that it was one of the good guys, a rookie called Walsh, first name Bradley. He was new enough to not be completely under Maguire's thumb, and he hadn't gotten on her case before. He'd always been nice to her. As a matter of fact, she strongly suspected he had a crush on her, the poor kid.

Apparently nobody had informed him that dating her would be fatal to his career, and somehow he hadn't yet figured out that she was, not to put too fine a point on it, a heartless bitch.

He stepped up quickly to her window, looking all spiffy in his uniform—but also, she thought, looking nervous as hell. The rain had let up for a minute, but he still got flecked with windblown spray as he leaned down to talk.

"Hi, Bonnie."

"Hey, Bradley. What law am I violating now? Dirty license plate? Improperly inflated tires?"

"Well, you did sort of roll through that stop sign." He smiled, but it didn't last. His boyish face was unusually grave. "That's not why I pulled you over. I've got some news for you. Some not-so-good news."

"Okay."

"I guess I'm sort of talking out of school. The chief doesn't want us putting the word out. But—well, I thought you had a right to know."

"To know what, exactly?"

He leaned closer, raindrops trickling off his hat brim. "The Long Fong Boyz are after you."

"Say again?"

"The Long Fong Boyz."

She squinted at him. "Are you coming on to me?"

"I'm serious. They're a Chinese-American outfit. The name means dragon gang boys."

"Dragon gang boys," she repeated, mystified.

"They spell 'boys' with a z," Bradley pointed out helpfully.

"Yeah, all the cool kids are doing that." She'd never heard of them. "They're not active around here, are they?"

"They travel. But mainly they operate in NYC and north Jersey."

"And they're after me? After me, how? Like, they wanna

hire me? They wanna talk to me? They wanna date me?"

"They want to kill you."

She puffed up her cheeks and blew them flat. "I was afraid that was it. Any idea why?"

"I sort of figured you would know."

"Not a clue." The Long Fong Boyz. Hell. It was like being hunted by porn stars—although at least that scenario offered the prospect of a happy ending. "Did they put out a contract for any takers, or are they keeping this in-house?"

"It's just them, for now."

She nodded. That was something, at least. Bad enough to deal with one gang. Way worse to deal with every freelance hitter in the tri-state area looking to score.

"And how long has my friendly neighborhood police department been in possession of this info?" she asked.

"Just since last night. A CI in Jersey City gave it up, and the Jersey City cops passed it on to us. Because, you know, you're local."

Jersey City. That was interesting. It suggested possibilities. "And Maguire wasn't planning to share this tidbit with me?"

"I don't think so."

"I'm guessing he won't offer me any special protection either."

"I asked the chief about that. He just looks at me like I'm a retard and says we can't spare the manpower."

"Sure."

"I've been cruising past your place pretty regular—you know, just to keep an eye on it."

"And scare off the riffraff."

"Well, yeah."

His instincts were right. Her home probably was where they would do it—there, or at her office. A drive-by, a few rounds expended as she walked to the door or stood at the window, a quick kill. And another notch in some hitter's gun. Not that she was in any position to criticize.

"You can't look after me all by yourself," she said quietly, "though it's sweet of you to try."

He actually blushed. He was younger than she was by a couple years, and he hadn't seen the things she'd seen. He was still a kid.

"Just doing what I can," he said modestly. "I can't figure the chief out. I almost think he *wants* them to ice you."

"Yeah, well, him and me haven't exactly been exchanging Christmas cards."

"Even so, he's got a duty to protect you."

Bonnie gave his shoulder a playful rap. "I like you, kiddo. But you might be better off in some other jurisdiction. Utah, maybe—you know, where the Osmonds live."

"The Osmonds?" He didn't get it.

"What I'm saying is, Jersey cops have a rep for not always playing it strictly by the book. Even the good ones. And Maguire—well, I hate to break it to you, but he ain't one of the good ones."

"According to the chief, you're the one who's the bad guy."

"Yeah. So he's told me."

"You telling me you're one of the good guys?"

That was a good question. She thought it over. "Let's just say I could be a lot worse."

"That's not a great answer."

"It's the best I can do. Look, thanks for the heads-up."

"You need to take this seriously, Bonnie." His earnestness was simultaneously touching and silly. "These gangbangers might have a funny name, but they're the real deal."

"Don't sweat it, pal. I'm taking it seriously. Believe me. Anything else I should know?"

He hesitated, looking up and down the street as if afraid someone might be spying on their little tête-à-tête. "I think the chief is building a case against you."

"For what?"

"I don't know. He's keeping it to himself. But I've seen the folder he carries around. It's got your name on it, and it's getting bigger and bigger. And last week he took a trip to Ohio. Buckington, Ohio—if that means anything to you."

It meant a lot. She did her best not to show it.

"Thanks, Brad. You're a stand-up guy. An officer and a gentleman."

She watched as he returned to his car. Once he was inside, she sketched him a wave and drove on.

What a mess. Of the two developments, the Asian gang clearly posed the more immediate danger.

But it was Maguire's foray into Buckington, Ohio, that really made her sweat.

8

IN THE KITCHEN, Frank laid his nephew's body on a countertop and stripped it bare—shoes, pants, shirt, briefs. The wet clothes went into a garbage bag. In one of the kid's pockets there was a cell phone, waterlogged, ruined. The SIM card, though, was salvageable. Frank removed the card and tossed the rest of the phone into the trash.

He spoke no words to the corpse. Too much time had passed; the spirit was no longer on this plane. The immortal essence of his nephew was already in the next world, facing judgment.

Frank didn't like to think about that. He had too good an idea what his own judgment would be.

He dried himself off and put on his clothes, then slung Alec's nude body over his shoulder and carried it to the beach.

The ocean was wild, a living thing. Frank deposited the body in a thicket of seagrass, where he piled up pebbles and shells in a makeshift cairn. He laid Alec's head atop the little monument. The kid's eyes were open. Frank shut them.

With a knife from the kitchen, he traced a thin line along the edge of his palm, opening a seam of flesh. He stood over the body, squeezing out a coppery trickle that pattered on Alec's face. The anointment complete, he bandaged his hand in a white handkerchief, which was instantly blotted with red. His hand hurt, but the pain didn't trouble him. Pain, like blood, was a thank-offering to his guardian angel, the patron saint of the outlaws and the dispossessed.

Frank Lazzaro had always been lucky. Twenty years in the life, and only two prosecutions, no convictions? He'd long suspected that some higher power was looking out for him. Two years ago his suspicion was confirmed. He'd been doing business in Mexico City when an associate suggested he attend a ceremony in a barrio—a rosary service for Santa Muerte, Saint Death, a cloaked hag with a skull face who looked after murderers and drug runners. Some wetback superstition, Frank figured.

Reluctantly he joined a couple of thousand worshipers clustered in the festering heat at dusk. He was prepared to leave early if the rites proved too boring or too crazy.

Instead he stayed until the end, transfixed by the ecstatic chants, the ribbons of smoke from votive candles, and the march of supplicants to the altar, where they offered up their homely treasures—a lock of hair, an heirloom ring, a family photo, a few coins, even small bottles of mescal and bags of cannabis.

Frank came away changed. He now had a name and an image for the spectral presence he had always dimly intuited. He knew whom to thank for his good fortune. No, she could not save him from his ultimate fate—he still expected to pass over to a place of bitterness and screams when his earthly sojourn was done. The outer darkness, where there was wailing and gnashing of teeth ...

There was a price to be paid for everything. A man

who'd done the things he'd done deserved nothing else. Still, the saint would safeguard her devotees as best she could while they were alive. It was all he could ask.

Back home, he had built a shrine to Santa Muerte in his bedroom, paying her nightly obeisance. Like the barrio congregation, he both loved and feared Saint Death. She was his helpmate and protectress, and she was a bitch and a man-eater, a stone killer who would turn on him in an instant if he ever let her down. That was okay. He could never have respected her if she'd been any different.

He had told none of this to his friends and colleagues. They wouldn't have understood. Only Victoria knew. She didn't understand, either—she thought it was all voodoo and witchcraft—but that didn't matter. Her opinion didn't mean a fucking thing.

Returning to the cottage, he rummaged in the garage until he found a can of kerosene for a barbecue grill. He emptied the can over Alec's corpse, letting the fuel mix freely with the cascading rain and spray of surf. Then he lit a match.

Alec Dante's mortal remains went up in a cough of flame that painted the beach in tiger stripes of orange. Frank watched from a respectful distance, unconcerned about witnesses. No one was left on Devil's Hook but himself and the dead man, and as he watched, the dead man vanished in a pillar of gray smoke and glittering cinders.

"Santa Muerte," Frank whispered. "Santa Muerte."

He needed her guidance now, more than ever. She would lead him to his nephew's killer. She would see that justice was done.

When the fire had diminished to a sputtering afterglow, Frank approached the charred ground. The seagrass had been burned away. Blistered shells lay scattered here and there, some cracked by the heat; during the ceremony he'd heard them pop and crackle like chestnuts.

With a stick of driftwood he poked among the parts of Alec Dante that hadn't burned, the teeth and some of the larger bones. He'd brought another trash bag with him for just this purpose. Heedless of the stinging rain, he collected the scraps, transferring them to the bag.

Done, he spent some time disarranging the sand so any small pieces he might have overlooked would be safely buried. An unnecessary precaution; at high tide, the beach would be awash, all remaining evidence swept away.

He carried the two bags and the empty kerosene can to his car, putting everything into the trunk. He left the Porsche parked where it was. Later he would send some of his guys to make it disappear.

He wanted nothing that would point to a crime, nothing that would bring in the police. At most, let them list Alec as a missing person—if there was anyone who would bother to file a report. Most likely there wasn't. Alec had been unsocial, friendless. A hard man to like. An even harder man to love.

But Frank had loved him. He might have found the kid exasperating, irresponsible, selfish, lazy, immature— he might have voiced a hundred similar complaints—but Alec had been his closest blood relative outside his own children, a kid he'd known since infancy, a kid he'd watched over and looked after just as the skeleton saint watched over Frank himself.

Somebody had murdered the boy. Shot him in the heart in the flooded basement of his own house, two days before Halloween.

And that fucker was going to pay.

9

BONNIE DROVE HOME to her duplex on Windlass Court, musing on what Bradley had told her and wondering just how worried she should be.

The detached garage alongside the duplex would be a good place for an ambush. And right now she was in the rare position of being unarmed. Well, *que sera sera.* She parked the Jeep and walked briskly to her front door, not really expecting to be shot, but not ruling it out, either.

No shots were fired. At the door she typed a six-digit code into the security system keypad, then went inside. With the door shut and locked behind her, she felt a little safer. But there was still a chance someone had found a way around the alarm and was waiting to take her by surprise indoors.

She made her way to the bedroom. In the past she'd stored her weaponry in a small safe by her bed, but last month she'd switched her entire arsenal to a floor trap in the closet. Kneeling, she pulled up a loose floorboard and surveyed the equipment hidden in the crawlspace. She chose a .32 and crammed it into her purse. Damn, she'd gotten used to carrying a gun. She felt naked without one.

Newly armed, she explored the premises, checking for signs of intrusion, finding none. In what might or might not have been an excess of caution, she shut the curtains so she couldn't be seen from outside. She was all for target shooting, but not when she was wearing the bull's-eye.

The power was still on in the duplex, though considering how the lights were flickering, she guessed it wouldn't stay on for long. The place was a mess, but she couldn't blame that on trespassers. She'd never had any illusions that her house was a showplace. It was located a few blocks from the railroad tracks and decorated in early garage sale.

Her neighbor, Mrs. Biggs, wasn't around; she'd left yesterday to stay with her daughter's family fifty miles inland. The usual noises of activity from next door were absent, but the storm more than made up for them—the thrash of leafy branches against the roof, the piston-pounding rain, the bagpipe skirls of the wind.

Satisfied that she wasn't risking a Bates Motel moment, she took a shower to wash off the residue of bloody water from the cottage's basement. She lingered under the spray, aware that it might be her last hot shower for days. Once the power failed, all bets were off.

Afterward, she changed into fresh clothes, choosing a T-shirt that bore the words *I'm A Classy, Sophisticated Woman Who Says "Fuck" A Lot*. Truth be told, she was neither classy nor sophisticated. But she did say "Fuck" a lot.

To go with the tee, she picked out a denim skirt and a smart little bucket cloche. Her ensemble was gray and black. She generally favored dark tones because they blended into the shadows, which was always helpful. You never knew when you might want to disappear.

Mindful of the coming blackout, she peered into her

fridge to see what might spoil. There was nothing inside except some takeout leftovers and a couple of tubs of Ben & Jerry's.

In the living room she switched on her TV, muting the volume, and tuned to News 12, which predictably was going crazy with the nonstop stormapalooza. Reporters planted themselves on beaches, defying wind and spray, and made faces at a foam-flecked camera lens. Weather maps displayed the menacing storm track. Harried public officials sweated under TV lights. New Jersey's governor, who in Bonnie's opinion bore a striking resemblance to Jabba the Hutt, was telling people to get out of harm's way while they still could. Either that, or he was ordering a Double Whopper and fries. With the sound off, it was hard to tell.

The silent images flickered past her, registering only on the periphery of her attention. Massive power outages. Regional airports closed. Beaches eroding. Plywood boards nailed up over windows and spray-painted with messages taunting the storm. Worries about voters' access to the polls next Tuesday. Bonnie didn't give a fig about politics. She never voted. She was half convinced the elections were rigged and the Illuminati ran everything. What the hell, it made as much sense as any other theory.

The Long Fong Boyz. That was what she focused on, while the rest of the stuff shuttled past her between commercials for car dealerships and pizza joints. What the hell could she possibly have to do with a bunch of Chinese-American gangsta types? She didn't even know any Asian people. Well, there was the proprietor of the Thai takeout place down the street, but his worst crime was using too much MSG.

Bradley had said they operated out of Jersey City. It couldn't be a coincidence. She'd spent a fair amount of time in Jersey City recently, tailing the late Alec Dante.

She remembered the first thing he'd said to her in the basement: *Did Chiu send you?*

Opening her laptop, she Googled the name Chiu in connection with the Long Fong Boyz. A handful of new stories came up. Twenty-four-year-old Patrick Chiu was the gang's head honcho.

The guy's age didn't surprise her. Gang leaders were younger than ever. Chiu, though, was a special case. According to one article, he was reputed to be smart, college educated, a young man who'd gone a long way toward a mainstream career before detouring into the gang scene. He'd been active for only three years and already commanded one of the toughest crews in north Jersey. Their strength was estimated at between twenty and thirty soldiers, and they were into the protection racket—lucky money, it was called in Chinese neighborhoods—and the drug trade.

Chiu was clearly an up-and-comer. Bonnie had never heard of him. But Dante had. He'd half expected Chiu to come after him. That was why he hadn't been all that surprised to find an assassin in this house.

Generally speaking, if you expected a visit from an assassin, you'd engaged in some violent misbehavior of your own.

She jumped to the website of the *Star-Ledger*, which covered Hudson County, and searched the archives for recent news items involving the Long Fong Boyz. She found one.

On October 22, a certain Joey Huang, believed to be a member of the gang, was shot to death in the Crossgate Gardens housing project in the Greenville section of Jersey City. Huang was described as a "willowy nineteen-year-old," reputedly active in heroin distribution. He'd been killed by a single shot to the face. Neighbors hadn't heard a thing.

Now it was starting to make sense. A little bit of sense,

anyway. Because Bonnie had been in that housing project on the evening of October 22—and so had Alec Dante.

She had followed Dante from his condo that night. He'd surprised her by taking his car; normally he used public transportation in the city. She'd tailed him into Greenville, a slum neighborhood at the south end of town, where he'd disappeared inside a multistory low-income project. Though she'd gone after him, she hadn't been able to track him down in the maze of corridors and stairways.

At first she had thought the location offered a promising opportunity to complete her assignment, but there were too many open doors, too many potential witnesses hanging out in the stairwells and hallways. She'd been seen by plenty of people, and she knew she stood out—white, blond, female—not somebody who'd ordinarily be wandering around the labyrinth of Crossgate Gardens, unless she was a cop or a fed.

Since she couldn't find Dante and wouldn't have been able to do anything even if she had, she left the building, returning to the parking garage where she'd dumped her Jeep just in time to scare off some layabouts who'd been eyeing her puke-green baby with the intention of swiping or stripping it.

She hadn't known why Alec Dante was slumming in Greenville. Visiting a whore? Buying drugs? But now she knew. He'd been killing Joey Huang—one shot to the face.

Why the hell Dante would do that, she couldn't guess. But he'd done it, all right; and the Long Fong Boyz, questioning the locals, must have gotten a description of a suspicious woman who'd prowled the project during the right time frame. The police wouldn't know anything about it; those witnesses would never talk to the cops about a gang shooting.

She didn't know how the Boyz had ID'd her by name. Maybe someone remembered her Jeep's tag number, or maybe her underground rep as a hitter had reached someone in the gang. Anyway, they thought she'd aced Joey, and they were out for blood.

And ironically, the only person who could clear her was Dante himself—and she'd just shut his mouth permanently.

"It's a pickle," she said grimly.

She was considering the implications when the lights went out.

And yeah, she jumped a little.

Of course, the power outage was no real surprise. Wind gusts had knocked down power lines, and storm surges had flooded switching stations, all along the Jersey shore.

There was zero likelihood the lights would come on again anytime soon. Before long it would be night, and she would be alone in the dark, listening to every rustle of leaves and slap of a branch, wondering if it was the storm she heard—or the footsteps of a ninja death squad. Wait, weren't ninjas Japanese?

Whatever. The point was, Bradley's story had spooked her. More than that, it had depressed her. Was this really all there was to her life—kill or be killed? She'd shot a guy to death this morning, and there was a crew of homicidal urban youth on her trail this afternoon. She could kill them, or they could kill her. And even if she survived, how long until the next threat presented itself?

And then there was Buckington, Ohio. Just thinking about it made her physically tired. With eyes closed, she wondered if maybe she should simply let Maguire build a case against her. Let him come for her with handcuffs and an arrest warrant. Let him frogmarch her to jail and make her pay the friggin' piper. It would provide closure, at least. An ending.

Things couldn't go on this way. Something had to give. She felt trapped like a wolf in a snare. Maybe she should try chewing off her own foot. Yeah, like that would help. Nothing would help. She could never be free. Never.

She listened to the wind toss the branches of the maple tree outside her living room. An ominous sound, like the flapping of monstrous wings. She shivered.

Oh hell. Life was tough enough without sitting around and waiting for a bunch of Bruce Lee wannabes to put a bullet in her noggin.

She threw a few items into a suitcase, locked up her place and reset the alarm, which would run on a backup battery, and headed over to Des's house.

He might be grateful for a friend tonight, anyway. Not that he needed her help to get around. That chair of his was maneuverable enough to pop a wheelie, and the fact that his upper body resembled the chiseled torso of a Greek god didn't hurt.

But nobody liked to be alone in a hurricane. Or so she told herself. It seemed as good a reason to crash on his couch as any.

The real reason was a whole lot simpler. Alone in the dark, she would have only her memories—and her fears. She wasn't sure she could deal with either tonight.

10

DES MET HER at the door and ushered her inside, out of the screaming wind. The sprint from her duplex to the garage and from the Jeep to his porch had left her drenched. She smelled like wet laundry. A thread of rain slithered into her nose, and she sneezed.

"Messy afternoon," Des observed from his wheel-chair. He was casually but impeccably dressed, and immaculately groomed. He lived alone and somehow did everything himself. She never had been quite sure how he got his shoes and pants on, and she had yet to find the right opportunity to ask.

"Sorry to barge in. I thought maybe you'd like company."

"Always welcome."

"Figured I could help out a little when it gets dark. Maybe stop you from stubbing a toe or something."

"One of the few advantages of my condition is that even if do I stub my toe, I won't know it."

"Point taken."

"You don't have to justify coming over, Parker."

"No. I guess I don't." She felt she did, though. She wasn't sure why.

His power was out, too. Everybody's power was out. They fixed tea in the kitchen, heating the water in a fondue pot over a can of sterno. She found herself talking about the hurricane.

"Sandy's not a good name for a monster storm. It makes me think of Sandy Duncan. Or is it Sandy Dennis? I always get them confused."

"What name would you pick?"

"Helga. Call it that, and you wouldn't need the governor flapping his chins about mandatory evacuation. Nobody would hang around if Hell Storm Helga was bearing down on them."

Des sipped his tea. "So I take it you prefer female names for hurricanes?"

"Oh yeah. All hurricanes should be girls. That's just common sense."

"Come to think of it, is Sandy male or female?"

"I don't know. Maybe ... transgendered?"

He lifted his mug. "Here's to transgendered hurricanes," he said grandly.

She studied him. "Someone's in a good mood."

"I like to entertain."

"No, you don't. You once told me having people over is a pain in the ass."

"Couldn't have been me. Ever since I flipped my Vette, my ass has felt no pain."

"Quit it with the lame jokes—and yeah, I'm aware I just made a pun. What's got you so freakin' cheerful?"

"Oh, I just made a little sale. Something I've been trying to unload for a long time."

He had a gallery, Luminaire, in downtown Brighton Cove and earned his living by selling art—his own paintings, and other people's. It was a hell of a lot more respectable livelihood than shooting people. Less dangerous too.

He didn't have a crew of crazed gangbangers after him.

The thought brought her down. "One of yours?" she asked, staring into her tea.

"No." He refilled his cup. "No, it's a piece I acquired years ago. Never liked it, really. Someone finally took it off my hands, and for a pretty penny too."

"A pretty penny? What are you, English?"

"I'm articulate."

"Hard to believe anyone would be shopping for art in a hurricane."

"It's not a hurricane yet. Actually, I was having the gallery boarded up when this guy from Englewood Cliffs waltzes in and makes an impulse buy."

"Cool beans." She lifted her mug. "Here's to the rich getting richer."

She heard the sour note in her voice and didn't like it.

He eyed her warily. "I'm not exactly rich. And you're in a shitty mood all of a sudden."

"Sorry."

"Something you want to talk about?"

"Oh no." She wagged a finger at him. "You're not putting me on the couch again."

He was always analyzing her psyche, and the really aggravating thing was that he was always right.

"Why not? The sessions are free. And I'm a distant relative of Dr. Freud, you know."

"Yeah, right."

"That's Dr. Bernie Freud, the proctologist." It was his turn to wag a finger. "I saw it. A tiny little smile."

"It was a wince of pain."

"I'll take what I can get. Come on, Parker. Open up. We've got all day, and there's nothing on TV. I mean that literally—the electricity's off."

"Well, okay." She sighed. "I guess there is something on my mind."

She told him about the Asian gang, omitting why

they suspected her—omitting any mention of Alec Dante at all. Des listened, his hand on his chin like that statue of the guy thinking; she forgot what it was called.

When she was through, he commented, "It's a pickle."

"Hey, that's exactly what *I* said. So what do you think I should do?"

"It's not my call. Whatever you come up with will be the right way to play it."

"I'd like to believe that."

"Don't kid yourself. You do believe it. You wouldn't have survived this long if you didn't trust your own judgment."

She stared out the window and listened to the groaning of the wind. "You're right. For a long time, I didn't trust anybody *except* myself. But now ..."

"Now?"

"I trust you, Des. You know I do."

He didn't answer.

"I trust you," she went on, forcing herself to say it, "and I'm starting to think you understand me. Which is a little scary."

"Why?"

"Because I'm no angel. Far from it."

"Who is?"

"*You* just might be."

"Me? I'm hell on wheels." He sounded uncomfortable. Apparently he wasn't any more accustomed to compliments than she was.

"I'm just being honest," she said. "Don't let it throw you."

It still amazed her that they could talk about this stuff. For a long time she'd held off telling him much about herself, because she was sure he'd freak out. Of course, he'd had suspicions—lots of people did—but suspicions could be ignored if you worked at it hard enough. Knowing for certain was a different story. After

Pascal, she'd told him openly that her sideline was killing people—but only people who deserved it, she was quick to add. She'd expected him to back up his chair and roll the hell away from her as fast as his wheels would carry him.

He hadn't. And that was the miracle of it. He'd only nodded and said, "I figured it was something like that."

Since then, she'd shared things with him. Not everything, but more than she'd shared with anyone else, ever. Having been alone for nearly her whole life, she was hardly in the habit of opening up. But she was starting to get the hang of it. What the hell, maybe it would even make her a better person, or at least slightly less of an asshole.

And for the first time, they'd begun circling the idea of intimacy, making jokes that weren't quite funny, and stray remarks that led nowhere. Neither of them wanted to broach the subject, but it was there, and they knew it.

"So ... just what exactly *are* you going to do?" he asked.

"Worry. Then worry some more. And when the bad guys show up—I'll improvise."

"Sounds like a plan."

"It's not a plan," she said irritably. "What part of 'improvise' don't you get?" She shook her head, dispelling the subject. "So ... you got anything to eat around here that doesn't require electric power?"

"I have steaks in the fridge, and a propane stove."

"You're my hero."

"I've also got wine. So I say we eat steak and drink wine and hope the Long Fong Boyz get washed away at high tide."

Bonnie smiled. "Now *that's* a plan."

11

THE GROVE STREET TOWER was a luxury high-rise in Jersey City's rapidly gentrifying downtown. Underground parking garage, twenty-four-hour security, on-site gym, indoor pool. Frank knew the building well. A couple of years ago, not long after the Tower had gone up, he'd plunked down more than a half mil for a two-bedroom unit, which he'd handed over to his nephew as a gift—the same ploy he'd pulled with the cottage on Devil's Hook. For Alec, it was a sweet deal; he could live in style, mortgage-free, with a view of the Manhattan skyline and a short walk to a PATH station. Frank had hoped the setup would help keep the kid out of trouble.

That was the problem with Alec. There was always trouble.

Frank parked on the street and approached the lobby, his body bent almost double against stinging sheets of rain. It wasn't even eight o'clock, and Sandy had yet to make landfall. The way things were going, the whole fucking state would be a wasteland by dawn.

The doorman saw him coming and flashed a look of

comical surprise. Frank knew the guy; Harry was his name. Played the horses, gave good tips on the thorough-breds at Monmouth Park.

"Mr. Lazzaro." Harry always called him that. It was a sign of respect. "What the hell you doin' out in this slop?"

"World don't stop turning just because of a little rain," Frank said with a shrug. "Alec in?"

"I don't think so. Didn't see his car in the garage when I came on duty."

"Weird. Where the Christ would he be on a night like this?" Frank assumed a cheery air. "Think he's shacking up with some nice young thing?"

"If he is, he ain't brought her around when I'm on duty."

"Maybe he's keeping her away from you. Afraid you'll make a move on her."

"Yeah, that's gotta be it."

Frank asked how the kid was doing, whether there were any problems—cops coming by, suspicious charac-ters, that kind of shit.

"Nothing like that," Harry said. "There was this one thing, but it was no big deal."

"What?"

"I guess Alec likes to party hard. Who can blame him? You're only young once, am I right? But his down-stairs neighbors started beefing about it."

"Nothing else?"

"That's all I know about."

Frank nodded, dismissing the information. He wasn't interested in a hassle over a loud stereo. Some uptight yuppie didn't do the hit.

He and Harry shot the breeze for a few minutes, talk-ing women and horses, the one subject leading naturally into the other, assisted by a little joke Frank told about a roll in the hay. Then Frank asked if he could get into Al-ec's condo, just to drop off the package in his hand. It was a bulging manila envelope, and in reality it contained nothing but today's newspaper; he'd picked up both the envelope and the paper at a 7-Eleven on his way over.

"I can take it," Harry said, "give it to him next time I see him."

Frank had anticipated this response. Since his name wasn't on the deed anymore, technically he wasn't allowed access to the unit when Alec wasn't there.

"Sure, we could play it that way," he said. "I'm just looking out for you, Harry. See, it might be better if you didn't have it on you. Get what I mean?"

Harry got it, all right. He regarded the package with unconcealed alarm. "Oh, okay, then. Sure, Mr. Lazzaro. You can go right up."

Frank rode the elevator to the eleventh floor and let himself into unit 1108 with a spare key that he'd never surrendered. The lights in the apartment dimmed now and then, but for the moment the power stayed on.

He surveyed the living room. Food containers lay everywhere, their contents starting to go bad. The walls were crowded with goofy paintings of melting clocks and people who wore their skeletons outside their skin. Modern art. Frank hated that shit.

He pulled on a pair of gloves and got down to business. He knew something about how to toss a place. He took his time, hunting through a disorganized file cabinet and sorting through the trash, sniffing out hiding places, reviewing the contents of the medicine cabinet, checking the phone log. He saved the computer until last, because he hated computers. Wished the damn things had never been invented. A pocket calculator was good enough for him. Google? Yahoo? It was like he was living in a goddamn nursery school.

Even so, he could find his way around a Windows system, though he'd never mastered that faggoty Apple shit. Fortunately his nephew owned a nice no-bullshit Hewlett-Packard and hadn't even bothered with a password. Frank inspected the files one by one. It took him more than two hours before he got to the kid's Twitter feed.

Twitter. Another stupid-ass kindergarten name. What the fuck was this world coming to?

But stupid or not, Twitter held the answers.

Alec had two accounts, one under his real name and another under the screen name SnatchSkilzXXX. Using this alias, he'd—what was the word?—tweeted some guy named Joey. Judging from Joey's camera-phone self-portraits, he was a skinny Asian kid, tatted up with gang symbols. Frank recognized the look. He was one of the Long Fong Boyz.

"Alec," he muttered with a slow shake of his head, "you dumb fuck."

His nephew, a.k.a. SnatchSkilzXXX, had sent Joey tantalizing shots of the female anatomy, claiming them as his own. He presented himself as a slutty tweener bimbo who'd seen Joey at the party and wanted to see him again, up close and very personal. A banquet of sensual delights was promised, with JPEGs of stiff nipples and a wet pussy as additional enticement.

Joey, who was just as stupid and horny as any other teenager, took the bait. After some back-and-forth teasing, in which Joey bragged about the dimensions and penetrating ability of his manhood, and SnatchSkilzXXX advertised her girlish charms in lascivious detail, they got around to arranging a rendezvous. The gang maintained an apartment at Crossgate Gardens. It might have been a safe house where they could lie low when the heat was on, or maybe a stash pad where merchandise was stored. Joey would meet his lady love there. A night of pornographic ecstasies would ensue.

Okay, they didn't phrase it exactly like that. The language was a trifle less refined. But that was the fucking gist.

Frank knew what had happened at the rendezvous. A few days ago, a kid named Joey Huang, a foot soldier for the Long Fong Boyz, had been shot dead in Crossgate Gardens.

Alec had set up Joey and taken him out. It had been neatly done, and on one level Frank admired it. But mainly he thought it was a stupid move. The Long Fong Boyz had made some forays into Frank's territory, moving in on their heroin trade, but it was nothing that couldn't be handled under the normal protocols. There was no need to take it to the level of a hit—not this soon.

Immediately after the killing, Alec had started pestering Frank with voicemails. The kid never had accepted Frank's decision to hold him at a distance from the business. Having decided to prove himself by going freelance, he'd been itching to brag about it in person, then sit back and wait for Frank to clap him on the back and welcome him into the organization.

You showed initiative, kid, Alec must have counted on hearing him say. *That's exactly what we're looking for. Looks like I've been underestimating you all these years.*

Christ.

Well, his nephew never had shown good sense. He was reckless—no impulse control. He took risks. So did Frank, sometimes. Like what he'd done to Proud American earlier today. But to get away with mayhem like that, you had to be lucky. You needed more-than-human skills and more-than-human protection. Alec had neither. The stupid kid never stood a chance.

To get ahead in this business, you had to take it slow. You had to prove you were reliable; you had to follow orders. You didn't make progress by freelancing, committing acts of reckless bullshit that would only complicate matters for middle management. Frank knew all about that. He'd come up the hard way, practicing patience, waiting for his chance.

Having made a little money in his teenage years and earning his nickname in the process, he'd established himself as a loan shark. Around that time he discovered he had a taste and a talent for violence. His clients were seldom late with their payments, and never more than once.

At first he loaned money mainly to other kids, but eventually he found a more lucrative client base consisting of small business owners who'd gotten in over their heads. Some were unable to make payroll; others had accumulated gambling debts. He was always happy to loan to those people; if they couldn't pay him back, he would simply become a silent partner in the business. By age twenty, he was part owner of a tow truck company, an auto detailing shop, a couple of junkyards, and an appliance store. Pretty good for a kid from the projects with an eighth-grade education and a drunken bum for a dad.

But he wanted more. So when a connected guy in the organization came calling, he was only too happy to listen. Though Frank was a minor player, he had come to the attention of the big boys. They believed he could be useful. They might want him to undertake the occasional odd job. "Think you can do that, Frankie?" the man asked.

He was still Frankie back then. No one called him Frankie anymore.

"I can do it," he said.

For a small cut of the action, he began picking up mysterious brown bags. Some of the bags contained money, some contained drugs, some contained other things. Frank never much cared what he was carrying. He didn't even care that much about his cut. He only cared about proving himself to his employers. A man who showed himself to be dependable was a man who could go places.

And then one day the same connected guy came to him again, this time with a more significant proposal. A troublemaker needed to be put out of the way.

"Think you can do it, Frankie?"

He had done it. He'd done whatever they asked. And now he was the underboss of the most hard-core, high-producing crew in Jersey City, in line to be a capo someday.

Alec knew about that, and wanted his piece of it. Hell, probably he wanted *all* of it. But the poor dumb kid just didn't know what was required. He wanted to take shortcuts. And one of his shortcuts had gotten him killed.

Somehow the Asians had found out who was behind the hit. They'd come after Alec and shot him twice in the chest. Frank was a little surprised they'd made it that easy on him. But maybe they'd been in a hurry.

Okay, mystery solved. But the story wasn't over, not by a long shot.

Frank might disapprove of what his nephew had done. He might not even blame the Long Fong Boyz for responding in kind. In their position, he would have done the same.

None of that mattered. A member of his family had been killed. The insult must be answered. Blood would have blood. It was the simple, inescapable logic of the animal, the predator's code.

Frank picked up the phone and got the party started.

12

Des's house came equipped with a gas fireplace, which kept the living room warm even as night came on and the temperature dropped outside. Bonnie sat with him on the couch by the fire, the two of them eating steak off plastic plates, while candles flickered on the coffee table.

"Gotta say," she observed between mouthfuls, "this is the first candlelight dinner I've had in a long time."

He smiled. "Not too keen on girly stuff, are you? Candles, flowers, fancy lingerie ..."

"I'll have you know, just this morning I was in a store that sells nothing but teddies."

"Victoria's Secret?"

"Paddington Station."

"The teddy bear place?" Des digested this information. "Is it wrong that I still find it sexy?"

"Whatever turns you on," she said lightly.

There was a pause in the conversation as they both drew back from where it was headed.

After a moment he asked, "What were you doing in there?"

"Working a case. Nothing interesting. No Jersey City bangers with long fongs were involved."

Des chewed his steak. "You seriously expect them to make a move?"

"Yeah. Yeah, I do."

"Then go after them first. Take them out before they can get to you."

She tilted her head. "Wow, Des. Bloodthirsty much?"

"It's merely a hard, practical application of realpolitik."

"I love it when you talk French."

"That was German."

"Close enough." She finished her meal and laid the plate aside. "I can't go after them because I don't know where to find them. Plus, I'd be outgunned like crazy. And speaking of crazy, these Asian gangs aren't known for being models of restraint. They dial it up to eleven."

"In what way?"

"Quentin Tarantino on crack. That kind of way."

He put aside his plate also. "You're really scared, aren't you?"

"I'm more ... antsy. I don't like waiting for someone else to make the first move."

"Well, in this weather, no one's making any moves tonight."

A sharp patter of rain on the window punctuated the thought. According to the news updates on Des's radio, Sandy was less than two hours from landfall. It was now expected to come ashore as a post-tropical cyclone, but the winds would still be hurricane strength, and the tidal surge would be massive.

"You're probably right," she said. "I'm not sure they could even get here from Jersey City right now. And if they did, they wouldn't know where to find me. Basically, everything's oo-la-la."

"I love it when *you* talk French. More wine?"

"Maybe a drop or two."

He poured. More than a drop. "So," he asked, "what's on the agenda for tonight?"

"I don't know. There's not a whole a lot to do in the dark."

"I guess that depends on what kind of entertainment you're looking for."

His eyes met hers. His gaze was bright in the candle-light, his implication unmistakable.

So there it was. The issue. Brought up as explicitly as either of them had dared. She could pretend she hadn't understood, but that would be the coward's way.

"What are *you* looking for, Des?" she asked.

"I think you know. But I don't know how you feel about it."

She took a quick, shallow breath. "I'm game, if you are. Only, we'll have to take it slowly, you know, step by step." She realized this was an unfortunate choice of words. "So to speak."

"Why?" he asked, smiling. "Is it your first time?"

"You wish. But, well, it *is* my first time ..."

With a guy who was paralyzed from the waist down, she meant.

He nodded. "Yeah, I got it."

"How about you? Have you been, um, active since you got into that chair?"

"Once or twice."

"Well, well—Des, the ladies' man. Even a cut cord doesn't take him out of commission."

"You sound almost jealous."

"Me? Nah. I'm not the jealous type." She thought about it. "Or maybe I am, a little. That's weird, huh?"

"It's sweet."

"Not an adjective that gets applied to me very often. Just who were my rivals for your affection?"

"Nobody you know."

"That's probably for the best. I wouldn't want to have to shoot 'em or anything."

"One of them was a pro."

"A bona fide lady of the evening?"

He nodded. "It was my first time after the accident. I needed some reassurance that I was up to the task."

"How'd you perform?"

"I didn't embarrass myself too much. You realize I'm not exactly functional south of the border."

"Hey, at least you won't get me knocked up."

"Glass half full."

"That's me. Rose-colored shades."

"So ... wanna go for it?"

"I've been waiting for you to ask. You'll just have to walk me through it." She winced. "Sorry. I keep making really poor choices."

"Not at all. Tonight you're making the perfect choice."

AFTER THAT, THEY did stuff in the bedroom. He showed her how to stimulate his erogenous zones. He couldn't have an erection, but every part of him above the belt line was hard as rock. At first, she was reluctant to climb on him for fear of inflicting some unspecified injury. But she got over her reservations in a hurry.

The best part was the laughter. When something didn't go as planned, they both found it hilariously absurd. She'd thought it would be impossible to get an orgasm from laughing too hard. She'd been wrong.

"GOOD FOR YOU too?" she asked when it was over. She lay beside him in bed and resisted lighting a cig, if only to avoid the cliché.

"Very good. Better than the pro I hired. Maybe you could consider this a whole new sideline."

"Just the kind of compliment every gal wants to hear."

"You mean you don't find it flattering to be favorably compared to a prostitute?"

"Oh hell, yes I do. I just don't like to admit it. It might endanger my society debutante status. So tell me, did you have a for-real orgasm?"

"Sure did. A full-body orgasm. It doesn't matter if the usual equipment is on the fritz. There are workarounds. And you know, ninety percent of an orgasm is mental."

"Where'd you read that?"

"Gimp Monthly." She heard him chuckle. "No, I just made it up."

"You're weird, Des."

"Says the female hitman who's being stalked by the Asian mob."

"Gotta admit, that was one of your better comebacks."

He pulled himself higher on the pillows. "Go on. Light one. You know you want to."

She sighed. He was right. She really did want to.

A match flared, and she started up a cigarette. Des, of course, didn't smoke. Healthy eater, workout addict—if he had any vices, she'd missed them. Well, until now. Some of the things they'd done tonight had to qualify as vices in somebody's book.

She nursed the cigarette in silence, trying to blow smoke rings, a skill she'd never mastered. Branches flogged the side of the house. Rain flung itself fitfully against the windows.

"So ... think we'll be doing this again?" he asked.

"On a regular basis, I'm thinking. Why not?"

"I just wondered if you might want someone who isn't, you know, half a man."

"You're *all* man, Des. Don't kid yourself."

"I'm damaged, though."

"Everybody's damaged. Everybody has issues. Look"—she heaved a breath—"I shot a guy today, for Chrissakes."

She wondered how he would take this news. To his credit, he didn't even flinch.

"He probably deserved it," Des said.

"Yeah, I think he did. But I haven't told you what his deal was, so you don't really know."

"Okay. What was his deal?"

She wasn't sure he really wanted to know. He didn't sound too enthusiastic about it. But she wanted to tell him. Wanted to justify herself, she guessed.

"The client approached me about three weeks ago. Not too long after I came clean with you about what I really do. This was my first case since then. I mean, my first ..."

"I got it." He sounded tense. She wondered if sharing the story was a good idea. Oh hell, she was committed now.

"He had medical records and a police report. His wife had been raped. The police report said it happened on a PATH train, late at night. Some vagrant. But, he says, that's not the real story. They made it up because they had to file a report when they got medical attention. The truth is, the wife was raped in the elevator of their condo building, and the rapist was their upstairs neighbor."

"Why all the deception?" Des had turned his head away, but at least he was asking questions. She took that as a positive.

"Because they're terrified of the guy. He's a psycho. And the rumor is, he's mobbed up. Everyone's afraid of him."

"Even so—"

"You haven't heard it all. In the elevator the guy made threats. He told the wife that if anyone found out, his relatives would see to it that both her and her hubby stopped breathing. And the cops wouldn't be able to protect them. Then he zipped up his pants and went on his way."

She remembered how Aaron Walling's voice shook as he delivered the details. Alec Dante had stopped the elevator between floors and raped Rachel Walling against the wall, then held a knife to her throat and whispered in her ear.

You know who my uncle is? Frank Lazzaro. Name mean anything to you? Look it up, bitch. He fucking owns this city. Talk to the cops, and he'll know. Talk to the building management, he'll know. Talk to anybody, and you're dead. You and the good doctor. Dead.

He'd nicked her with the blade for emphasis, drawing a single teardrop of blood.

"Sounds like a real charmer." Des's voice was low and bitter.

"Yeah, he's a regular Don Juan. He made it clear that if they went to the cops, they'd be asking for a mob hit. So the husband came to me."

"How'd he even know about you?"

"That's a question I never ask. It's not like I can advertise on Craigslist. Somehow word gets around."

"Could you be sure he was telling the truth? Maybe he was, you know, setting up this other guy for some reason."

"You have a suspicious mind, Des. I like that. Truth is, I wasn't completely convinced, even though I saw the medical file. And as you know, I won't whack just anybody. I've got standards. So I looked into it, did my own research. It's what they called due diligence."

"And it checked out?"

"Oh yeah. The guy's a loser from way back. His rap sheet could be a friggin' miniseries. Bar fights, sexual assaults, reckless driving—drag racing or some shit. Drugs too. The works. He was a human hand grenade, and it didn't take much to pull the pin."

"Why wasn't he in jail?"

"Good lawyers, supplied by his relatives."

"He really was mob-connected?"

"Yeah. Not in the organization, but looked after, taken care of. I think this guy was too unstable for them to actually use. Think about that. Too unstable for La Cosa Nostra. Anyway, he did the deed, all right. It would be doing the world a solid to take him out. And I was in a charitable mood."

"Did the wife know? About you, I mean?"

"No, hubby was keeping it on the down-low. He didn't want his wife in on it. Which was fine by me. That's one less person who might be tempted to blab." She took a breath. "So ... you still think he probably deserved it?"

He turned to her. She wasn't sure, but she thought he was smiling. "There's no 'probably' about it."

It was what she'd needed to hear. Until this moment, she hadn't realized just how badly she needed it.

"Hold me," she whispered, surprised by the urgency of her voice. "Just hold me, Des."

He held her in the dark, and the storm raged.

13

FRANK'S CELL PHONE rang at ten o'clock, giving him the news he'd been waiting for. A couple of his guys had picked up one of the Long Fong Boyz. The young man in question was currently being detained in an industrial distribution warehouse in the Heights district at the north end of Jersey City.

"What's this all about, Frank?" the caller, a none-too-bright goombah named Belletiere, inquired in a wheedling tone.

"Never mind about that. It's something personal. Just hold him there and wait for me."

Frank left Victoria sitting up with the twins, who were restless tonight, disturbed by the storm. He made it from his home to the warehouse in twenty minutes, shooting through rainswept intersections with dead traffic signals, laying his fist on the horn.

Belletiere's partner, Jimmy Rocca—known to all as Firehose, an only slightly exaggerated tribute to a portion of his anatomy—stood in the doorway of the big brick building, partly shielded from the hard downpour. Frank took a moment to confirm that no one had seen his guys make the snatch.

"Nah, we did it clean. You know the alley, runs behind Golden Duck?" Golden Duck was a Chinese restaurant that doubled as a gang hangout. "We was watching it. Hour ago, one of the assholes comes out to take a piss. They do that when the toilet backs up."

"Remind me never to eat there."

"The kid was tweaking on something, all fucked up. We grab him with his dick in his hand before he can say boo. Bundle him into the Caddy's trunk and bring him here."

Rocca was smarter than his partner, and he didn't ask what was up. He knew Frank would tell him if he needed to know.

Before long, it might be necessary. The Long Fong Boyz, having hit Alec, would be expecting retaliation. But Frank didn't want to escalate the situation any sooner than he had to.

He'd spent the past few hours mapping strategies for a gang war. Going to the mattresses, the old-timers would call it. Like in *The Godfather*.

Frank hadn't seen street combat in years. He was looking forward to it. But there was no need to rush into things. First he had to have a little talk with a kid who'd chosen the worst possible place and time to take a pee.

He and Rocca went in the front way, through a security door—bullet-resistant, fabricated of 16-gauge steel with a 10-gauge armor plate welded inside. The door opened onto a small lobby with an office at the far end. Right before the office there was a doorway to the main room of the warehouse, a single windowless space two stories high. The place was fucking huge. What was the word? Cavernous. It was also pretty empty just now. The storm had indefinitely delayed Frank's latest shipments, leaving the rows of shelves and yards of poured concrete floor ominously bare.

At the far end, Belletiere loitered by the Cadillac, parked near the freight door. He and Rocca had driven inside and shut themselves in before hauling their prisoner out of the trunk.

The power was out, of course. It was out almost everywhere. The two goombahs must have raised and lowered the freight door by hand. Around the warehouse they'd set up a few kerosene lanterns, which threw big wavering shadows on the towering ladders that ran on rails along the shelves. Outside, the rain hammered and the wind made ghost-story sounds.

In the center of the room sat a small, solitary figure, a solo actor on a giant stage.

Tommy Chang had been stripped naked and ducttaped to a straightback chair, his arms secured to the armrests. Tattoos crawled all over his body. Columns of Chinese characters ran down his neck. Dragons growled from his chest and thighs. Buddha scowled out of Tommy's six-pack abs, frowning harder whenever the kid sucked in a breath. Gang tats, spell tats—powerful mojo. Every drop of ink was black, without a touch of color, except for the blood red face of an evil chink sorcerer riding Tommy's shoulder like a bearded gnome.

Ugly shit. Fucking primitive, tribal. Sometimes Frank felt like civilization was being overrun by zoo animals.

The kid was scared, obviously. Whatever he'd huffed, snorted, or mainlined had lost its effect, and he was lucid enough to know he was in some real pretty shit. His skin, oiled with sweat, glistened in the overhead light. His bare feet bumped restlessly on the floor.

But he tried playing it cool as Frank walked up to him. "So here he is, the big fuckin' man. What you gonna do to me, Guido? Gonna fuck me up, pizza boy?"

"Something like that," Frank said quietly.

"Bring it. Play your fuckin' games. I got nothin' to say, so fuck you."

Frank had heard it all before. He leaned over Tommy, studying his hands. Even the kid's fingers were tattooed; miniature skulls glared up from his knuckles.

"Nice art," Frank said. "But mine's got more power."

Loosening his necktie, he withdrew a necklace from inside his shirt and let it dangle like a hypnotist's watch before Tommy's face. Hanging from the chain was a small gold ring engraved with the image of Santa Muerte.

Tommy seemed to know that image, or maybe he merely sensed its meaning. A shudder moved through him. But his voice was steady when he said, "Eat shit."

Frank smiled. "I already had dinner. But I know somebody who hasn't." He nodded to his guys. "Bring out Virgil."

Belletiere went through a side door into the office. He didn't look happy. Him and Virgil, they didn't get along so good. And like most people, he hated rats.

Rats had a bad rep, in Frank's opinion. It was because of that plague shit. Hell, everybody was diseased in the fucking Dark Ages. There was no reason to single out rodents for abuse.

Frank liked rats, and he liked them mean. There was nothing meaner than a damn wharf rat. Every so often, he set traps down by the docks, cages that would snare the greedy creatures without harming them. They were good and frantic by the time he picked them up—he always did the job personally—and his practiced eye could judge right away which ones had the true killer spirit. The weaklings and layabouts he drowned. The fighters went into the ring.

The ring was an arena of sorts, an oval of sand fenced in by chicken wire, in the cellar of a dry-cleaning establishment in which Frank had a half interest. The ring was where Frank sicced his rats on each other in paired match-ups, fights to the death.

As a kid he'd gotten his start with rat fights. The

MICHAEL PRESCOTT

venue was a shuttered bowling alley on 16th Street near the projects where he grew up. On a nightly basis he attracted a respectable crowd—respectable in size, if not in other in any other way. Wagering was done. Frank charged an admission fee; later he garnered greater profits by participating in the betting, typically with the help of a proxy who placed bets for him. He improved his odds by rigging the matches, dosing a long-shot contestant with PCP to make him especially savage, or weakening the favorite with a nonlethal swallow of warfarin. It was his first business venture and, in terms of his percentage of profit, still one of his most lucrative; outlay was minimal, and there was no limit on the return.

Frank didn't arrange rat fights for spectators anymore. It was too small-time. But he still enjoyed watching the animals go at it, so he staged fights for himself. The contrasts were a Darwinian competition, a vivid illustration of survival of the fittest. Frank knew about that stuff. He'd made it through the eighth grade, even if at sixteen he'd been the oldest kid in his class. When he wasn't busy sneaking blow jobs from whores in training in the girls' bathroom, or running a numbers game in the neighborhood, or catching and exhibiting his rats, he learned about electron shells and George Washington, isosceles triangles and *The Catcher in the Rye*, and Darwin. A lot of that shit didn't stick with him any longer than the next test, if even that long, but Darwin made an impression. It felt true. It matched what he'd seen for himself. The earth belonged to those who would claw and tear and kill and never fucking quit. That old line about the meek inheriting the earth was just a con, a way to soften up the marks so they'd offer their throats to the knife. The meek inherited nothing. They didn't even merit respect, and without respect, a man was so much garbage. And respect was always grounded in fear.

Frank might not have been exactly an A student, but

that was one lesson he'd learned well.

In the rat fights, the weaker and more cowardly specimens were inevitably weeded out, until only the strongest were left. The survivors of many fights were something akin to super-rats, small miracles of ferocity and cunning. They made your average rat, even your average wharf rat, look like a fucking Chihuahua. And at the moment, the best of them was Virgil.

Belletiere brought out Virgil from the office, where he lived in regal isolation from the other rodents. Being a superstar had its perks. Virgil dined on raw ribeye steak and liver pâté. After each victory, he was allowed a sip of champagne.

But for all that, he wasn't going soft. He was huge, nearly two feet long from nose to tail, a giant among rats, weighing in at a hefty two pounds. His coarse brown fur was streaked with gray, and his evil eyes always spoiling for a fight. Even now he was scrabbling at the bars of his cage as Belletiere carried it by its handle. Belletiere looked nervous. So did Tommy Chang.

The kid squirmed like crazy when Belletiere and Rocca pulled up a crate and set the cage on top, directly abutting the left armrest. Virgil shifted restlessly inside. A low metallic clanking could be heard, the sound of a chain that ran from a harness around his neck to a spindle at the back of the cage, controlled by a hand crank outside the bars.

Tommy Chang was taking in all this, but the bewildered expression on his face suggested he didn't quite get the picture. Frank could have explained, but he'd never been real big on speeches. Anyway, a demonstration would be more effective.

"Do it," he said.

Rocca lifted the cage door. Belletiere turned the crank, unspooling the chain.

Virgil, straining at his leash, emerged from the cage.

The rat's black-button eyes were fixed on Tommy's hand, trapped on the armrest, secured with multiple turns of duct tape. Another creature might have hesitated to attack larger prey. Virgil would never have survived his many bouts in the ring if he'd been capable of fear. For him, there was no hesitation.

He set to work on Tommy's fingers, biting and gnawing voraciously, reducing the tattooed knuckles to knobs of bleeding flesh.

14

SHORTLY AFTER TEN at night, Bonnie woke up with a plan.

Alec Dante's Porsche was an awfully expensive set of wheels to park in a crime-ridden shit hole like Greenville. He had done his best to minimize the chances of having the car stripped or swiped by leaving it in the same multistory parking structure where Bonnie had parked. On her way out, she'd tossed her ticket stub into the backseat with the rest of the litter.

This simple fact gave her an idea.

The ticket was stamped with the time and date. She could plant the stub in Dante's car, then hope the police checked out the cottage to see why the owner's vehicle had remained there during the storm. They would find Dante's body in the cellar and the ticket stub in the Porsche; the ticket would place him near Crossgate Gardens on the night of Joey Huang's murder. With any luck they would make the connection and pin Dante's murder on the Long Fong Boyz.

Bonnie didn't care about that. What mattered was that word about Dante was sure to get out, either officially or through backchannels. With any luck, the Boyz would learn that he looked good for the hit on Huang, and maybe, just maybe, a certain small-town PI would be off the hook.

It could work. She only had to hope the police would be smart enough to put it together. She didn't have much confidence in the investigative smarts of the authorities, but if she laid it out nice and obvious, even the dumbest lawman ought to catch on.

She was throwing on her clothes when Des opened his eyes, squinting in the dark.

"Running out on me?" he asked. She couldn't tell if it was a joke.

"Something I need to do. I may be gone awhile."

"Gone where?"

"Devil's Hook." She adjusted the cloche on her head.

"You can't go out in this weather."

"Sure I can. I'm crazy, Des. Haven't you figured that out by now?"

"You'll never make it. The roads are a mess, and according to the radio the island's been sealed off to traffic. Half of it's probably underwater by now."

"Hey, if it was easy, women 'n' children would be doing it." She'd picked up that expression somewhere, and kinda liked it.

She leaned over and kissed him, noticing a faint stubble on his cheek. Never before had she seen him less than perfectly groomed.

"Keep the bed warm," she said in what she hoped was a voice of seduction. "I'll be back."

His voice stopped her at the bedroom door. "Why Devil's Hook?"

"I'm dropping in on a friend. He won't know it, though."

"Why not?"

"'Cause he's the one I killed."

Rain was falling heavily as she left the house and ran

to the Jeep. Des's one-car garage was occupied by his handicap van, so she'd had to park in the driveway, leaving the Jeep exposed to the elements. She was relieved to see that no debris had landed on it, though a couple of walnut trees had come down across the street.

Climbing in, she rooted around in the backseat litter until she found the ticket stub, half hidden among fast food cartons and empty water bottles. At least it hadn't gone into a trashcan. Sometimes being a slob paid off.

She settled into the driver's seat. The Jeep's fuel gauge showed more than half a tank—a good thing, since finding a working gas station might be tricky for a while. The power outage was predicted to last a week or more. People always said they wanted to go back to nature. It seemed like nature was taking them at their word.

She backed out of the driveway, maneuvered around the fallen trees, and headed down the street.

As Des had predicted, the roads were a mess. Several times she had to alter her course to bypass a flooded street or avoid downed trees and utility lines. The local ponds had overspilled their banks, flooding streets and homes. Even the drier roadways were checkered with clumps of seaweed and hills of sand. Most residents of Brighton Cove had evacuated; they would be returning to waterlogged carpets, shattered windows, and collapsed chimneys.

Finally she reached Garfield Avenue, the main route to the highway. Just past the railroad station, the lightbars of scattered squad cars rotated like disco balls.

Shit.

The cops had set up a checkpoint. They must have blocked off all other access points, and now they were protecting the one available means of entry or exit. For any other resident it wouldn't have been a problem, but Maguire's troops had been told to ride her hard, and she could expect a once-over at the roadblock. If they wanted to look in her purse, they might find the unregistered .32.

She pulled to a stop, thinking she ought to hide the gun under the driver's seat, and then Sammy came to life, singing a Beatles tune.

It was another of her preprogrammed special alerts. The song was "Help!," and it meant that the silent alarm in her duplex had just gone off.

"Fuck," she said, steering the Jeep into a U-turn. Somebody was breaking into her place.

If she was lucky, it was just some looter. But lately it seemed she was all out of luck. The way things were going, it was probably the Long Fong Boyz, or maybe somebody else with murder in mind.

The cops wouldn't be responding. Her alarm wasn't linked to a monitoring service. She'd never wanted to give the authorities an excuse to go sniffing around her place. Which meant, as usual, she was on her own.

Well, she'd never been one to run from a fight. She only hoped she could get there before the bad guys amscrayed.

She stomped on the gas pedal and plowed through deep puddles, sending up hissing sprays of rainwater. Twice she had to swerve around detached tree limbs blocking the street; once, she veered onto the sidewalk. What the hell, there were no pedestrians.

She only wished she hadn't had so much wine with dinner. At times like this, it helped to have a clear head.

Her duplex was a mile away. She reached it in two minutes, slowing only as she turned onto her street. By then she'd turned off Sammy to make the Beatles shut up.

No unfamiliar vehicles were parked by her place. No strangers were inside. But her front door hung open, proof that someone had been inside.

And maybe was still there. She didn't think so, though. Had it been an ambush, the door would have been shut. There was no point in advertising a break-in if you were trying to take the homeowner by surprise.

She parked curbside, aware that she was putting herself in an ideal position to be shot by anyone lying in wait. Once out of the Jeep, she would be exposed to fire, with no cover or concealment until she was inside the house. And even then, she might be walking into a trap. On the plus side, it was this kind of situation that kept life interesting.

Gripping the gun in her purse with one hand, she stepped onto the street. If someone was drawing a bead on her, she could only hope they weren't a very good shot. If they missed with their first attempt, she could throw herself flat and try to return fire.

Slowly, ignoring the stinging rain, she moved around the Jeep, reluctant to part with it until she had to. The vehicle might be her last chance of refuge if gunfire broke out.

But no one was shooting at her, and the open door continued to beckon. She made a run for it.

The distance to the door was short, less than fifty feet, but it took her forever to get there. She seemed to be moving in slow motion, like an astronaut on a spacewalk. The rain fell in surreal silence. All she heard was the distant slap of her shoes on the walkway and the answering beat of her heart in her ears.

Then the door came up, and reality shifted back to normal speed. She pivoted inside, dropping into a half crouch, the gun out of her purse and swinging in a half circle as she panned the room.

She crept forward, leaving the door open at her back in case she needed to beat a retreat. Her flashlight would have been helpful, but she kept it off, not wanting to make herself a target.

Little had been disturbed. Her laptop sat on the dining table where she'd left it when the power went out. Some drawers and closets had been opened, but the job was sloppy, haphazard, rushed. Most likely the intruders had seen the alarm keypad by the door. Realizing they had no choice but to trigger the alarm, they'd gone in fast. Not finding her, they hadn't stuck around.

Given how cursory the search had been, she wasn't surprised to find the floor trap undisturbed. She lifted the loose floorboard and took inventory. Four unregistered guns. Two silencers. Extra ammo—magazines and loose rounds. Two telescopic sights. One long gun, specially modified and broken down. One tripod. One night vision scope. Two flashbang grenades. Three sets of fake ID. A bunch of cheap flip phones she'd picked up to use as burners. Assorted bugs and related gear.

Given the high probability that her new friends would make a repeat appearance in the near future, she decided the best course of action was to arm herself to the teeth. She found a tote bag in the closet and dumped all the guns inside, along with the night scope and most of the ammo and, what the hell, the flashbangs too. She didn't know what she might need, but she intended to be ready.

With her bag of goodies in tow, she left the duplex, rearming the system and locking the door.

It was a safe bet the Long Fong Boyz had paid her a visit. But they hadn't done any real harm. Maybe they weren't as hard-core as advertised. Anyway, if her ticket stub ploy worked, she might be able to throw them off her trail.

She returned to the Jeep, settling behind the wheel. It would be a good idea to hide the tote bag under the blanket in the rear compartment, in case the cops at the checkpoint gave her a hard time. She added the .32 to the bag, turned in her seat to push the bag under the blanket in back, and found herself facing the muzzle of a gun.

"Don't do anything stupid, Parker," a male voice said from the shadows. "Be cooperative."

It didn't look like she had much choice.

15

AT FIRST, TOMMY CHANG didn't scream. Even as his forefinger was stripped down to red bone, he kept silent, jaws clenched, eyes squeezed shut. His feet beat a manic drumroll. The Buddha on his belly scowled more fiercely than ever. His self-control was impressive to witness.

Rocca and Belletiere did their best not to look. They were made men and tough bastards, but even they couldn't stand to watch too much of this show. Frank never blinked, never turned away. He could take it. Like Virgil, he was harder, crueler than his peers. That was why he was number one. He ruled over his personal rat pack, his teeth ands claws the sharpest, his glittering, alert eyes never missing a thing.

After several minutes, Frank made a cutting gesture, and Belletiere reversed the chain, reeling Virgil back into the cage. The rat's whiskers and claws were dyed a deep carmine. The top joints of two of Tommy's fingers had been chewed clean off. Naked bone showed through a patchwork of lacerated skin. Blood pooled on the armrest and pattered in a red rain on the floor.

Frank gave the kid a few minutes to recover. While waiting, he stepped into the office and phoned home. Victoria answered.

"You put the kids down?" Frank asked.

"Finally." She sounded tired. Lately she always sounded tired.

Frank had thought having kids would help his marriage, bring back some of the old spark, but it hadn't worked out that way. His wife had little to say to him these days. She seemed scared all the time. And fuck it all, she'd dared to mention divorce. She had to know it was impossible. Frank Lazzaro did not surrender the things that were his, and his wife was one of those things.

"Well, get some rest yourself," he said, playing nice.

"Are you coming home soon, Frank?"

"Not for a while."

"What could you possibly have to do so late on a night like this?"

He bristled. "Like that's any of your fucking business? Like you get to tell me how I spend my time?"

He heard her nervous intake of breath. "I'm sorry, Frank. I didn't mean anything."

"I'll be there when I feel like it. You start giving me orders, maybe it's time for another attitude adjustment." The last such adjustment, inflicted after she'd uttered the d-word, had sent Victoria to the ER.

"I'm sorry," she said again. Her voice dragged lower with hopeless weariness. "Really ... I'm sorry."

"You need to stop riding me."

"I'm sorry, Frank."

"I got a lot of shit to deal with, and I don't need any fucking bullshit from you."

"I'm sorry."

"You just keep your mouth shut and look after those babies. It's all you're fucking good for."

"I'm sorry."

"Stop saying you're sorry. It's fucking annoying."

She was silent. He gripped the phone and thought about smashing things.

"We'll work this out later," he said finally. "Count on it."

He ended the call, satisfied that he'd given her something to think about.

First the crack about divorce, and now she was questioning his business. Jesus. When every damn day he was busting his hump to provide for his fucking family. Did she think it was easy, moving the products he specialized in? On this end, he had to supervise the street crews who were out every night boosting luxury cars for export to the port of Aqaba in Jordan. The cars needed dealer invoices and transporter plates and die-cut VINS, and any built-in tracking system, like LoJack, had to be disabled. And there were rules. Leather seats weren't ideal; a lot of Arabs didn't like leather. Sedans were better than coups; a fair number of the vehicles ended up as taxis or cop cars. Light colors were better than dark; the merciless desert sun was hard on a car with a dark color scheme.

At Aqaba, his freighters would take on new cargo for the return trip—granite blocks hollowed out with a diamond-tipped drill and packed with Moroccan hashish, rope carpets cleverly interwoven with heroin from a lab in Istanbul. Plenty of legitimate merchandise, too. All of it was destined for a pier in Newark, where Frank maintained three Customs agents on a private payroll. Their only job was to look the other way.

He'd built all that from the ground up, starting with the rat fights in the projects. And still she didn't respect him. That was the problem.

But she would. Oh, yes. He would see to that.

He returned to the kid duct-taped to the chair.

"Feel like talking, Tommy?"

"Blow me."

Frank batted him across the face with the back of his

hand. His wedding ring left a long bleeding gash in the bastard's cheek.

"Do not disrespect me. I am life and death to you. You got that? You will bow down to me."

"Suck my cock, guinea."

Frank raised his hand for another blow, then remembered that he had a better option.

"Your call," he said with menacing calmness.

With a nod, he let his boys know that it was time for round two.

This time Tommy did scream. His head whipped back and forth, and crazed cries erupted from his throat. But when Virgil was withdrawn, the kid remained defiant. Though his middle finger had now come off entirely, severed at the third knuckle, he wouldn't beg or give in. On the contrary, he rattled off an inventive string of ethnic slurs, many involving grease.

In round three he lost his ring finger. After that, his voice started to crack like a twelve-year-old's, but he went on trying to mock.

"You can't hurt me, you fuckin' wops, fuckin' greaseball apes. You can't make me talk."

Frank kinda liked him. The little slant had guts. Frank wasn't prejudiced—well, no more than anybody. He respected the Asians, especially the Vietnamese and the Chinese. Tough, wiry little bastards. They were ruthless, showed no mercy, took no prisoners. Nowadays his own organization had grown semi-legitimate, and he had to watch his step, maintain a degree of respectability, but these young chinks were reckless and crazy and they didn't give a shit. They expected to die before they made it to twenty-five, and they only wanted to make as much mayhem as possible while they could. Santa Muerte would have approved, and so would the black beast.

But nobody could hold out indefinitely against this kind of pain. When Rocca and Belletiere moved to the cage to face the other armrest, where Virgil was poised to go to work on Tommy's right hand, the kid began to cry.

"Okay, don't do it no more, I'll talk to you, I'll fuckin' talk ..."

People said torture wasn't effective, because the victim wouldn't tell the truth. This was bullshit. Break a man's spirit and he would tell you everything. He would be too beaten down to lie. You just had to know when the breaking point had been reached. It was an intuitive thing. Frank could sense it. Smell it, almost. He knew when a guy was shamming, and when he was sincerely broken.

Tommy Chang was broken. No fucking doubt.

"Sorry about your art," Frank said after ushering his subordinates out of earshot. All the skull tats were gone, along with most of Tommy's left hand.

Tommy said nothing, only shivered.

"What do they call you, kid? What's your nick?"

"Fish Face."

"Heh. It suits you. Okay, Fish Face, let's talk." Frank bent close. "I want to know about Alec Dante."

"Who?"

"My nephew. Devil's Hook. Don't play dumb, fish-fuck. You got a lot more parts you can lose."

Tommy shook his head miserably. "Ain't shinin' you, man. I dunno any Dante or any Devil's Hook."

"We can butt that cage up against the chair seat, let old Virgil have a go at your junk."

"Swear to God, I don't know what you're fuckin' talking about."

"I guess you don't know any Joey Huang either."

"Joey?" The kid's eyes lifted in relief. "Sure, I knew Joey. Is that what this is about? The PI?"

Frank cocked his head to the left. He was a little deaf in his right ear, a consequence of a firearm that had gone off a bit too close, and he wanted to be sure he heard every word. "What PI?"

"The hitter. The bitch."

"What the fuck you talking about?"

"She did the hit on Joey. We got witnesses."

"Who did? Give me a name."

"Parker. Bonnie Parker. She's a PI in one of them little beach towns. Brighton Cove, it's called."

Bonnie Parker. The name meant squat to Frank. And he knew she hadn't aced Joey. His nephew had done that job. But the Long Fong Boyz seemed to think otherwise.

"The wits saw her pull the trigger?" Frank asked dubiously.

"No, man. But they saw her at Crossgate at the right time. And she's a pro. She calls herself a PI, but on the side she takes on contracts."

It sounded crazy. "You're shitting me."

"Swear to fuckin' God, man. She's got a rep. Couple of our guys heard of her. Patrick says she's a stone killer."

He meant Patrick Chiu, the generalissimo of this private army. Frank hadn't met him, but from what he'd heard, Chiu was smart and plugged in. If he bought the story about the PI, there must be something to it.

So there was a small-town PI moonlighting as a hitter. A fucking lady hitter at that.

She hadn't killed Joey, but it looked like she'd been in the building when Alec was there. No way it was a coincidence. And if she hadn't been after Joey Huang, she must have been tailing Alec.

It was the only answer. It explained why Tommy Chang didn't know shit about what had gone down in Devil's Hook. The Long Fong Boyz hadn't had anything to do with it. This PI, Parker—she was the one who'd put two .38 slugs in Alec's chest.

If the PI had done the job, then it wasn't likely to be any kind of gang hit. Somebody with a personal beef had hired her.

"So if you know who hit Joey," he said to Tommy, "what are your people doing about it?"

The kid managed a sickly smile. "We gonna put her deep under the soil. Parker doesn't know it, but she's one dead bitch."

Frank nodded. She was dead, all right. But he didn't want Patrick Chiu's merry band of dragon-fuckers taking her out. He intended to reserve that pleasure for himself.

"Okay, Tommy. I'm gonna let you go now."

A moan shuddered through the kid, the complaint of a beaten animal. "No, man, you're gonna kill me. I fuckin' know you are."

"Chill out. All I wanted was information. I was never gonna kill you."

"Seriously, man? Seriously?"

"Seriously," Frank said, and from inside his jacket he pulled out a big black HK .45, the kind of gun known to aficionados as a manstopper, and he shot Tommy Chang in the face.

16

IN THE TIME it took her to hitch in a breath, Bonnie understood. One of the people who'd invaded her home had hidden in the Jeep's backseat. That person was now pointing a gun at her face.

"Turn around, Parker," he said, "and drive." His voice was uninflected and strangely calm. It was the voice of someone accustomed to obedience. A leader, not a follower. An educated voice.

She turned to face forward. The gun's muzzle kissed the nape of her neck.

"You're Chiu," she said, "right?"

"Just drive, please."

She noticed he didn't deny it. "Where?"

"Not very far."

"What direction?"

"East."

The beach. That wasn't good. Nobody went to the beach during a hurricane.

She put the Jeep into gear and pulled a U-turn, heading east. Behind her, headlights flared. Another vehicle was following. A Cadillac Escalade, black.

"Your friends?" she asked with a nod at the rearview mirror.

"That's right. I always have backup. Too bad you don't."

If not for the other car, she could have tried something desperate—steer the Jeep into a skid, hope to throw Chiu off-balance long enough for her to grab a gun from her bag. The odds weren't good, but she might stand a chance.

The Escalade changed all that. Even if she took out Chiu, she could never defend herself against his goons. She was outgunned, hemmed in. All she could do was talk. Chiu seemed rational enough. He might be open to persuasion.

"I thought you guys had cleared out," she said.

"The break-in was only a ploy. We were pretty sure you weren't home."

"Why?"

"No vehicle in your garage."

"Oh."

"We took a quick look around, just in case we were wrong. Incidentally, your place is a sty."

"Hey, gimme a break. It's not like I was expecting company."

"When we confirmed you weren't there, we waited on a side street to see if the alarm reeled in members of the law enforcement community—or you."

"I'm not real tight with the cops."

"Neither am I."

"We've got a lot in common. It could be the basis for a beautiful friendship."

"I wouldn't count on it. You've been messing with us, Veronica Mars. That wasn't a very intelligent thing to do."

"Veronica Mars? Seriously?"

"You prefer a different pop-culture reference? Nancy Drew? Buffy? Snooki?"

"Definitely not Snooki. You know, you don't sound like a gangsta type."

"I went to Towson University in Baltimore. Got a bachelor's in business administration. But I can talk street when I have to. What's in the bag?"

The change of subject took her by surprise.

"Guns and stuff."

"Arming for battle?"

"I just like to be prepared."

She heard him rummaging in the tote, but the gun never left her neck.

"Hit kits, extra-capacity mags. This is some quality gear, Annie Oakley."

"Glad you like it."

"Are these grenades?"

"They're flashbangs. You know, for—"

"Distraction and disorientation. I know. Now what would a nice girl like you be doing with a pair of concussion grenades?"

"I picked up three of them for a job last year. Turns out I only needed one."

He set the bag aside and leaned forward. "How old are you, Parker?"

"Twenty-eight. Why?"

"What's your birth month?"

"June. I'm a Gemini. You?"

He ignored the question. "You were born in the Year of the Rat. According to the Chinese zodiac, that makes you smart, adaptable, and unstable."

"Fits me to a T."

"I was born in the Year of the Dragon. Which makes me ambitious, energetic, arrogant."

"You believe in horoscopes?"

He laughed. "I believe in nothing. Except loyalty to my associates. You know, like Joey Huang."

"Look," she said, keeping her eyes on the windshield

wipers as they beat rivers of rain off the glass, "I know you think I hit Huang. But I didn't."

He didn't bother to acknowledge her denial. "Those grenades remind me of a gambit used by old Sing Dock of the Hip Sing Tong. He was a highbinder in the Tong Wars. The great Mock Duck hired him. That led to the Chinese Theater massacre of 1905."

"Can we focus on me, please? You know, the girl with the gun to her head?"

"Sing Dock didn't use flashbangs, of course. He used firecrackers. Tossed them into the audience in the middle of the show. Chaos, panic, everybody running for the exits. In the confusion, Sing Dock's men gunned down four of the On Leong Tong and got away clean."

"I don't care about that."

"I do. It's my history. And history has a way of repeating itself. Mock Dock has been gone a long time, but people still know his name. I intend to be what he was. And when I'm gone, people will know my name too."

"Will you just listen to me?"

"Why should I? There's nothing you can say. Taking out one of ours—did you really think we'd let you stay alive after that?"

"I was there, in Crossgate Gardens. I admit it. But it had nothing to do with your guy." She talked fast, trying to get it all in before they reached the beach. "I was tailing Alec Dante. He went into Crossgate Gardens. He must've killed Joey."

"You should have known we would identify you. And once we did, your life would be forfeit."

"I told you, it was Alec Dante who did the hit."

"Who is Alec Dante, and why would he touch one of my people?"

"He's Frank Lazzaro's nephew."

"If Lazzaro were starting a war, he would target all our soldiers. Bodies would be dropping. We wouldn't need you to tell us about it."

"I think Alec was freelancing. He was doing it on his own."

"One man taking on my whole crew?"

"He was trying to get in good with his uncle."

"I don't think so, Squeaky Fromme. It might make sense if Joey wasn't our only casualty. But he is."

"I can't explain it. My only interest was Alec Dante. I took care of him this morning. It was something personal for a client. It had nothing to do with you or Joey."

"You never messed with us?"

"No. Never."

"Then how do you know who I am?"

"The local cops told me the Long Fong Boyz were after me. I researched you online."

The gun didn't waver. "You're feeding me a line, Princess."

"Everything I've said is true."

"Can you prove this pretty story?"

"I'll give you Dante's mug shot. You can show it to the people at Crossgate Gardens, see if they saw him there that night."

"And meantime, you continue breathing?"

"Breathing's always been real high on my agenda."

"Sorry, Parker. I call bullshit. At this moment you'd say anything to keep your heart pumping. You'd tell me the man in the moon did the hit. Or Elvis, maybe. Was Elvis there? Is he here right now?"

She swallowed. "I'm pretty sure Elvis has left the building."

"Yes, I think he has." He waved the gun. "Pull in there."

They'd arrived at Ocean Drive. A line of empty parking spaces stretched along the east side of the street. She steered the Jeep into the nearest space. The Escalade glided in next to her.

She gave it one last try. "Just look into what I'm saying."

Chiu sighed, bored with her. "I don't need to look."

"What if you're making a mistake?"

"What if I am? What difference does it make?"

"It makes a hell of a difference to me."

"Then you're looking at it wrong. Your life, Parker, isn't anything special. You're no more important than a dog or a rat. Everything dies. Tonight it's your turn."

"Is that, like, Buddhism or something?"

"It's reality. Exit the vehicle."

She killed the engine, leaving the keys in the ignition. She cast a sidelong look at the tote bag on the passenger seat. A small-arms arsenal lay within reach. Going for it might be her last chance.

"Don't." Chiu was watching her. He couldn't see her eyes, but he must be good at reading body language. "That's not the smart play."

"It's not like I have a lot to lose," she said quietly.

"From what I've seen, nobody willingly shaves even a few minutes off their time."

Bonnie couldn't argue. He was right.

She opened the door and got out of the Jeep, abandoning the tote bag. She left her purse behind also. Somehow she didn't think she'd be needing it.

The wind was fiercer here, so close to the sea. The storm slapped her face and knocked her hat off her head. It flew away into the dark. Instantly she was soaked to the skin.

Two young men emerged from the Caddy flanked her. They wore loose pants and sleeveless black shirts that bared their wiry tattooed arms. Their hair was long and unruly, pulled back by red and black do-rags, gang colors. Their hard, expressionless faces looked ridiculously young. They walked with a swagger, kids showing off.

Patrick Chiu joined his men. Like them, he was clad in black, but he didn't sport a do-rag. He wore a suit jacket and an open-collar button-down shirt, and he was older than his companions—twenty-four, she recalled from her reading.

None of them was taller than five foot five, which gave her an inch or two advantage in height. Somehow she failed to take comfort from this fact, possibly because one of Chiu's pals was carrying a Cobray MAC-11 assault pistol, which shot 1200 rounds per minute. It was the kind of weapon that tended to minimize physical differences.

"Get moving, Wonder Woman," Chiu said. "We're taking a walk on the beach."

"Not a great night for it."

"Not a great night for you, period. Walk."

Chiu might not be tall, but he was handsome as hell, and he moved with languid grace, his lean, muscular body hugging her like a shadow. Up close he looked gravely serious, almost bookish. But he was a stone killer. She could tell.

Takes one to know one, she told herself.

Head down, she made her way to the boardwalk. She was about to be killed for a murder she hadn't committed, but she couldn't say it was unfair. There had been other murders, starting in Ohio, continuing here. Murders that might have been justified—she thought so—but then, Patrick Chiu thought her death was justified, didn't he? She was dying by the whim of someone who, like her, had taken the law into his own hands. Hoist by her own petard. Poetic fucking irony. And what the hell was a petard anyway?

She thought she might be crying, a little. With all the rain on her face, it was hard to tell.

Pretty fucking undignified, Parker. The words floated through her mind, spoken in Des's voice.

Des ... She'd just gotten close to him, really close. Too late. Should have trusted him sooner. They could have had more time.

She came to a flight of wooden steps that led to the

beach. The staircase wobbled, already coming loose under the pressure of wind and rain.

As she descended the stairs, Chiu leaned in close enough to be heard over the storm. "You can make this easier on yourself."

"I'm listening."

"Tell me what happened to Joey Huang."

"Already did." The words were hard to say. Her teeth were starting to chatter from the cold. At least she liked to think it was the cold.

"Be straight with me, and I'll do you with one bullet, back of the head. Bang, and it's over. Nice and clean. You won't feel a thing."

It would be easy to tell a lie, any lie. Say Frank Lazzaro hired her. Let the Long Fong Boyz go after him. He was no innocent. He deserved whatever he got.

Just lie, and take a bullet, and be done.

She sucked in a lungful of air. "Dante killed Huang. I killed Dante. That's all she wrote."

"You're a fool, Parker."

It was tough to argue with that.

She stepped onto the beach. The surf licked her sneakers. The storm had pushed the tide right up to the boardwalk, drowning the sand.

Chiu shoved her forward, away from the stairs. The sand beneath her was a boiling mass of grit, thick and grasping like quicksand. She splashed deeper into the surf, her feet slip-sliding in the muck, forming long runnels that were instantly filled in. A sign floated past: *No Dogs On Beach*. Not an issue now. There was no beach.

The water was up to her calves now. Cold. The rain poured down, a sleet of needles. Everything was roaring fury, thundering chaos, the boardwalk groaning, the wind screaming. A hell of noise and water, and no escape.

"Stop here," Chiu said.

She turned, intending to say something—she had no

idea what—and Chiu seized her forearm, his slender fingers digging into her muscles painfully hard. He gave a slight twist, and an electric wave of agony radiated through her arm, weakening her. She fell to her knees in the surf, sending up a white shout of foam.

Jesus, that hurt. Was that what they called a kung fu grip? She'd thought that was just a GI Joe thing.

Chiu stepped back. Wordlessly he signaled to the kid with the gun. The kid handed it over. Chiu hefted the MAC easily in one hand, training it on her.

Bonnie stared up through a mist of spray at the three figures in black. Chiu's face was closed, unreadable. The kid who'd surrendered the gun looked excited. The other kid, too. Their blood was up. To them it was just a game. They were like children at a carnival. Killing her was like taking a ride.

I took that ride too, Bonnie thought. I'm not any different.

She waited for Chiu to open up on her with the automatic. At this range the gun would cut her in half.

Confused thoughts spun through her mind. Year of the Dragon. Stolen fish in a cooler. Alec Dante: *You are about to make a very big-time mistake.* Gunshots in a flooded cellar. Blood in the water ...

It would be her blood now, as soon as Chiu pulled the trigger.

But he didn't. He only snapped his fingers in a peremptory command. The two kids moved away, sloshing through the surf.

A wave rolled in, a big comber, detonating around her, blasting her with spray like shrapnel. It receded, and Chiu was still there, drenched but uncaring, rigid despite the insults of the storm.

One of his men fished a stick of driftwood out of the tide. Another found a short length of pipe, part of the boardwalk's railing, which was already coming apart.

They returned, weapons in hand.

She got it now. Chiu didn't want her shot. He wanted her beaten. His boys would whale on her with the plank and the pipe until she told whatever she knew. And even then, she wouldn't get a bullet. They'd beat her to death or leave her crippled in the surf to be batted around by the storm surge. Her remains would be recovered eventually, but by then she would look like a victim of the hurricane, not the Long Fong Boyz.

Smart. She couldn't help but admire the elegant simplicity of the plan.

The two kids looked to their boss. He, in turn, looked at her.

"How you doing, Parker?"

"Never better." She forced out the words past the tightness in her throat.

"You look like a drowned rat."

She tried to laugh, choked on the effort. Year of the Rat, she thought. That's me.

"You going to talk?"

"Got nothing to say."

"Last chance."

"I've already told you. You just don't want to hear it."

Chiu's head inclined in a barely perceptible nod. His boys started forward.

This was where it would get rough. She could lie, but it wouldn't help. They'd gone past the point of letting her off easy. She would just have to take the beating and go on taking it until she was dead, or as good as dead. It wasn't the way she wanted to go out. But there weren't a whole lot of good ways to die.

They were almost on top of her when Chiu said, "Hold it."

The two kids stopped, looking confused.

Peering past them, Bonnie saw Chiu cradling something under his chin. A cell phone. He'd gotten a call.

Reprieve from the governor, she thought numbly.

She knelt in the surf, waiting. Her two assassins stared down at her with cruel, hungry faces. They wanted blood. She could almost feel the itch in their palms.

They weren't going to wait much longer, word or no word. Bonnie could see it in each one's shifting stance. They were like little kids who had to take a pee. They could hold it for only so long.

Chiu folded the phone. The call was over.

"Back off," he said, just loudly enough to be heard over the background roar.

The two kids exchanged questioning glances. For a moment, caught between bloodlust and obedience, they didn't move.

"Back the fuck *off*!"

This time they retreated. Reluctantly they threw aside their makeshift weapons and returned to Chiu's side.

Bonnie stared at him through a tangled net of hair.

"It's possible you've been truthful," he said.

He turned and walked away, striding easily through the tide. His men followed, black ghosts dissolving into darkness.

Then they were gone, and she was alone. And alive.

Somehow, still alive.

17

PATRICK CHIU SETTLED into the backseat of the Escalade, listening to the rain.

He liked rain. He appreciated its cleansing qualities. As a child he would sometimes imagine a hard steady rain washing away the grit and garbage of the streets, making the world new and shiny.

Childhood was far away now. He no longer dreamed of immaculate streets or new beginnings. But he still enjoyed the rain.

The Cadillac's front doors opened, and Lam and Eng climbed in, dripping, the tote bag from the Jeep in Eng's hands. "We did what you told us, dai lo," Eng said.

"You left the handbag?" Chiu asked.

Eng nodded. "There was hardly no money in it anyway."

Chiu didn't want his guys in possession of Parker's credit cards or anything else that could tie them to her. But he was willing to bet the guns and other gear couldn't be traced.

Lam sat behind the wheel, keys in hand. But he didn't start the engine.

"You sure we want to book?" he asked.

Chiu leaned forward in the backseat. "Why not?"

There was a tense silence in the car, punctuated by the beat of rain on the roof.

"My man," Eng said finally, "I don't see why we didn't blip that cooch. I thought that was the fuckin' plan."

"Plans change."

"She gonna bang on us, we not gonna do nothin'?"

Lam nodded his agreement. "We need to take this shit all the way. Every second she keeps breathing is fuckin' unacceptable."

"We was all ready to get it on," Eng said, "and you make us stand the fuck down. It fuckin' sucks."

They had both turned to look at him. Chiu stared them down. There were times when it helped to talk their language. This was one of those times.

"Who's running shit here?" he asked calmly. "You bitch-made punks wanna take over? You wanna coach this team?"

Lam shook his head. "Nah, dai lo. It's not like that."

"Then shut up. Keep your fucking mouths shut."

Grudgingly they faced forward. Lam cranked the ignition and put the Caddy in gear, reversing out of the parking slot.

Chiu had learned many secrets of power as dai lo of the Long Fong Boyz, and one of those secrets was to withhold information from his subordinates whenever possible. Volunteer nothing. Leave others in the dark. This inevitably placed them in a position of weakness.

Sometimes he thought he could write a book about the things he'd learned. *Management Secrets of a Tong Warrior*, maybe. He was ideally positioned to do so.

His father was Chinese, an immigrant from the Szechuan province. His mother was a dark-eyed Latina. She'd raised him while his dad was off drinking and whoring and finding excuses not to send money home.

Though his mother meant well, she never knew what to say to him, so for the most part she said nothing at all. With no real family of his own, he'd found a sense of belonging among the older kids who roamed the streets, jacking cars and shaking down massage parlors. To placate his mom, he'd stayed in school, at least enough of the time to earn a diploma, even qualifying for the honor roll on occasion; but his real education had been on the streets.

He was jumped into the Panlong Fong at sixteen—a ritual that required taking a beatdown from his gang brothers. He got three of his ribs kicked in, suffered two black eyes and a busted ankle. It was no big thing. He was in.

But he didn't stay in. At eighteen he went to college in Baltimore, graduated with a BBA, and spent four months in New York City, occupying a cubicle and following orders.

Then he quit and returned to Jersey City, taking up the life he'd known.

The nine-to-five world wasn't for him. He couldn't tolerate the boredom, the conformity, the kowtowing to people he could have defeated in any contest of wits or strength. Though it reduced his mother to angry sobs and mystified his former teachers, he would follow his own path.

Not as a member of the Panlong Fong, though. He set about organizing his own crew, spending money and buying credibility. It was a risky game. The Panlong Fong didn't like competition, and one of their shotcallers, an OG named China Dog, put a price on Chiu's head. Luckily, China Dog was arrested in an FBI-DEA sting a few weeks later, the Panlong Fong were broken up, and the contract lapsed, leaving Chiu alive and in control of his own crew, perfectly positioned to move in on territory that had been suddenly vacated.

Chiu was selective in his recruiting; so far he'd limited the gang to twenty-six members and a few hangers-on. The Long Fong Boyz were an independent set, unaffiliated with any tong or dragonhead, though willing to get in on a joint venture when the money was good. Currently they occupied a small apartment complex in Hoboken, formerly used by a Guatemalan crew who'd been persuaded to relocate by the judicious application of force. All his men hung there, watching kung-fu movies, eating take-out, drinking and getting wasted. Girlfriends came and went.

It took brains to run a crew. It took strategic thinking. Consider his approach to Bonnie Parker. When word reached him of a blond female who'd visited Crossgate Gardens on the night of Joey Huang's murder, Chiu had put out feelers, inquiring about any known or reputed hitter who matched the description. Parker's name had come up.

A less prudent man would have moved on her immediately. Chiu knew that killing a white woman in a small town entailed greater risk than knocking off a rival gangster on the city streets. He'd taken the trouble to confirm Parker's identification as the hitter. One of his contacts was a police officer with a gambling problem, who was on the hook to the gang. Chiu persuaded this individual to obtain Bonnie Elizabeth Parker's Department of Motor Vehicle records, which included her driver's license photo, home address, and vehicle registration. The photo was shown to the witnesses in the project, garnering positive responses. It was all very neat and methodical. A jury trial could not have been fairer.

Then there was the challenge of actually carrying out the hit. While his subordinates saw the storm as an inconvenience, Chiu recognized it as an opportunity. Without power, Parker would be more vulnerable to a surprise attack in her home. The police checkpoint, which had been easily circumvented by taking the Escalade off-road through a cemetery and a patch of woods, would provide plausible deniability.

His years on the streets and his years as a student had come together for Chiu in one great truth—that all of life was a battleground. Everything was strategy and tactics, perseverance and discipline. The long-range planner prospered. The shortsighted fell by the wayside. The race was not to the swift, but to those who could see farthest and persist longest.

Chiu was smarter and better educated than his rivals. And he intended to go far. Someday, people in Chinatown wouldn't be telling stories about Sing Dock and Mock Duck. They would be telling stories about him.

The Escalade hummed south, skirting rubbish in the streets. Up front, his men were disturbingly quiet. Chiu knew they would never openly challenge him. They were soldiers, supremely loyal, and they would follow him straight into hell. But they needed reassurance sometimes. Like children—and they were barely older than children—they required a soft voice and a comforting hand.

"Listen up, little brothers." This was a term of affection, one he knew they appreciated. "Parker's story ain't been told yet. From here on, we decide her quality of life. You get that? She don't know it, but right now she's just a cunt hair away from being dead."

"She coulda been dead already," Eng said petulantly. He held the MAC in his lap, stroking it like a puppy.

"Yeah, she could've. But what we need right now is discipline. We gotta play the long game."

"What game?"

"I got a call from Lee at the Golden Duck. Fish Face is missing."

Eng turned in his seat. "Tommy? Shit."

"He's probably just off gettin' his knob gobbled by some skank," Lam said.

Chiu wasn't so sure. "Parker and I had a parley in her Jeep. She said the Italians were behind the hit. I called bullshit, 'cause why would they drop only one body? But now ..."

Eng blinked. "You think those fuckin' pasta shitters coulda clipped Tommy?"

"Could be." Chiu smiled. "Or Parker could be lying to save her *lo faan* ass."

Lam's voice was low, thoughtful. "Maybe she's in it with the wops. Maybe they, you know, outsourced the hit."

Chiu nodded. The same thought had occurred to him. "She gave up the Italians real fast. She might've been straight with me, or she might've been spinning a story with just enough reality in it to play me for a fool."

"How we gonna know?"

"We keep an eye on her. If she's tight with the Cosa Nostra crowd, she'll do a sit-down with them before long."

Lam made a sound signifying understanding. "That's why you had us plant the thing."

"Now you're catching on, Monkey."

The nickname was affectionate. Every member of his crew had a gang name. Eng was Kicker. Chiu himself was Yellowjacket.

And Joey Huang—he'd been Cricket. The name had suited him. A small, inoffensive creature.

"If Parker killed Joey," he said quietly, "with or without the Italians, we'll know soon enough. Then we come a-knockin', and her life takes a turn for the worse. We use harsh measures. We get fucking extreme. And we put Barbie in a body bag. She will be girl, interrupted. You feel me?"

Heads were nodding. "I feel you, dai lo."

"Good. Then drive." Chiu laid his head against the back of the seat. "I want outta here. I don't like this shitty hick town."

18

BONNIE FOUND HER JEEP unlocked, the key still in the ignition. Her purse was there, but the tote bag full of weapons was gone.

She'd been effectively disarmed. Terrific.

Come to think of it, she did have one more firearm. And she wanted it now, because she felt extremely naked without it.

She climbed into the Jeep, instantly soaking the seat cushion. With the engine running, she turned on the dashboard blowers to dry off and warm up. Her teeth were still clacking, and unpredictable shivers racked her body. She remembered the blanket in the backseat, draped it around her like a shawl, and hugged herself, slapping at the patches of numbness in her lower legs, willing herself back to life.

Then she got the Jeep moving and left the boardwalk behind.

Downtown Brighton Cove was only three blocks from the beach. The streets were still navigable. She made it to her office in two minutes, parking in the alley between her building and the one next door. She let herself into the lobby and climbed the stairs in darkness to the second floor, her waterlogged sneakers squeaking with each step.

By habit she flicked the wall switch in her office, before remembering that the power was out. She beamed her keychain flashlight into the kneehole of her desk and there it was, a Smith 1911 semiautomatic pistol ducttaped to the side panel.

It had occurred to her that a girl in her line might attract a few enemies. If one of them showed up at her place of work while she was seated at her desk, she wanted a loaded gun within reach.

She peeled off the tape and removed the gun. It was a .45, too big and noisy for a hit kit. When doing a hit, she preferred a smaller caliber gun that could be more effectively silenced.

She checked the magazine. It was fully loaded—eight rounds. She'd had more ammo at home, but it had gone into the tote bag.

Eight rounds wasn't a hell of a lot when you were going up against people who toted machine guns, but it sure beat nothing at all. She felt better with the gun in her hand, and better still when she'd shed her wet clothes, toweled off with a sweatshirt, and donned a spare outfit she kept at the office—shorts and a maroon tee with the words *Jersey Girl* printed across the breasts. Not that she was particularly proud of living in New Jersey; she just liked the shirt.

She even had a second pair of sneakers at hand, and another hat, a gray newsboy cap with a certain turn-of-the-century charm. Never let it be said she was unprepared for a sartorial emergency.

Dressed and newly armed, she felt almost like herself again. Only one thing remained to be done. She pulled a wastebasket into the center of the room, leaned over it, and calmly and deliberately threw up.

She'd been so goddamn sure it was all over. And she'd been afraid. As tough as she liked to think she was, as cool and heartless, she'd been so very afraid.

Not afraid merely of dying. Afraid of missing out. What she'd discovered with Des just this evening was something worth preserving and exploring. Something that could really go somewhere, maybe lead her out of the dark maze of her life. Maybe take her to a place where dealing with death and facing torture weren't the costs she paid for being alive.

Or maybe not. She might be fated to stay on this course till the end. Her flashlight beam moved to the photo of the original Bonnie Parker on the wall. Her namesake grinned at her, a stogie jammed defiantly in her mouth, a gat in her hand. That other Bonnie seemed to say that you could pretend to yourself all you liked, but there was no way out except the way she herself had found, when she and Clyde were torn apart in a bloody fusillade.

Fuck that. Clyde's Bonnie was dead, and today's Bonnie was alive. That was enough for now.

She locked up her office. At the end of the hall there was a washroom. She checked herself out in the mirror in the glow of her flashlight. Her hair was a tangled mess peppered with bits of debris. She brushed it clean, then dried her windbreaker with hand towels and shrugged it on.

Returning to the Jeep, she stashed the .45 under the driver's seat, then headed for the checkpoint at the edge of town. She was still intent on getting to Devil's Hook. If anything, planting the ticket stub in Dante's car was more urgent than ever. It would confirm the story she'd told Chiu, and maybe get him and his crew off her back for good.

Three squad cars, their light bars flashing, were stationed at the checkpoint. The role of the police was to keep looters out of town, not to keep residents in, so logically there was no reason for her to be stopped. But she expected to be, and she was. Maguire's troops were always on her case these days.

Tonight it was the chief himself who took the lead. He waved her to a stop with an imperious hand and strode up to the Jeep through the shimmering downpour.

"Hello, Parker," he said with his customary malicious bonhomie. "Surprised to see me?"

"Not really. I always knew you were too dumb to come in out of the rain."

She noticed Bradley Walsh loitering in the background, obviously eavesdropping.

Maguire aimed his flashlight at her. "Where are you off to?"

"Sunday drive."

"It's Monday."

"I'm getting a late start."

Bradley smiled at this.

The chief was unamused. "You're heading out of town shortly before midnight in the middle of a hurricane. You won't say why. Why shouldn't I believe you've got trouble in mind?"

"What kind of trouble?"

"A lot of houses are standing empty right now. They make tempting targets for looters."

"Gimme a break. You got nothing to tie me to any burglaries. All those donuts have clogged the arteries to your brain."

The flashlight explored the Jeep's interior, the cone of light falling on her purse. "That handbag of yours looks pretty heavy. What are you carrying?"

"Lady products."

"I never know what women mean by that."

"Tampons, moisturizers, a vibrator for those lonely nights."

"Mind if I take a look?"

She did mind, actually. She had just remembered that her set of lockpicks was inside the purse. If Maguire wanted to hold her on suspicion of burglary, the pick set would be just the ticket.

"You've never seen a vibrator?" she asked, stalling.

"Not one of yours. I'm guessing it's designed to withstand extreme cold."

"Sorry. You don't have a warrant."

"I don't need a warrant. This is a public street."

"You need probable cause."

"With you, Parker, there's always probable clause. You've always lived up to your name."

"It's a perfectly good name. I can't help it if Clyde Barrow's main squeeze used it too."

"No, it's more than a coincidence. It's something spooky. You're just like her. You're like her in every way."

"Am I?" She leaned toward him. "They say she shot a lawman once."

Maguire's face puckered up in a squinty scowl. "That sounds like a threat."

"Just a historical observation."

He gave her a long look. The rain had picked up, but he didn't seem to notice.

She wondered if he'd forgotten about the purse. She hoped so. If he found the lockpicks, he would search the rest of the car and turn up the unlicensed .45.

"I've been finding out about you, Parker. You've led an eventful life. Did you love your parents?"

"What kind of question is that?"

"I think you did. At least you were loyal to them. Loyal enough to avenge their deaths."

"You've gone off the deep end, Dan. That's a dangerous move for a guy as shallow as you."

"They were murdered. You saw it. And you made sure the killers didn't get away with it. Didn't you?"

"Seriously, you gotta stop fortifying the cough syrup with Night Train."

Bradley was studying her, a quizzical expression on his face. He hadn't heard this story before, it seemed. And now he had some idea of why the chief had flown to Buckington, Ohio.

"Truth is," Maguire said, "a jury might take pity on you. Orphan girl, all alone in the world, taking the law into her own hands. They might not send you away for too long. Not for that. But it opens up a whole can of worms, doesn't it, Parker? I mean, all the things you've done since?"

"Can of worms, barrel of monkeys—it's just a matter of perspective."

"Once the door's open, even a little, all the rest of it will come out. Your clients will start to talk. We'll *make* them talk. We'll have leverage. How many people have you killed by now? A dozen? More?"

Bradley turned away. At first she thought she couldn't look at her. Then she realized she was talking into his portable radio.

"I've never killed anybody, Dan," she said with a smile. "I'm a law-abiding citizen."

He snorted. "You can't even say it with a straight face."

"I just think it's funny how obsessed you are with me. You're like a dog chasing its tail."

"I see myself more as Captain Ahab hunting the white whale."

"Yeah, that worked out great for him."

"Keep riding me, Parker. It's not going to help. I'm on to you. Now let me see that purse."

Bonnie blew out a breath. "Sheesh. We back on that again? A girl can't leave her own home—"

"You weren't at your own home. You were at 113 Chestnut Avenue, the home of Mr. Desmond Harris. Your Jeep was parked out front until about an hour ago."

"You're so observant. It's what I love about you."

"What's in the purse?"

Things were getting dicey. She couldn't put him off much longer.

"Chicf." Bradley holstered the radio on his belt. "We got an alarm ringing at Jay's Deli."

"Aw, shit." Maguire gave up. "Stay out of trouble, Parker."

"Always do."

Maguire huffed toward his car, and Bonnie allowed herself to relax.

Close one. She kept betting against the house. One of these days, she was going to lose.

Before joining his boss, Bradley risked a moment of conversation with her.

"So, uh, you were staying with Mr. Harris, the art gallery guy?" He looked pained.

"He's an old friend."

"You know him before he was a cripple?"

She didn't like that word. "Yeah," she said a little too sharply. "But not as well as I do now."

It didn't take an expert in body language to see that he was itching to ask just how well she did know him.

"Walsh!" Maguire glared at him in the rain. "Get a move on!"

"Yes sir."

The kid trotted off, and Bonnie revved the Jeep and got out of town.

19

DAN MAGUIRE WAS feeling pissed off. He always got like that when he dealt with Parker. She had this way of getting under his skin like a damn deer tick. But before long, he would be uprooting that tick once and for all. He would perform a Parker-ectomy.

"Parker-ectomy," he muttered, pleased with his own wit.

"What's that, Chief?"

That was Bradley Walsh, riding shotgun. Maguire had almost forgotten the kid was there.

"Nothing."

Maguire steered the cruiser onto Main Street, heading for Jay's Deli, where an alarm was ringing on backup power. Rain tap-danced on the windshield. The wipers beat in long, steady strokes.

He threw Walsh a glance. "What were you saying to Parker back there?"

"I just asked if she was being more careful. She rolled through a stop sign yesterday. I gave her a warning."

"You didn't ticket her? God damn it, I told you to put heat on that bitch."

"Sorry, Chief. I figured with the storm and all, we had bigger fish to fry."

Maguire shook his head. It had been a mistake to hire Walsh. The kid didn't understand how things worked in this town. He wasn't local; he'd grown up in New Hampshire, for Christ's sake.

It was different for Maguire. He'd been raised around here and had served under Brighton Cove's previous chief, a good man but too easygoing. Maguire's dad, now deceased, had been a cop in Algonquin. Dan Maguire had risen higher in the ranks than his old man, but he still felt he had something to prove. And Parker was his ticket to proving it.

Bigger fish, hell. For him, there were no bigger fish. He hadn't been kidding when he compared himself to Captain Ahab. And Bonnie Parker was his white whale.

And yeah, maybe he was a little obsessed. He could admit it. He'd had a bug up his butt about Parker for years, and even more so since August. He *knew* Parker was involved in that mess—the shooting at the pavilion, the craziness in the Coach House, and whatever had gone down at the airport. But there was no proof. The damn girl had covered her tracks too well.

But not about everything.

Through relentless digging into the PI's past, Maguire had tentatively identified her parents as Tom and Rebecca Parker, both murdered in a motel room in central Pennsylvania in 1998. The motel clerk had reported that they'd had a girl with them, a girl of about fifteen or sixteen, the right age for Bonnie. A girl who'd never been found.

The Pennsylvania state police had worked the case. Evidence at the scene had identified the killer, a certain Lucas Hatch, though indications were that more than one perpetrator had been involved. Hatch couldn't be found, and probably the authorities hadn't looked too hard. The

MICHAEL PRESCOTT

two victims had been drifters, the wife a high school dropout who'd gotten pregnant at sixteen, the husband a small-time crook with a lifelong history of making trouble. No great loss. And the girl? Well, nobody could say what had become of her.

Six months later, Lucas Hatch turned up dead in Buckington, Ohio, along with two other losers who might have been the guys from the motel. The Ohio authorities got nowhere. But something caught Maguire's eye when he went through the old police reports. Two days before the killings, Hector Samuelson, owner of a Buckington gun shop, spotted a teenage girl shoplifting a box of ammunition. He chased her down in the parking lot outside, at which point the girl turned, calmly finished loading an antique .38, and aimed it at his face. Prudently, Samuelson backed off. In his statement to police he described the girl as approximately sixteen, blond, blue-eyed, and "fierce."

Maguire obtained a copy of Bonnie's PI photo, on file with the state, and had a computer guy age-regress her to sixteen. He put it in a six-pack with five mugshots of teenage female offenders, all blond and blue-eyed. He flew to Ohio and showed Samuelson the photo array. It was a long shot—the encounter had taken place twelve years earlier, and the witness was in his sixties now. But it paid off. Samuelson unhesitatingly selected the photo of Parker. No doubt, he said, none at all.

The best part was that one of Hatch's pals had been shot with a .38. The other two had been shot with 9mm rounds, but that could be explained easily enough. Little Bonnie had killed the first guy with her antique gun and then lifted the victim's own piece before going after the remaining pair. The police hadn't connected the shoplifting with the murders, because who would suspect a teenage girl of being the triggerman in a bloodbath?

Maguire would. He knew Parker. She was a bad seed.

Hatch and his gang had made a mistake not finishing her off in the motel. Somehow she'd tracked them down and taken them out.

He was certain of it. Dead certain. But Samuelson's word on the basis of a computer-altered photo and a twelve-year-old memory wasn't enough.

Maguire's next move would be to persuade Ohio law enforcement to depose Samuelson. Armed with an affidavit, he hoped to get a court order to exhume one of Parker's parents. He would do a DNA test on the remains, and another one on Parker herself. If she could be confirmed as Tom and Rebecca's daughter, and as the armed shoplifter who stole ammo in Buckington just two days before the killings, then he could put some serious pressure on her.

All he needed was an opening, and he could make her crack.

He slant-parked at the curb outside the deli, beaming his headlights at the shop, where the alarm was still clanging frantically. Right away he could see there was no break-in. One of the plywood panels nailed up over the storefront windows had blown free, and a loose awning had punched through the glass. Even so, he'd better check it out.

He left the car and tramped through puddles, the rookie at his side. While the alarm screamed in monotone, Maguire angled his big steel flashlight through the opening in the window and let the beam explore the interior of the deli. The cash register appeared untouched, and there was no sign of intrusion.

"Call Jay," he told Walsh, yelling to be heard over the alarm. "Tell him to get down here and board it up again before something worse happens."

"Right, Chief."

They were back in the squad car, returning to the checkpoint via a roundabout route, when Walsh spoke up. "So Parker and Desmond Harris—they're an item?"

The question came out of nowhere, asked with phony casualness. For the first time it occurred to Maguire that Walsh might have the hots for the PI. The idea wasn't so far-fetched. Parker was comely enough in a chain-smoking tough-gal kind of way. To a rookie like Walsh, barely old enough to shave the peach fuzz off his cheeks, she might exude an aura of glamorous mystery.

"That's how I figure it," Maguire said, watching the kid's reaction. "Weird, huh? She's got a thing for a fucking paraplegic. Maybe they do it in his wheelchair."

Walsh nodded in a distracted way.

Maguire stared straight ahead. "Look, kid. I don't want you getting close to that girl. She's bad news."

"I know that, sir." The words came out a little too fast.

"I'm not shitting you. The stuff I found out about her—it's serious. She's a bona fide sociopath. Violent and crazy, deeply messed up. And she will be going away for a long, long time."

"Okay."

"Keep your distance, is what I'm saying. For your own good."

"Yes, sir, Chief. I understand."

Maguire grunted, unconvinced.

The kid would bear watching. Everyone had to be part of the team.

20

THE DRIVE TO Devil's Hook Island was all kinds of hell, and not just because of the weather. She kept flashing on Alec Dante's face just before he hit the water. That stupidly surprised expression.

In the past she never would have been haunted by a thing like that. She had done her job and moved on. Now it was different. After Pascal, she knew what it was like to be in the crosshairs. What it was like to be hunted. And if she'd been in danger of forgetting, tonight's little tea social had served as a timely reminder.

She didn't like these thoughts, these issues. She didn't like feeling damaged and scared and—hell—guilty, even. But while she might not be happy about it, she didn't know what she could do.

Except quit. Or die.

The first wasn't an option. The second—well, that one was very much in play.

Cohawkin Bridge was impenetrably blocked. She wasn't surprised. The population of Devil's Hook had been cleared out, and the police didn't want anyone sneaking onto the island to loot the empty houses. Still, there might be another way in.

She swung around to the island's southern tip, where a second bridge allowed access from the mainland. It was an ancient, narrow structure barely wide enough for two vehicles, and while she didn't think the authorities would have forgotten about it, she hoped they'd made less of an effort to blockade it.

She reached the bridge. Inexplicably, the entry was clear. No barrier at all.

Weird. There should have been something.

She slowed the Jeep, suddenly wary. She had learned not to trust good fortune.

Close by, a big SUV was parked sloppily on the dirt shoulder. The side window was broken.

She parked behind the vehicle, got out, and took a look inside. A mess of wires hung below the steering column. Someone had hotwired the ignition. She didn't think they had taken it for a joy ride. Her guess was that the SUV had been parked at the entry to the bridge, straddling both lanes. Someone had moved it out of the way.

If so, she wasn't the first one to trespass on Devil's Hook tonight. The other visitor could be a looter, of course. But she wasn't counting on it.

She returned to the Jeep and crossed the bridge, uneasily aware of the whitecaps sloshing at the girders. From here it was only a short distance to Alec Dante's cottage. Most of the streets were awash; her tires jetted up hissing plumes of spray. Nearing the house, she killed her headlights. Dangerous move in a storm, but she had her reasons.

She glimpsed the driveway as she coasted past. The Porsche Boxster, Dante's car, was still there; but another car had joined it. She was willing to bet the new arrival had everything to do with the hotwired sport utility.

As before, she parked the Jeep in the woods. She retrieved the .45 from under her seat. Through a whirl of windblown leaves, she made her way to the edge of the woods, where she crouched low, hidden by holly bushes, studying the driveway.

Two figures were visible through the rain. One leaned into the Porsche, while the other stood watch.

She had a pretty good idea of who had sent them, but she needed to be sure. When the sentry's back was turned, she sprinted across the open lawn to a row of arborvitae fronting the house. She slid behind the hedges like a runner sliding into third and listened for any indication that she'd been seen.

The one pulling guard duty was talking. "... So the manager says, 'That's great, but you gotta be bilingual.' And the dog says, 'Meow.'"

The guy in the car laughed. "Heh. Fuckin' meow."

"Hurry it up, will ya? I'm gettin' soaked out here."

"It's not as easy as the SUV. The security system in this thing is state-of-the-art."

"Just shake a leg, for Chrissakes."

A cell phone chirped. The sentry answered.

"Hey, Frank. It's Lou ... We had a little trouble getting onto the island. Cops replaced the prowl car you bulldozed with a big-ass SUV. Too big to push, so we hadda hotwire it ... The Porsche? Same deal. Paulie's working on it now ... We looked, but the keys weren't in the house, at least no place we could find. It's pitch dark in there ... Don't sweat it, Frank. We're getting it done."

Two of Frank Lazzaro's people. Sent here to move the Porsche. Something Lazzaro wouldn't want to do unless he knew about his nephew. The only reason he would go to all this trouble to conceal someone else's crime was that he didn't want the police involved. He was treating Dante's death as a personal affront, and he meant to handle it himself.

"I'll let you know, Frank," the one named Lou said.

125

"Ciao." He ended the call.

"Still no word on what's going on?" the other man, Paulie, asked from inside the Porsche.

Lou shrugged. "He'll tell us what we need to know, when we need to know it."

So Frank was playing it close to the vest for now. Good. That was better than having the whole organization on the case.

Bonnie crept closer, staying behind the shrubbery. She was within fifteen feet of the men on the driveway when Lou asked, "The name Parker mean anything to you?"

She froze, a small, huddled shape hidden in the shifting hedges.

"Parker? Nah. Should it?"

"I thought I heard the Chang kid say something about somebody named Parker. And Frank was gettin' real interested."

Okay, so Lazzaro had already talked to one of the Long Fong Boyz and gotten her name. That had to be why Chiu had spared her; Lazzaro's actions supported her story. That was the upside. The downside was that Lazzaro would be gunning for her. He might be doing it on his own, without bringing his men up to speed, but he was still doing it.

"I don't know no Parker," Paulie said. "Okay, I think I got it."

The Porsche's engine revved to life, and the headlights flashed on. With the car parked at an angle, the beams sliced directly into the stand of arborvitae where she was hiding. Instinctively she pulled back.

"Hey," Paulie said. "You see that?"

"See what?"

"I think something moved in those bushes there."

Shit.

In a situation like this, the old saying definitely applied: He who hesitates is fucked.

Bonnie didn't hesitate. She plucked the .45 from her purse, aimed it at Lou, and pulled the trigger.

Click.

Misfeed.

She racked the slide and squeezed the trigger again. Nothing happened.

A gunshot cracked like a whip, blowing into the aluminum siding at her back.

The bad guys' guns were working fine.

On hands and knees she retreated along the front of the house, using the hedges as cover. While on the move, she ran through the procedure for clearing a jam. Slap the bottom of the magazine to seat it firmly, pull back the slide, and fire. Tap, rack, bang.

No good. Goddamn slide was stuck.

"There!" Paulie yelled.

Another shot sounded, spraying her with bits of pine needles from the closest hedge.

She ducked behind the corner of the house, pushed herself to her feet, and broke into a run, fighting to keep her footing on the sodden ground.

She was betting the pistol's malfunction was a double feed—two live rounds trying to occupy the chamber at once. She could probably clear it, but not while she was running for her life.

Behind her, the first pursuer rounded the corner.

"Holy shit"—Lou's voice—"I think it's a woman!"

He took a shot, but she'd already swerved to throw off his aim. The bullet didn't touch her, and then she turned the corner and found herself at the rear of the house, where the battered remains of the patio butted up against a flat expanse of beach and crashing surf.

She wasted a second trying the back door. Locked. She kept running.

If they caught her alive and saw her ID, they would

know she was the Parker their boss was after. Then she would take a trip to see Frank Lazzaro, whose methods would make the Long Fong Boyz look like amateurs.

A bullet would be better. But staying alive would be better still.

As she rounded the far corner, it occurred to her that Paulie might have doubled back to cut off her escape. If so, she was running into an ambush.

But no one was there. She had a straight shot to the driveway if she wanted it. She could jump in the Porsche and take off—

And they would gun her down before she could back out of the driveway. In the car she'd be an easy target. Like Clyde and Bonnie, she thought distractedly. Shot to pieces in an automobile on a rural road.

Halfway along the side of the house, she nearly bumped her head on the broken branch that had speared the kitchen window and started the flood in the cellar. The window had been smashed, and whatever stubborn shards might have clung to the frame had been swept away by wind and rain.

She grabbed the branch, hoisted herself up, and slipped through the window feet first, landing on the wet floor.

Outside, she heard Lou shout, "She went in the window!"

They weren't giving up. But she had the edge now. They were in full cry, not thinking clearly. They had sized her up as prey. They weren't expecting her to fight back.

She retreated to the cellar stairs, sinking into a crouch, and went to work on the gun. She locked back the slide and tugged at the magazine. It wouldn't budge.

Lou appeared, swinging a stubby leg over the window sill.

She slammed the magazine against her thigh, hard enough to leave a bruise, but it still wouldn't pop free.

His other leg was over the sill now.

She slammed the magazine down again. This time it loosened. She stripped it out. Two crushed cartridges spilled onto the steps.

Lou's feet thumped on the kitchen floor.

She shoved the mag back into place and cranked back the slide to cycle a new round into the chamber—hopefully without a misfeed this time. She couldn't be sure, though.

Lou took a step forward, squinting in the dark.

If the mag was defective, the gun still might not fire. There was only one way to find out.

Bonnie stood, took aim, and squeezed the trigger twice.

The .45 was a big gun, and it made a big noise. Lou went down in a clumsy heap.

There had been no other sound. She hadn't given him time to scream.

She moved forward, the gun in both hands, and glanced out the window. Paulie wasn't there. She was wondering what happened to him when she heard the thump of the front door swinging open, probably caught by a gust of wind.

Reaching down, she took Lou's piece, a K-frame Smith .357 Magnum with three rounds left in the cylinder. The .45 went into her purse. Until she knew why it had malfunctioned, she couldn't trust it.

She left the kitchen and approached the living room, hugging the wall. In the darkness she heard footsteps and ragged breathing.

Then a whisper:

"Lou? You get her?"

"He didn't get me," Bonnie said, and gripping the gun in the Weaver stance, she fired twice into his center mass.

He fell backward and didn't get up. She closed on him and checked him out. He was alive, though just barely. Like a half-crushed cockroach, he twitched feebly.

She took him out with a head shot. The .357 did a vicious job, opening the man's skull like a cantaloupe.

Her wrists were numb. The Smith had a wicked kick. But it had done the job.

Kneeling, she pried the pistol out of the dead man's hands. In his pocket she found a spare magazine. She checked him for an ankle gun, but he wasn't carrying one. Too bad. She could have used a new ankle gun.

The driver's license in his wallet identified him as Paul Belletiere of Jersey City. She wondered if he'd been married, had kids. Probably. The thought didn't reach her, didn't mean anything.

She was feeling okay. More than okay. She'd beaten them in a contest of life and death—beaten them cleanly, by speed and skill. They were bona fide bad guys, probably made men in the organization, which meant they had killed before. She had no regrets, no second thoughts. Not now, anyway. Those thoughts might come, but not this soon.

She returned to the kitchen. The second man, thankfully, did not require another bullet. One of her shots had caught him in the face, wiping out most of his forehead and all of his nose. She took a speedloader from one pocket and his cell phone from another, depositing both items in her purse. Then she checked his ID. Louis Rocca, also of Jersey City.

Two dead mobsters. Working for Frank Lazzaro, a man who knew her name.

At least she didn't have to worry that the shots had been heard by the neighbors. The whole island had been evacuated. Even if anyone had stayed behind, the noise of the storm would have drowned out the gunfire.

In no hurry to leave, she took the time to wipe down any surfaces she'd touched. There was a good chance these killings would be covered up the same way Alec Dante's had, but if the police did investigate, she wasn't giving them any leads.

She was on her way out the front door when it occurred to her that Alec Dante was the type of guy who just might keep a few guns of his own lying around. Right now she needed to rebuild her arsenal, and she wasn't choosy about how she did it.

If he was anything like her, he'd want a gun in his bedroom. She always took the gun from her purse and slipped it under her mattress at bedtime. She'd found this policy made for sweet dreams.

Detouring into the bedroom, she conducted a quick search by flashlight. In the nightstand drawer she found a nice shiny Walther .22 with eight rounds in the ten-round magazine and one in the chamber.

The missing round might have been the one that killed Joey Huang. A careful assassin would have disposed of the murder weapon, but Alec Dante hadn't been careful.

She dumped that piece into her purse also. As she was turning to go, her flashlight's beam shifted to the wall over the bed. A painting hung there, a stylized interpretation of a wolf on a rocky bluff, the moon big at its back. Lambent eyes swirled with miniature whirlpools. Silver fangs gleamed. Other wolves shimmered in the background, ghostly shapes, a silent army. More and more of them came into focus the longer she looked, until she was left with the impression of a limitless horde materializing out of the darkness—predators everywhere in an unending parade of death.

Bonnie stared at the painting, and stared and stared. It said a lot of things to her, and none of them was good.

21

BEFORE RETURNING to the Jeep, Bonnie planted the ticket stub in Alec Dante's Porsche. The cops would show up eventually. When they found the stub, maybe she could get the Long Fong Boyz off her ass for good.

She drove off the island and headed north on the state highway. Along the way she spotted a bar called Finnegan's that was somehow open despite the storm and the power outage. A drink sounded pretty good right about now. She parked out front and stashed her newly acquired guns under the blanket in the rear compartment, leaving only Alec Dante's .22 in her purse.

The bar was lit by candles. A boom box played some kind of Top 40 bullshit. The barstools were occupied by a motley assortment of yuppie burnouts and *Duck Dynasty* rejects. They looked pretty much like the kind of patrons you'd expect to find in a bar at one thirty on a Tuesday morning during a hurricane.

Bonnie couldn't criticize. She was there too.

"Yeah, we're open," the bartender said in answer to a question she hadn't asked. "No power, so no ice, and the beer is warm."

"Suits me fine. Jack 'n' Coke, and make sure it's got a kick."

She would have liked a cigarette to go with it, but you couldn't smoke in bars anymore. Whole damn country was going to hell.

As she was waiting for her drink, Sammy started singing "A Hard Day's Night." It was her standard ringtone, and it had never seemed more appropriate.

The caller was Des. "I was getting a little worried," he said. "You okay?"

"Never better."

"How'd your trip to Devil's Hook go?"

"Uneventful." This was perhaps not entirely truthful.

"You coming back here?"

"Um, I dunno. Things have gotten complicated."

"What do you mean, complicated?"

She meant a lot of things, but all she said was: "There's a lot of heat on me coming from all directions. It wouldn't be safe."

"I'm willing to chance it."

"I'm not. The volume on this situation just got turned way up."

"You can't be more specific?"

"Not here."

"Where's here, anyway? And what's that music? Are you at a bar?"

"No, I'm at a friggin' symposium. Look, I got stuff to do. I'll be in touch."

She clicked off, aware that she hadn't been quite civil. At the moment she didn't have the energy to practice the social graces. She needed to think. And she did her best thinking with some hard liquor in her system.

Fortunately the bartender chose that moment to serve up her drink. She raised her glass to him. "Here's to swimmin' with bowlegged women."

He didn't even reward her with a grin. Not working for tips, evidently.

She sipped the cocktail—okay, chugged it—and reviewed the problem before her. Having done her homework on Alec Dante, she knew a good deal about his uncle, and it was all coming back to her now.

Frank Lazzaro, a legitimate businessman operating out of Jersey City, was involved in a variety of money-making ventures that included gunrunning, narcotics distribution, and auto theft. He was a stone killer with a pronounced paranoid streak, a guy whose fixation on eliminating all real or potential enemies made Thuggee stranglers look like Hare Krishnas.

Desmond had told her that scientists these days looked on evolution less as survival of the fittest and more as mutually beneficial cooperation. She couldn't remember what point he'd been trying to make—something about why she ought to be less of a hard-ass, probably. Anyhow, whatever the latest theories, Frank Lazzaro was definitely a throwback to the survival-of-the-fittest model. Peaceful cooperation was not in his DNA.

You could ask George Fratto. Except actually, you couldn't, unless you had a Ouija board. Frank had gotten pissed off at Fratto for some reason no one seemed to know, and had exhibited his displeasure by having Fratto kidnapped and taken apart, piece by piece—first an index finger, then a middle finger, and so on, until all the fingers were gone, at which point he'd continued disassembling the man bone by bone—arms, legs, ribs. Kind of like a Lego set. At some point in this ordeal, which evidently had lasted longer than a month, Fratto must have expired. No one could say just when. All that his friends and business associates knew was that parts of him kept turning up, day after day—an envelope pushed through a mail slot, bearing a severed thumb; a gift-wrapped box left on the doorstep, with a lower leg inside; a collarbone surreptitiously planted in the fish tank at his office. By the time his head made its appearance, nested in a Halloween pumpkin on his wife's front porch, nobody was really surprised. Well, maybe the wife.

"Buy you a drink, honey?"

She glanced up. An unshaven guy with a rhinestone ear stud had taken the barstool next to hers.

"Fuck off," she said tonelessly.

He wasn't deterred. "You're trouble, huh?" He leaned closer. "I like trouble."

"This kind?" She opened her purse and let him see the Walther.

He moved off without a word.

And some people said a well-armed citizenry was no longer necessary in the modern world.

So anyway, that was Frank Lazzaro. He was, not to put too fine a point on it, bad news. Bonnie didn't know how smart he was. Tough, yeah; psycho, sure—but it didn't necessarily take a lot of brainpower to make money moving heroin, which was the principal import in Lazzaro's import-export business. Exactly how he obtained it and got it past customs wasn't clear, but he was doing a bang-up job of distributing the product—cut with quinine, or sometimes baby powder—to Jersey City and parts south, all the way to Atlantic City.

Lazzaro was believed to be the underboss of the mob's Jersey City faction, meaning that the capos reported to him, and the foot soldiers in the street reported to the capos. He was a big brawling bear of a man, and he was reputed to be lucky. In his entire career he had spent not more than four hours in a jail cell. Twice he'd been brought up on charges; twice he beat the rap, making the prosecutors look like fools. He did not lack for confidence, and he was greatly feared. One former associate was quoted as saying, "He kills people the way the rest of us go take a shit."

He lived in a mansion in Saddle River, a very high-rent district. He was forty-nine years old and had a thirty-two-year-old wife and two baby boys. She forgot the kids' names. Didn't matter—it wasn't like she was going to be added to his Christmas card list.

She sighed. It had all gone to hell, hadn't it? If not for the hit on Joey Huang, the Long Fong Boyz would never have had any reason to find out about her, and Frank Lazzaro would never have had any reason to talk to the Boyz. Now that he had talked to them—or to one unfortunate kid named Chang—he'd connected Bonnie to the hit on his nephew, a connection he could not have made otherwise.

Best laid plans of mice and men, she thought soberly, or maybe not quite soberly at this point.

The worst of it was that there was nothing she could do except wait and see what Frank would do next. And meanwhile she had the Long Fong Boyz still suspicious of her, not to mention Chief Maguire's stroll down memory lane.

She finished her drink and ordered another. She had a feeling she was going to need it.

22

BONNIE SPENT THE NIGHT in her Jeep, parked behind Finnegan's, sleeping fitfully in the driver's seat as the storm howled. It wasn't the greatest arrangement, but she knew she wouldn't feel safe at home or in the office, and she still didn't want to go back to Des's place.

When she woke at daybreak, the storm had passed. There was a strange stillness everywhere.

Mindful of the checkpoint in Brighton Code, she took the Walther .22 out of her purse and stuck it under the seat. It occurred to her that at least three of the firearms she was carrying—the .45, the .357, and the .22—could be linked to homicides. Ordinarily she would have tossed any gun used in a killing, but under the circumstances she couldn't afford to give up any of her arsenal. She would just have to take her chances. Arrest was not at the top of her list of worries right now.

On her way into town, she remembered some unfinished business—Mr. Brown's Fish Market. She called the owner's cell phone. She thought she might wake him, but he was already up and frantic. There was still no power in his shop, and the fish were in danger of spoiling.

"Sorry to hear that," she said, not actually giving a damn. "I thought you'd like to know your pilferage problem has been resolved."

She expected him to inquire as to the culprit's identity, but he was too stressed out to ask. "This is a disaster. I could lose my whole inventory."

"Throw a block party. Fry up all the fish and invite the neighborhood."

"I'm not running a soup kitchen, for Christ's sake."

"Then you figure it out. Not my circus, not my monkeys."

That was another expression she'd picked up somewhere. She'd been waiting for a chance to use it.

Two minutes later, the cell she'd lifted from the late Louis Rocca started to buzz. The screen identified the caller as Frank Lazzaro.

"Getting worried about your boys, Frankie?" she murmured.

She didn't take the call.

BONNIE EXPECTED THE WORST at the checkpoint, but she got a break. Maguire wasn't there. Bradley Walsh was handling it. He gave her Jeep a perfunctory once-over, not even asking for her ID. Then he leaned into the open window and produced a thick manila envelope from under his windbreaker.

"Some light reading," he said as he handed it over. She started to open it. He stopped her. "Not here."

A suspicion took shape in her mind. "What is this?" she asked slowly.

He looked away. "The police station was pretty much deserted last night. Everybody was out on patrol. The place was running on generator power. Not a lot of juice, but enough for the copy machine in the chief's office."

"You didn't."

"Burn after reading. We never had this conversation."

He cocked a finger at her and sauntered off, leaving her amazed.

It was Maguire's file on her, obviously. His investigation into Buckington, Ohio. Something she never could have gotten hold of on her own.

The best place for it was probably her office. She could hide it there until she'd digested the file and figured out what to do about it. She headed into downtown, driving slowly to avoid scattered branches and wind-blown shingles.

Millstone County was one of nine New Jersey counties that were now federal disaster areas. In daylight the reasons were obvious. Streets were strewn with seaweed and driftwood and blocked by hills of sand; others were cordoned off with sawhorses and traffic cones because of fallen power lines. The whole south end of town was off-limits and flooded out. She saw toppled chimneys and caved-in roofs, heaps of waterlogged furniture stacked up along curbs, concrete benches that had once lined the boardwalk now lying two or three blocks inland, cast there by the tidal surge. Patrol cars prowled everywhere. Sirens blared in the distance. National Guard helicopters fluttered overhead.

According to the radio, more than eight million people were without power, a situation that might last as long as ten days. Gasoline was becoming scarce; the service stations couldn't use their pumps without electricity. Oh, and most of the boardwalks, including Brighton Cove's, had been completely destroyed.

That was kind of a sucker punch. The town's boardwalk had been obliterated by Hurricane Irene just last year, and now, after a massive rebuilding effort, it was gone again. It sort of spoke to the pointlessness of the human condition. Or the pointlessness of building flimsy wooden structures along the coastline, at least.

Twice Bonnie circled the building that housed the Last Resort office, checking for any sign of unwanted visitors. It was possible the Long Fong Boyz had changed their minds, or that Frank Lazzaro was waiting for her at her place of business. She didn't think a hit was likely in daytime, but she wouldn't bet her life on it.

She saw no unfamiliar vehicles, no loitering strangers. She parked in the alley, as usual, and replaced the Walther in her purse.

The building door was unlocked—not surprising, since some of the more optimistic tenants were open for business. Before climbing the stairs, she checked out the second floor hallway, partly visible from the lobby.

Someone waited there, hanging back, in the shadows.

All of a sudden she was awfully glad she'd brought the Walther along.

She retreated into the niche under the staircase, where the visitor couldn't get a clear shot at her, and called out, "Who's up there?"

She might have expected almost anything in reply—a man's voice, a hail of gunfire, dead silence. Anything but the answer she got.

"Miss Parker?" A woman's voice. "My name is Victoria Lazzaro."

Frank's wife.

Bonnie took a moment to register this development. She doubted Frank had sent the missus to do his dirty work. Cautiously she emerged from under the stairs.

The woman in the hallway had moved forward into clearer view. She looked tired and wet and windblown, much like Bonnie herself.

"Hey, Mrs. Lazzaro," Bonnie said. "You bring your husband along?"

She shook her head. "He doesn't know anything about this."

Bonnie was pretty sure this was true. It was the head shake that convinced her. In that one reaction Victoria Lazzaro had conveyed a habitual, reflexive anxiety that couldn't be faked.

"Okay, I'm coming up." She took the stairs, keeping one hand on the gun in her purse in case someone had followed Victoria here. It was possible she was being used as bait without her knowledge.

Up close Victoria looked younger than her age—which, as Bonnie recalled from her research, was thirty-two. She was red-haired and pale, with good bone structure and sad eyes. And she was scared. That was obvious.

She unlocked her door and ushered Victoria through the small anteroom into the office. The place was too small to offer more than a couple of hiding places, and a quick, surreptitious inspection established that no bogeymen were present.

"Gotta say, I wasn't expecting to see you this morning." Bonnie tossed her purse onto the desk. "How'd you get past the checkpoint?"

"I parked outside town and hiked in."

"That's about two miles in wet weather."

"I'm a determined woman, Miss Parker." Victoria took a chair facing the desk.

"How could you be sure I'd even show up for work?"

"I was prepared to wait. Your home address is unlisted. This was the only address I knew."

"Had breakfast?"

"No."

"I think I can scrounge up a candy bar or something."

"I'm not hungry."

"I am. It's been kind of a rough twenty-four hours."

Victoria studied her in the light from the window. "You do look a bit disheveled."

"I'm always disheveled. I'm more Sam Spade than Kate Spade." She stuck the manila envelope into a drawer.

It would have to wait. "So how do you know about me?"

"A couple of weeks ago I was parked outside Alec Dante's condo building. I saw someone else watching the place."

"Someone being me." Bonnie seated herself at the desk, pulled open the bottom drawer, and discovered a small stash of edibles. A couple of Snickers bars, a package of peanut butter and crackers, and a long-forgotten banana that had deteriorated into something horrible.

"Yes, it was you. I saw you follow Alec on foot when he left the building. When you got back to your Jeep, I—well, I followed you here."

"That story raises more questions than it answers." She chose a Snickers bar and peeled off the wrapper. "It also doesn't explain why you're here."

"This morning Frank told me Alec was dead. I'm reasonably certain you're responsible. Why else would you have been tailing him that night?"

"Just for argument's sake, let's say you're right. Aren't you a little put off by the idea that I killed your nephew?"

"I expect you had a good reason. And he was Frank's nephew, not mine. Nothing of my husband's is mine."

Even so, Bonnie felt the need to justify herself. "The kid was a rapist. He attacked a woman and threatened her and her husband to keep them quiet."

"It doesn't surprise me. All the Lazzaro men are comfortable with violence. It seems to be a family trait, like brown eyes or hammer toes."

Bonnie started on the Snickers, talking around a mouthful of chocolate. "If you feel that way, why'd you marry into the family?"

"I was stupid. I thought it would be glamorous, being married to a man like him. I must have seen too many Martin Scorsese movies." She removed something from her purse and started playing with it nervously. Rosary beads. "In my defense, I didn't know the whole truth then. About his enterprises, I mean—and what he's capable of."

"But you knew he was connected?"

"Yes, of course I knew. But the details—even today I know only parts of it. He exports stolen cars, you know, through a holding company. Sends them to the Middle East—to Jordan, I believe. On return trips, the freighters carry various legitimate goods, along with black tar heroin and other commodities."

Commodities. Not a word Bonnie would have used. Mrs. Frank Lazzaro had an education, and probably some money in her background.

"Your husband grew up in the projects," she said, polishing off the Snickers. "I'm guessing you didn't."

"I grew up in Litchfield, Connecticut. Riding lessons, debutante balls. I suppose that's how I could be so painfully naïve about Frank." She went on fingering the beads, unconsciously counting them. "I met him at a political function; he's a legitimate businessman, they said, and a pillar of the community. I quickly learned otherwise. But what he did—it wasn't real to me. It was a fantasy, a role for Robert DeNiro or Al Pacino, someone like that."

"And now that you're married to the mob, it's not what you expected."

"No. Not what I expected at all."

Victoria rose from the chair and started pacing the room, still counting on the rosary.

"Let me tell you what it's like to be with Frank Lazzaro. You know how some people say they can read auras? I never used to believe it. I do now. Frank has an aura, and it's pitch black, like smoke. Like fire and brimstone."

Bonnie watched her from her chair. "He's not the devil."

"Don't be so sure. He lives for money and power ...

and violence ... and death. It's all he cares about. He doesn't love me. He doesn't love the babies. He *owns* us. We're his possessions, like his Mercedes or his hunting knife, the one with notches in the handle. I know what those notches mean. Maybe there'll be a notch for me someday."

"Victoria—"

"Frank was at the supermarket yesterday. On the news they said a man was killed in the parking lot. Stabbed. It happened in the right time frame. I checked Frank's raincoat. There were spots on it. Blood spots, possibly. He could have killed that man."

"What motive would he have?"

Victoria released an odd little laugh, as if a child had said something unintentionally funny.

"You don't get it. He doesn't need a motive. Giving him a dirty look is a motive. Burning dinner. I've been married to him for five years, and he's broken my nose three times. Three trips to the emergency room, three lies about walking into a door. Everybody knows I'm lying. They pretend to believe, because they know who my husband is."

Bonnie took out a pack of Parliament Whites. "If it's that bad—"

"It's worse. You don't know what it's like. To sit there and watch him smash every piece of china in the house ..." She hitched in a breath, remembering. "I didn't move a muscle, even when he threw some of the dishes at me. You know what I did?"

"Recited the rosary?"

Victoria blinked. "Yes. Silently, of course. How did you—" She become aware of the beads in her hand. "Oh. Well, what else can you do in the presence of pure evil?"

Bonnie didn't have an answer for that. She tapped a cigarette into her hand and lit it.

"The babies cry all the time. They sense it too. They

know I'm afraid, and they know why. And I'm afraid for them. A few weeks ago I came into the nursery, and Frank had scrawled words on the wall with a black felt marker, words three feet tall. HATE ... KILL ... DEATH. In our babies' room."

"Why?"

"Stop asking why. He'd had some kind of breakdown, I guess. An episode. I told you, anything can set him off. Anything."

"So he's overly fond of Cocoa Puffs. That's what you're saying."

"No, it's *not* what I'm saying. Frank's not insane. Insanity is a disease. It's no one's fault. Frank is ..." She searched for the right word. "He's a monster."

"You're making him out to be something more than human."

"No. Something less. The beatings he gives me, that's nothing, I can live with that. It's not knowing what he'll do next, when you know he's capable of anything. And he's been getting worse. Ever since Santa Muerte."

"Santa what-now?"

"Santa Muerte."

"I'm guessing whoever that is, he ain't as jolly as Santa Claus."

"It's a peasant superstition. A skeleton woman who stands guard over drug runners and murderers. Frank found out about it a couple of years ago. Now he's obsessed. He built a shrine to Santa Muerte in his bedroom. He prays to that thing, that voodoo idol. Sometimes— sometimes I think he's actually possessed. It sounds crazy, I know, but you haven't *seen* him. He can be almost normal, and then it's as if a switch has been thrown and he's ... I don't know what he is. An animal."

Bonnie took a long drag on the cig. "You don't think he'd let you leave him?"

"I told you, I'm his *property*. I broached the subject of

145

divorce not long ago. He nearly put me in the hospital again. He'll never let me go. He'll kill me first. In our marriage that's the only way out. Till death do us part ..."

She stood at the window, looking out, a caged bird forlornly contemplating the sky.

"I thought having children might make it better somehow. Soften him, give him something to love. Something we could share. My God, I was such an idiot. The children have only made it worse. Now I've got them to worry about, as well as myself. And it's not just that he might ... hurt them. The worst of it is wondering what they will become. His sons. He'll make them into carbon copies of himself. He'll make them into monsters, and I'll be the breeder of monsters ..."

She leaned against the sill, head down, crying silently.

Clearly some words of solace and comfort were required. Unfortunately Bonnie didn't have that gear. Empathy was not her gift.

She gave it a shot. "Mrs. Lazzaro—Victoria—you need to get a grip."

It didn't land. Victoria raised her head, disappointment and outrage on her face. "That's all you can say? Get a grip? As if I'm being hysterical over nothing—"

"I didn't mean ..."

"You haven't heard a single thing I've said, have you? Or you just don't care. Well, maybe you'll care about this. You killed Frank's nephew. That's the kind of insult he takes very personally. He may or may not be on to you yet. But he has a way of sniffing out the truth about these things. He's smart like that, supernaturally smart. It's as if he has a sixth sense. He *will* find out about you."

Bonnie expelled a rippling feather of smoke. "He already has."

"Has he? You're sure of that? Good. That makes it easy."

"Makes what easy? Just what is it you want me to do?"

"Isn't it obvious? I want you to kill him."

Bonnie fixed her with a cool blue gaze. That stare had been known to unnerve some people, but Victoria Lazzaro was apparently accustomed to dealing with hard cases. She returned the look, unflinching.

"Kill your husband," Bonnie said finally.

"Of course. You're an assassin, aren't you? A hit man, or hit woman ...?"

"Hit man is still the preferred term. Not too many of us gals have cracked the glass ceiling."

"Well, why else would I be here? Why would I have been sitting in a car outside Alec's building that night?"

"That was something I kind of wanted to ask you about."

"I was trying to work up my nerve to go in and see him. I wanted to see if I could talk him into killing Frank."

"What made you think he'd have been up for that?"

"He was a violent man. And he resented his uncle for keeping him out of the business."

"It was still a high-risk play. What if he'd told your husband?"

"That was a chance I was prepared to take. I was desperate. But then I caught sight of you, and I decided to wait and see what you were up to. Now I know."

"You don't know I killed Dante. It could be a coincidence that I was following him that night and he was bumped off a couple weeks later."

"I don't think so. I think Alec crossed the wrong person, and that person hired you to take him out. Tell me I'm wrong."

Bonnie said nothing.

Victoria nodded. "All right, then. Now I'm hiring you. We need to move quickly. You can do it tonight."

"Not that soon. Things like this take time. Especially in this case. Your husband is what's known in the trade as a hard target."

"He doesn't have to be. I'll give you the security code

for our house and the combination to the padlock on the gate. You'll wait for him to go to sleep and then ..."

"Shoot him while he's in bed with you?"

"We sleep in separate rooms. I'm with the babies in the nursery down the hall. He's alone in the master bedroom."

"How about servants?"

"There are none who live at the house. They work from eight to six. They're gone at night."

"Dogs?"

"We don't have any."

"Cats, ferrets, boa constrictors?"

"No pets. No staff. I can walk you through it, every step of the way."

Bonnie expelled another jet of smoke. "I don't think so, Mrs. Lazzaro. As tempting as your offer sounds, I can't let you do it."

"But why on earth not?"

"Because the way you've set it up, the police will know it's an inside job. And they'll be all over you like ugly on an ape."

"I won't tell them anything."

"Even if you don't, Frank's business associates will know. For both our sakes, it's gotta be worked out so you're not the obvious suspect."

"How can you arrange that?"

"This ain't my first rodeo. I'll think of something."

"Well, think fast." Victoria rummaged in her purse and handed over a slip of paper. "This is the number of my cell phone. I have it on my person at all times. Call me when you're ready. And don't wait too long."

She crossed to the office door, terminating the dialogue. Bonnie waited until the woman had her hand on the doorknob before saying, "I'll do what I can. But sometimes these things can't be rushed."

Victoria turned. "If he knows your name, you're already a target. Either he has you in his sights or he will soon. If you don't take action tonight, it may be too late."

Bonnie leaned back, smiling around the cigarette in her mouth. "Trying to scare me, Mrs. Lazzaro?"

"Miss Parker, if you're not scared already, you're a bigger fool than I ever was."

The door shut after her, leaving Bonnie to think about that.

23

FRANK LAZZARO HAD never needed a lot of sleep. Three or four hours would do it for him. He had shut his eyes around three in the morning and awakened at seven. He checked his cell, thinking he must have missed a call from Rocca and Belletiere about Alec's car. But there hadn't been any call.

"What the fuck is up with those clowns?" he muttered.

He tried Rocca's cell, then Belletiere's. Both calls bounced to voicemail. He tried Belletiere's home phone. His wife Sophie said he hadn't been home all night. She wasn't worried; Paul didn't exactly keep regular hours.

But Frank was getting a little concerned. It occurred to him that the boys might have run into some trouble with the police. They'd been trespassing on the island, after all. If they'd been arrested, they would have called Frank's attorney, Howie Springer. Frank got in touch with him. Springer hadn't heard a thing.

This was starting to get spooky. Something wasn't right.

Over breakfast, Frank tracked down DiRosario and Costello and told them to go to Devil's Hook and see if the car had been moved. Victoria, washing dishes in the sink, overheard his end of the conversation and had to be told about Alec. She didn't exactly break down in tears. She'd never been a fan of the kid, or of any of Frank's family members. Ordinarily, Frank might have taught her a little respect, but at the moment he had other things on his mind.

He shaved, showered, and dressed in his trademark Armani suit and Charvet necktie. He was reviewing some paperwork when Costello got through to him on his cell. He and DiRosario were at the cottage, and they had bad news.

"It's a goddamn crime scene," Costello said. "Cops all over the place. Paulie and Lou—they're dead, Frank."

He shut his eyes, feeling suddenly winded. "How?"

"Dunno the details. It's not like we can go up to the cops and ask. But Paulie's Impala is there, and we seen two body bags being loaded onto a morgue wagon. You got a TV signal at your place?"

"Yeah, the dish is still working."

"Turn on channel four. They got a news van here and they're gonna go live in a minute."

Frank switched on the set in the den and watched the live update from Devil's Hook. Two reputed mobsters killed in a shootout. A car linked to a third party, the cottage's owner, Alec Dante, currently a person of interest to the authorities.

Frank stamped at the remote, killing the TV. He put his head in his hands and tried to make sense of it. How the fuck ...?

Maybe that little scrote Fish Face had been jerking him off. Maybe the Long Fong Boyz knew about Alec all the time and were keen on having a war. It had to be something like that. He couldn't believe this woman,

Bonnie Parker, was behind it. One gun-toting twat couldn't do that much damage, and why would she have been back on Devil's Hook anyway? For that matter, what would the Long Fong Boyz be doing there?

None of it added up. He was feeling itchy and antsy, and he could sense the black beast stirring in its cave.

That was when he'd left the house in Saddle River, heading into Jersey City in search of answers.

The drive was rough, and not just because the roads were fucked. He had trouble concentrating. Rage and sorrow competed for his attention. He couldn't believe Rocca and Belletiere were gone, just like that. They'd been with him for years. Not the brightest bulbs, but loyal and dependable and always good for a laugh. Dead now—killed while running a stupid errand, picking up a car. After all the shit they'd been through, all the threats they'd survived.

The last he'd seen of them was when they left the warehouse, having helped Frank put Tommy Chang into the drum.

No body, no murder—that was Frank's motto. Without a corpse, a murder prosecution was nearly impossible. So unless you wanted to send somebody a message, the corpse had to disappear. A drum was the easiest way.

Along one line of shelves in the warehouse stood a row of 55-gallon steel drums. Together he and Rocca had upended one of them and rolled it over to the chair, where Belletiere was busy cutting Chang's body loose. They stuffed the kid inside, headfirst, and stood the drum upright. Chang's bare feet stuck up like flowers in a vase. Frank pushed them down, bending the corpse's knees.

Rocca and Belletiere handled the rest, while Frank returned Virgil to the office and fed him some chopped liver as a treat. By the time he came back, the drum had been filled with five bags' worth of Sakrete instant concrete and water from a hose. The hose also proved useful in washing down the blood-flecked floor.

The concrete would take twenty-four hours to set. At some point down the line, the drum's lid would be sealed, and the whole thing would be trucked to a landfill, where it would join a million tons of garbage. And Tommy Chang would never be found.

They had locked up the warehouse, and Frank had dispatched Rocca and Belletiere to collect Alec's Porsche, because he didn't want the local cops asking questions about it. What had happened after that was a fucking mystery. And he had to admit, it unnerved him a little. He'd been sure to pay his respects to Santa Muerte at his bedroom shrine before leaving the house.

Jersey City was mostly without power, and the waterfront was a flooded mess. Luckily, Alec hadn't lived on the water. The gate to the building's underground garage stood open, presumably because it wouldn't operate without electricity. No one was guarding the garage, so Frank drove in and found a dry spot to park. He could have parked on the street, but he preferred to keep the Mercedes out of sight. There was no telling exactly what was about to go down, and he didn't need an eyewitness placing him at the scene.

Ever since interrogating Tommy Chang, Frank had been recalling his conversation with Harry the doorman. One detail in particular kept coming back: Alec had gotten into a dispute with his neighbors. At the time Frank hadn't asked for details, but he wanted the details now. A pissed-off neighbor with surplus disposable income might be just the person to hire a PI with a reputation as a triggerman.

Frank took the Ruger from the gym bag, along with a screw-on silencer, slipping both into a pocket of his raincoat, then pulled on black gloves. It paid to be careful when there was trouble afoot.

He found Harry at his post. The doorman was surprised to see him back so soon, and clearly uneasy about the look in Frank's eyes. Maybe he'd seen the news. Maybe not. Frank didn't give much of a shit either way.

"Hey, Mr. Lazzaro. You just can't stay away."

"Got an inquiry for you, Harry." No small talk this time. "You said my nephew, he got into a situation with his downstairs neighbors?"

"Uh, yeah. This have anything to do with why the police were snooping around?"

"The police were here?"

Harry nodded. "I had to give them access to Alec's unit. They had a warrant," he added defensively. "They weren't there too long, though."

"They're gone now?"

"Left about a half hour ago."

That was lucky. Frank didn't want to waste time dealing with the police. "You tell them anything about the neighbors?"

"No sir."

"Tell me. Tell it all."

"Well, it happened a couple months ago. I don't really know the details."

"Just tell me what you *do* fucking know." Frank was in no mood for bullshit.

"Uh, okay. It was the Wallings in number 1008. Well, Dr. Walling, anyway. I saw him and Alec get into it in the lobby once."

"A fight?"

"Nah, just the two of them getting in each other's face. Dr. Walling says Alec's been making a lot of noise in his place and it's coming right through the ceiling. He's pretty hot about it. Then Alec leans in close and says something real quiet, and Walling backs off."

"This Walling sounds like a goddamn pussy."

"You know it. Your boy scared the shit out of him. He must've crapped his cotton Dockers."

"Did it go any further?"

"I'm pretty sure the Wallings reported the noise situation to the condo board. A formal complaint, that kind of thing. You know, violation of the rules, lowering their unit's resale value, blah blah blah."

"The board take action?"

"They might have sent Alec a letter. No big deal."

"Other neighbors complain?"

"Not that I know. Most of them—well, they know who Alec is. They're smart enough not to make trouble."

"Yeah. But this Walling, he's not so smart. What kind of doc is he, anyway?"

"Aaron Walling? He's an orthodontist. Married. No kids."

"They around now?"

"The wife's not. She went to Philly to get away from the storm. Hubby's still in town. I saw him this morning ... Um, why d'you ask?"

"Not important."

Harry didn't seem to like where this was going. He tried to pull in the reins. "I don't think it amounted to anything, Mr. Lazzaro. You know, just a little dustup between neighbors. Happens every day."

"Yeah. Okay."

Frank returned to the garage, thinking hard. It seemed incredible that anybody would put Alec out of commission on account of a fucking noise complaint. But there could have been more to it. Who knew what Alec had said to this clown Walling, what kind of threats he'd made? Anything was possible.

Walling could have hired Parker—or the whole scenario could be wrong. Frank still didn't know. But there might be a way to find out.

From his time as owner of Alec's condo, he knew that residents garaged their vehicles in assigned spaces, and the numbers of the spaces corresponded to the unit numbers. Walling would park in space 1008. Frank checked it out. A black BMW was sitting there.

Okay, it was a safe bet Walling was home, which made sense, since who would be out and about on the day after a hurricane? The whole Eastern Seaboard was a fucking disaster area.

Back in his Mercedes, Frank found the SIM card he'd salvaged from Alec's cell phone. He took a throwaway cell from his glovebox, tossed the SIM card that came with it, and installed Alec's. Now the throwaway was a clone of his nephew's phone, and when he made a call, Alec's name would show up on caller ID.

From an online directory he obtained Aaron Walling's home number. Smiling fiercely, he punched it in.

Walling's phone rang five times—long enough, Frank estimated, for Walling to have lifted the handset and seen the caller's name.

Six rings, seven. It would go to voicemail if the son of a bitch didn't pick up soon. If the guy had been really spooked by Alec, there was a chance he would be too much of a wuss to take the call.

Frank had almost resigned himself to failure when he heard a click and a strangely hesitant, rather throaty, "Hello?"

Though he was no mimic, Frank believed he could match his nephew's voice well enough for a word or two.

"This is Alec Dante," he said, pitching his voice an octave higher than normal. Alec had been a tenor, a pretty good one. Frank had heard him do "Ave Maria."

Walling's response was deeply satisfying. There was a sibilant intake of breath, then the beginning of a reply—just one stammered syllable: "Wha—wha ..."

It was all Frank needed to hear. He ended the call.

The guy's reaction was as good as a confession. He should have had no way of knowing that Alec was dead, yet he'd sounded just like a man who'd been tapped on the shoulder by a ghost.

The little ass-suck was behind it, all right. He'd had Alec killed—because of the loud parties, or for some other reason.

And he hadn't even had the stones to do it himself. He'd hired Parker. A woman, for Christ's sake. What kind of man hired a fucking cooch to do his dirty work? What the hell was he made of?

Frank intended to get an answer to that question. He intended to open up Aaron Walling and see just what was inside. After which, he would pay a visit to the crazy bitch gunslinger who'd offed his nephew.

Then things would get really interesting.

24

"HE'S ALIVE."

The voice on the line belonged to Aaron Walling, but fear had made it almost unrecognizable.

"Aaron?" Bonnie pushed aside the pile of photocopies Bradley Walsh had given her, and pressed her cell closer to her ear. "What are you talking about?"

The phone—the special burner she'd used exclusively on the Dante case, a phone that couldn't be traced to her—had started chiming just seconds ago as she sat at her desk, reviewing the early portions of Dan Maguire's investigation.

She'd known it was Aaron calling; no one else had the number. But she couldn't imagine what he wanted, and she wasn't prepared for what she heard now.

"Dante," Walling said, the word crackling with terror. "He's *alive*."

She flashed on a memory of a body adrift in a widening circle of blood.

"He's not," she said. "Trust me."

"He just called. He called me on the fucking *phone*."

"That's not possible."

"Don't tell me what's not fucking possible. The phone rang, and caller ID showed his name. *His name*. And when I picked up, it was him. 'This is Alec Dante'—that's what he said."

Without thinking, she spun her desk chair to face the window. It was an automatic reaction. Suddenly the room was too small, the walls too close. She felt confined. She couldn't breathe.

"It wasn't him," Bonnie said slowly. "Someone's playing games."

"Games? You call this a fucking *game*?"

"Aaron, calm down. You're okay. You're in Philly, right? At a hotel or something? No one can find you there."

"I'm not at a hotel. I'm not in Philly. I never got away."

"Oh." Definitely not what she'd wanted to hear. "What happened?"

"I had to stay late at work. Last-minute stuff. By the time I closed up, it was too late to start for Philadelphia. The weather was already bad. So I decided to ride out the storm at the condo."

"How about Rachel?"

"She got away. I told her to go without me."

"All right, Aaron. I want you to listen to me."

Lazzaro must have put it together. It was the only explanation. How he'd done it, she couldn't imagine. It almost gave credence to Victoria's claim that her husband had supernatural powers.

Whether by black magic or by other means, Frank had made the connection to Walling and used his nephew's phone to place a call to Walling.

"Aaron, did he call your cell or your landline?"

"Landline. The phones are still working, even with the power out."

That was bad. It meant Frank knew Walling was at home.

"Okay. Here's what I want you to do. Leave your condo and get out of town. Do it *now*. Don't stop to pack. Take the back stairs to the garage. Try not to let anyone see you—"

"What the hell is this? What do you think is going on?"

"I don't know. But if somebody's on to us, you need to get to Philly and hole up there."

He was hyperventilating into the phone like a prank caller, his breath fast and shallow. "What I *need* to do is call the police."

"That's not an option, Aaron. You know that."

"It's all gone to shit, Christ, all gone to shit ..."

He would pass out if this went on. Or he would call 911 or do something equally stupid.

"Aaron," Bonnie snapped. "For fuck's sake, get it together."

She might not be much good at giving comfort, but she knew how to slap somebody out of a panic attack.

She heard him rein in his breath. "Right. Right."

"Now listen. The two of us need to get together face to face so we can talk things out. I'll fill you in on what's happening. You know any place where we can meet halfway?"

She could have suggested a location, but she needed to get him thinking. Fear was funny that way; if you could distract yourself, you'd forget you were afraid.

"Umm ... there's a hotel in Edison that's running on a generator. A friend of mine called last night to tell me about it."

"Good. What hotel?"

"The Sheraton. At Raritan Center. You know it?"

"Sure," she said. She didn't, but she could find it. "Go there. Wait in the lobby. I'll get to you as soon as I can.

Hopefully by noon. Got it?"

"Right. Okay," his voice was starting to break up again as fear crept back in. "Shit, this was a mistake, such a big mistake. I never should've done this—"

She didn't have time for regrets, and neither did he. "Quit dicking around and get out of there. And don't stop for anything. You hear me? Aaron?"

No answer. He wasn't there.

She couldn't be sure if he'd hung up or if the call had been dropped. It didn't matter. He knew what he had to do. And so did she.

And so, apparently, did Frank Lazzaro. That was the thing that had her scared.

25

AARON WALLING WAS in his bedroom, a suitcase open on the bed, a mess of clothes and toiletries scattered everywhere. Bonnie Parker had told him not to take the time to pack, but he couldn't go without a change of clothes and his laptop and other essentials. There was no telling how long he would be away.

The sheer weight of what had happened, the magnitude of what he had set in motion, pressed down on him like an avalanche. He was a murderer. Maybe not personally, maybe he hadn't pulled the trigger himself, but he'd ordered it done and paid for it. He had violated one of the Ten Commandments; he could never remember which one. If there was a hell, he was going to it. Probably there wasn't. Even so, the rest of his life would be different now. He had a secret, and he would have to carry it to the end of his days.

Weird how his strongest impulse right now was to tell somebody. To drive straight to the nearest police station and confess all. He felt an almost irresistible compulsion to talk and talk and talk until everything had been said and it was out in the open and he could feel clean again.

He wouldn't, of course. He would be betraying Parker, who had only done what he'd asked. More important, he was a coward. He knew that about himself. Long ago he had come to terms with it. He even took a certain perverse pride in it. He understood his limitations. He was not going to consign himself to prison merely to clear his conscience. Guilt was an abstraction, and a steel cage was very real.

He wouldn't talk. But he would know. For the rest of his life, he would know.

Strange how things had worked out. He'd considered every possible consequence of his choice to hire an assassin, except the one that mattered most.

An insistent knocking sound interrupted his thoughts. It came from the front of the apartment. Someone was at the door.

He wouldn't answer. He would just sit tight until whoever it was went away. That was the intelligent move.

But suppose the person picked the lock, or had a master key, or just broke down the door. What then?

He had to know who was there. A remote, superstitious part of him actually pictured Alec Dante, dead but alive, standing at the door with a decomposing face and a red grin like a smear of blood.

He left the bedroom, approached the front door, and dared a look through the peephole. The face that greeted him in the fisheye lens belonged to Harry the doorman.

Aaron let out a slow breath. He trusted Harry.

Still, he wasn't ready to open up. The man didn't look quite right. He seemed nervous, flushed.

"What is it?" Aaron called out.

"Dr. Walling? It's Harry. We—we have a situation here."

"What sort of situation?"

"The police caught a man breaking into your car in the garage. He had the keys to your upstairs neighbor's unit. Now he's making some pretty wild accusations against you."

"Accusations?"

"You'd better come with me, sir. The cops want to talk to you."

Oh Christ. This was the worst possible development. Whoever had called him was in police custody, and there was no telling how much he knew or what he could prove.

These thoughts crowded his mind in the two seconds it took him to open the door. His hands were shaking, and he found it difficult to get a grip on the knob. With effort he pulled the door wide, and Harry was there.

Behind him stood another man. A big man, a stranger, in a buttoned-up raincoat and black gloves.

Aaron just had time to take in the possible implications of this fact, and then the stranger bulled his way forward, ramrodding Harry through the doorway. The doorman blundered into Aaron, and both of them went down in a pile. The door slammed, and the big man was standing over them, and Harry was begging.

"I did what you said, Frank. I did what you said."

"You sure did, Harry."

The man named Frank raised his arm, and Aaron saw a long-barreled gun in his hand. It was the first time in his life that he'd seen an actual gun—not an image on a screen, but the genuine article.

"You and me, we're friends, Frank." Harry's voice broke with a sob. "Friends."

Frank nodded. "That's why I'm making it easy on you."

There was a pop like a champagne cork bursting free, and sudden hot stickiness everywhere.

Harry the doorman slumped across Aaron's chest, a dead weight. His head an exploded melon. Aaron heard a hiss that was a strangled scream begin to claw its way out of his throat.

The man called Frank swatted him with the gun, as casually as he might have swatted a bug. "Shut the fuck up."

The gun lowered, and the man slowly unscrewed the barrel, which was not a barrel after all, but a silencer or something. The kind of thing a professional killer used. And a professional would leave no witnesses.

"Don't hurt me." Aaron's voice was small and pleading. It scared him because it was the voice of someone who had already lost, someone with no hope and no chance.

Frank put the gun and the silencer into a pocket of his raincoat, then kicked the doorman, rolling the body roughly off Aaron. It was sickening to see the boneless sprawl of the dead man's limbs. Had Alec Dante flopped like that after Parker shot him, like a stuffed dummy, a rag doll ...?

Another kick, this one directed at Aaron's rib cage.

"Up."

"Who are you?"

"Up."

There was something awful in the calm implacability of the man. He seemed to be playing a part he had enacted many times before, always with the same outcome.

Aaron found the strength to struggle to his knees. The big man grabbed him by the collar and assisted him to a standing position.

"Bathroom," he said.

Aaron didn't understand. "You want to use the bathroom?"

"Go into the bathroom," the man named Frank explained with frightening patience.

Aaron wanted to ask why, but he was afraid of the answer, and anyway his throat was seizing up on him and if he tried to force out any more words, he just might be sick.

He stumbled through the condo and found the bathroom. The room was windowless and, with the power off, nearly dark. Frank sat him down on the toilet and leaned over him, producing a flashlight from another pocket of his coat. The light burned into Aaron's vision, dazzling, blinding, and even when it went away he could see nothing but a blue haze.

With a thump Frank set down the flashlight on the sink, where the glow painted the bathroom walls and reflected off the mirrored doors of the medicine cabinet. He still hadn't removed his raincoat or even unbuttoned it.

"You had Alec Dante killed," Frank said.

Aaron didn't answer, merely shivered all over while the bile rose higher in his throat.

"Alec was my nephew." The flashlight's glare lit his face from below like a Halloween mask. "I take shit like this real serious."

Aaron had to say something now, summon some kind of excuse or explanation or defense. He opened his mouth and tried to speak, and a rush of vertigo overcame him, dropping his head between his knees. He threw up.

When he raised his head, Frank was looking down at him and smiling.

"Figured you was gonna do that. That's why you're in the bathroom. No point messing up the carpet any more than it already is."

Aaron wiped his mouth, tasting acid.

"Plus," Frank added, "this room don't share any walls with the neighbors. Just in case any of 'em are around."

"They're not," Aaron whispered, then wondered why the hell he'd said that.

"Good to hear. You hired Parker." It was not a question.

"You—you know about that?"

The big man smiled. "I know a lot of things."

Aaron saw a chance. A small chance, a desperate chance, but a chance. "I hired her, but I didn't know she would kill him. I only asked her to talk to him, that's all. I swear."

"Shut your yap."

"It's true. She's a loose cannon. She's crazy. She went off on her own. I had nothing to do with–"

Frank's gloved hand caught him hard across the face. "Shut it."

Aaron fell silent.

"Why'd you do it?" the man asked.

"He—he raped my wife."

"Yeah? Harry said your beef was about noisy parties and property values."

"No. No, it wasn't that. He attacked her in an elevator. He held a knife to her throat."

"Well, that's the kind of thing a husband has a right to resent."

Aaron experienced a moment of relief. This man understood. But the relief faded when he head Frank's next words.

"It won't help you, though."

"But you said—"

"Fuck what I said. You killed a member of my family. He was my blood. You get that? My *blood*."

Aaron didn't like hearing that word. It seemed to speak to his future.

"Now you're going to get in touch with Parker," Frank said, "arrange a meeting."

"I ... I already did."

"What?"

"I just called her. We agreed to meet at noon."

"Where?"

Aaron knew it was a death sentence for Bonnie Parker if he told. But somehow he couldn't let himself think about that.

"The Sheraton in Edison. They're running on emergency power," he added pointlessly.

"Where in the Sheraton?"

"The lobby."

"What does she look like? Describe her."

"Take me there, and I can point her out to you."

The hand came up, and Aaron's skull rang with another slap. "Tell me."

"She's blond. Pretty. In her twenties. Average height. Trim. She, uh, I don't know. She wears a hat usually. She likes hats."

Frank shut his eyes momentarily as if painting himself a picture. "Blond girl in a hat. Got it."

The toilet seat was cold. The room smelled of disinfectant. Aaron didn't want to die here, in the room where he came to take a crap. It was so ... undignified.

"Please let me go," he breathed. "I have a wife."

"What the fuck do I care?"

"I never meant for any of this to happen. Really."

"You're a shitty liar, Dr. Walling. It's doctor, right? You're a, whatchamacallit, orthodontist." He put the accent on the first syllable.

"Yes."

"You work on teeth."

Aaron nodded.

Frank reached into his coat pocket and brought out something small and metallic. Blinking in the flashlight's glow, Aaron identified the thing as a pair of pliers.

Frank tapped the pliers slowly against his open palm.

"Me too," he said.

26

ON MAIN STREET in Brighton Cove, a pair of handymen were taking down plywood planks from the storefront windows of Luminaire. Bradley Walsh surveyed the gallery from outside and saw no obvious damage. But it wouldn't hurt to check with the owner, and he knew the guy was there. His special van, the handicap-accessible kind, was parked out front.

He found Desmond Harris inside, taking photos of a large water stain that had discolored a corner of the showroom wall. Harris looked up from his wheelchair and gave Bradley a friendly nod.

"Hey," Bradley said, "how's it going?"

"Could be better. Of course, it could also be a whole lot worse."

"I hear that." Bradley pointed at the stain. "This the worst of it?"

"Far as I can tell."

"You didn't lose any of the art?"

"Nope."

"Lucky."

"Yeah."

Bradley did his best not to stare at the guy. He'd never been up close to Harris before. He'd always had the idea that the guy was sort of a dweeb—you know, him being an artist and all. But the truth was, Harris was pretty damn cut, at least as far as his upper body was concerned. From the waist up, he could have passed for a goddamn Navy SEAL. Bradley wasn't necessarily too happy about that.

He poked around the showroom, searching for something to say. "So, uh, what do you call this stuff anyway? Modernistic?"

Harris wheeled his chair after him. "Postmodern, actually. For my own work, I use the term semi-abstract magical realism. As for the rest, well, there's some Stuckism, some neo-Expressionism, some massurrealism. And some that's harder to categorize."

The words meant exactly zero to Bradley. He was more interested in the price tags. Harris sure wasn't giving this stuff away. Some of the paintings cost more than a small-town cop earned in a week.

"How much of it is your own stuff?" he asked.

"About half the pieces." Harris gestured to a rainbow-hued portrait of some freaking thing that seemed to be a cross between a caterpillar and a Chinese dragon. "Like this one here."

Bradley studied it. "Huh." He attempted to muster some enthusiasm, though to be honest his appreciation of art didn't extend much beyond the latest X-Men comic. "Kinda looks like Frank Frazetta."

"Yeah, that's what I was going for."

He wasn't sure if this was sarcasm. He decided it was better not to find out.

"Mind if I ask a personal question?" Bradley said.

Harris shrugged. "Feel free."

"How long you been in that chair?"

"Since I hoisted myself out of bed at seven AM." He smiled at Bradley's discomfort. "I know what you mean. Five years."

"Accident?"

"No, I did it on purpose." Another smile. "Got you again. You're easy."

"Sorry, I—"

"No, my bad. People get a little ill at ease talking about it. They never know what to say. For some reason I find that funny. Which, I think, speaks very poorly of me."

Bradley wasn't quite sure he followed all that. "Uh, okay."

He pretended to be interested in a painting called *Vortex*. It was a series of green swirls spattered with thick crusty globs of yellow paint. It cost $950 and looked like something a monkey might vomit up after eating a bad banana.

"To answer your question," Harris said, "assuming you're still interested—it was a car accident. I flipped my Vette on Nighthorse Road. And yes, Officer, I was exceeding the posted speed limit."

"Guess you learned your lesson."

"So you'd think. But I still speed sometimes." He held up a hand in mock defense. "Never within borough limits."

"Okay," Bradley said again. He was feeling a little flustered. He just didn't know what to make of this guy. "Was there another vehicle involved?"

The question seemed to catch Harris up short. For a second he hesitated. "No. I was alone on the road. Spun out, flipped over, and barreled into a power pole. They say I was lucky not to be electrocuted."

"Yeah. No one else in the car with you?"

"Thank God, no." No hesitation that time.

"Where on Nighthorse was this?"

"Just north of the intersection with Route 329."

Bradley knew that stretch of road. It was treacherous as hell. Ran straight as a shot for a couple miles, and then a curve came up fast.

"Lot of accidents out there," he said. "Kids, mainly. Drag racing."

"Yeah."

"You ever talk at schools? You know, the dangers of reckless driving?"

"I don't relish being put on display," Harris said tersely.

"Okay."

"I'm not an object lesson."

"Right. Sure. Sorry." Bradley moved for the door. "Well, gotta get moving. Tell Bonnie I said hi."

"You know her?"

"Slightly." Bradley decided to test him just a little. "Not as good as you, I guess."

"We've been friends a long time," Harris said neutrally. "Six years now."

"That's good. I, uh, I don't think she has all that many friends."

"How many does she need?" The words were spoken lightly, but the undercurrent was cold.

Bradley summoned a smile. "That sounds like something *she* would say. Hang in there, Mr. Harris."

"You too," Harris said, but he didn't return the smile.

27

F<small>RANK STEERED HIS</small> Mercedes into the vast outdoor parking lot sprawling around the Sheraton and hunted for a space. He was in no hurry. He had arrived well before Bonnie Parker could possibly get here, assuming she was driving up from Brighton Cove.

It was good that he'd had extra time; it had allowed him to clean himself up in the Wallings' condo before leaving. He'd even had a bite to eat from the fridge. Even without power, the food was still cold. He'd enjoyed a roast beef sandwich on rye. And a pickle.

That was after he'd killed Dr. Aaron Walling, of course. The procedure had not lasted quite as long as he'd hoped, but he'd made it memorable.

He remembered the doctor's pleading terror when the pliers were produced. "What more do you want me to tell you?" the guy whispered.

That was funny. Frank actually laughed. "If I wanted you to talk, asshole, I wouldn't do this."

Quick as a snake, the pliers were thrust into Walling's mouth, closing over his tongue. Frank gave a hard yank, and the tongue came out by its roots, a long, slithery, slimy thing, followed by a spectacular gout of blood. He shoved a hand towel into the doc's mouth to stanch the flow.

Walling did a lot of moaning after that, and a lot of crying, and a lot of kicking and flailing. None of it did him any good. Frank found it easy to hold him down as the pliers went to work on his teeth. He excised them one at a time, leaving bloody gaps in the gums. Dentistry, gangland style.

The noise Walling made wasn't too bad, though his shoes did beat like the dickens on the tiled floor. Still, he'd said there was no one around. And even if there was, the black beast didn't give a shit.

At some point Walling stopped struggling and the blood stopped jetting. That was when Frank knew the man was dead. Heart failure, stroke, some fucking thing. Too bad. He'd suffered, but not enough.

Though he was now working on a corpse, Frank removed the last of the teeth. There was no point in doing the job halfway.

Anticipating wet work, he'd worn an old nylon raincoat and buttoned it up to his chin. As expected, the coat and his gloves had taken most of the spatter. He stripped off those garments and stuffed them into a plastic garbage bag retrieved from Walling's kitchen cabinet. His suit and tie were unspotted. His shoes had sustained minor damage, but he scrubbed them clean. Then he washed his face, drying himself with a hand towel, and disposed of the towel in the same trash bag. A sensible precaution. Who knew what clues the CSI weenies could recover from a cloth that had touched his face?

Frank ate his lunch, thinking about what he'd done to Harry. He felt a little bad about that, but it couldn't be helped. Casualty of war.

He considered what the police would make of the

crime scene. There would be a record of a call from Alec's cell to Walling's apartment. At that point, the homicide squad would be thinking it was a murder spree. Their guess would be that Alec Dante, a young man with a history of impulsive violence, had finally snapped. He'd killed Rocca and Belletiere at the cottage, killed his downstairs neighbor and the doorman at his condo building. Why he'd done it, no one would ever know. It was just one of those things.

The authorities would search for Alec—he might even make the FBI's Ten Most Wanted—but Frank wasn't concerned about that. His nephew would never be found. The few parts of him that hadn't burned had already been scattered by the storm.

Anyway, he didn't care about Alec. He cared about Bonnie Parker.

A blond girl in a hat. Soon she would be a blond girl in a drum. Then a blond girl in a landfill.

For it to work out the way he wanted, he had to take her alive. It shouldn't be hard. She would be looking for Walling, not him. She might not even know what he looked like. Frank had never been too keen on having his picture taken. Not many photos of him were in circulation.

He would come up behind her in the hotel lobby and stick the gun in her back. Escort her to his car. Knock her out, stuff her in the trunk, and take her somewhere for a nice quiet talk. Like the kind of talk he'd had with Dr. Walling.

Finished with his meal, Frank added the plate and napkin to the trash bag. He was worried about saliva.

Regrettably, Aaron Walling was considerably smaller than Frank, and none of his coats was likely to fit. Frank would have to proceed without a raincoat. Well, a little moisture wouldn't kill him.

He returned to his car, stowed the trash bag in the

trunk, and drove south to Edison, bypassing a section of the turnpike that had been washed out by the storm.

At the hotel he found a parking space and took it, beating out some asshole in a Ford minivan. The .22, salvaged from the pocket of his raincoat, was snugged in his waistband, Mexican style, under his suit jacket. He did not take the silencer; its bulk made the gun too difficult to carry concealed.

He crossed the parking lot in a patter of rain. At the lobby door, a valet was offloading luggage from a steady stream of arriving cars. As Walling had said, the hotel was running on emergency power. The surrounding neighborhood was still blacked out, along with much of the tri-state area. People were decamping here to escape lightless, heatless homes, or taking shelter in the hotel because all flights out of town had been indefinitely delayed.

The lobby was crowded. A restive queue faced the check-in desk. More people huddled in the hallway waiting for an elevator; a sign said that only one of the three elevators was running in an effort to conserve power. About half the lights were on. The restaurant was serving some kind of hotplate stir-fry meals; no electricity in the kitchen. The bar was open and doing a brisk business. Frank was tempted by the prospect of a scotch, but he needed to keep his head clear.

He chose a seat in the lobby near a window. From there he could scan the entrance and lobby itself. The time was 11:32, and Parker wasn't expected to arrive before noon.

In his jacket he had a copy of *People Magazine* that he'd purloined from the Wallings' apartment, having taken the precaution of peeling off the subscription label. He opened it. Celebrity bullshit. He didn't care about that crap, but it provided him with cover.

Truth was, nobody in America was more invisible

than a middle-aged white guy. Plop him down in a chair, stick a newspaper or magazine in his hands, and he just ceased to exist.

He sat there, reading about the Kardashians. In a strange way he admired those girls. They were talentless bimbos, yet they'd conned the public into following their every move. They were richer and more famous than cancer doctors or astronauts. It was one hell of a scam.

But mostly he didn't think about the Kardashians. He thought about the PI who'd killed his nephew.

When she came in, he would see her. Then he would make his move. If she offered any resistance, he might just shoot her dead right there. The black beast had fed once today, but it was hungry still.

28

BONNIE'S RIDE NORTH from Brighton Cove was all kinds of crazy. With the power out, the traffic lights along the county highways were dead, prompting a dangerous game of chicken at every intersection. Flooded streets forced unplanned detours.

The parkway was open, at least. Bonnie sped north, relying on her E-ZPass sticker to barrel past the toll booths.

Around Cheesequake, she passed a bunch of boats at a marina tossed together like castoff toys. The cross-hatched masts resembled a pile of toothpicks.

She wondered how the hell anyone ever came up with a name like Cheesequake. It always made her hungry. Especially today. That Snickers bar hadn't really done the trick.

As she drove, she thought about Maguire's file. She had skimmed enough of it to know about Maguire's hole card. The Ohio witness, the gun shop guy. Hector Samuelson.

Bonnie remembered Samuelson. And all too obviously

he remembered her.

Reading the file, she'd felt it all come back—the day she'd arrived in Buckington courtesy of a big rig driver who'd tried to feel her up. The weight of the .38 in her hand, a rusty relic she'd bought on the street in Harrisburg for twenty bucks. The hour she'd spent firing practice shots in the woods, trying to get the hang of the weapon; she'd never used a gun before. By the time her practice was concluded, she was out of ammunition, and with no money left in her pocket, she couldn't buy any.

So, necessity being the mother of larceny, she stole a box of .38 cartridges from the local gun shop, stashing it under her jacket when she thought nobody was looking. She believed she'd played it cool, but the owner was on to her. She heard his fast footsteps in the parking lot at her back. If she was arrested, she would be remanded to Pennsylvania, and she couldn't allow that, not when she was so close.

He was almost on top of her when she turned, the revolver newly loaded, and aimed the gun at his face. She said nothing, only glared. She watched his righteous anger dissolve into fear.

It was the first time she'd ever felt really powerful, and she liked it.

Now, twelve years later, Samuelson was the one gunning for her. He could be a problem. Hell, maybe she should've just shot the son of a bitch when she had the chance.

She thought she was probably joking, but sometimes she couldn't quite tell anymore.

SHE ARRIVED AT the Sheraton and dumped the Jeep into the first parking space she could find, in a distant corner of the lot. She hiked to the hotel and went in through a side door. Experience and paranoia had taught her never to use the entrance that was expected.

Peering out from the hallway, she scanned the lobby. The place was a mob scene. A whole bunch of foreign airline personnel had just swarmed in. They looked Slavic. Russians or something. Hell, maybe they were invading. Rows of public computer terminals were fully occupied by folks checking their email, while the bar was rapidly filling up with less businesslike folks intent on getting drunk.

She didn't see Aaron. And that was bad. He should've been here by now.

If he'd made it at all. It was possible he hadn't gotten out of the condo building in time. If Lazzaro had gotten hold of him, Aaron was sure to have spilled everything, including the details of this rendezvous. Bonnie had no illusions about his ability to hold up under pressure.

All of which meant Frank just might be here now, in Aaron's place.

She did not actually know what Frank looked like, at least at his present age. The only photo of him she'd ever seen had been taken during an unsuccessful criminal prosecution fifteen years ago. Scanning the crowd, she didn't see anyone who matched her memory of the photo. But too many faces were hidden behind bodies and other obstructions. And a person could change a lot in fifteen years.

It occurred to her that she still had Louis Rocca's cell phone in her purse. And Frank wasn't the only one who could make fake phone calls.

She took out the phone, which happily was not passcode-protected, and pulled up the call log. The last incoming call was the one Frank made this morning, the one she hadn't answered. She dialed the number, then watched the lobby, waiting to see if anyone answered.

Over by a window, a copy of *People Magazine* dropped into an ample lap, and a heavyset gray-haired guy pulled out his phone and spoke into it. Simultaneously the phone in her hand crackled with a rough masculine voice. "Yeah?"

She pressed the phone to her cheek. "Hey, Frankie boy. How's tricks?"

"Who the fuck is this?"

"I think you know. If you need a hint, I can tell you your nephew's last words."

"Parker," he breathed.

"You're waiting for me, right, *paisan*? Okay, I'm coming over, and we're gonna have ourselves a chat. I'm carrying, and I'm in a shitty mood. Try anything and you'll be sorry."

She dumped the phone into her purse and pushed her way through the lobby, walking directly toward him. What the hell. He couldn't shoot her in a public place. Or so she hoped.

As she approached, she compared him with his photo. He was fatter than before, with less hair and more chins. But he was still imposing. Tall, scowling, and impeccably dressed.

He was ensconced in a little conversation nook with a good view of the lobby and the driveway. She took the chair opposite him and waited, forcing him to start the dialogue.

"So you're the PI," he said finally.

"And you're Alec Dante's uncle. I'm guessing you're kinda pissed off at me right now."

Frank studied her. "A woman hitter. That's new."

"It's the twenty-first century. Glass ceilings are shattering everywhere. Try to keep up."

"You a dyke?"

"Do I gotta be a dyke to pull the trigger on somebody?"

"How many bodies have you dropped?"

"Enough."

"What are you, like, twenty-two years old?"

"I'm twenty-eight. And a half."

"Yeah? 'Cause you look about thirteen."

"Quit it with the alpha dog bullshit." She shook a cigarette out of the pack and lit up.

"They won't let you smoke in here," Frank said.

"I figure I can get in a couple of good puffs before they shut me down." She gave a careless wave. "I know, I know—these things'll kill me."

"I can pretty much guarantee they won't." Frank settled back in his chair. "Tell you one thing, you got a pair on you."

"Tits or balls?"

"I meant balls."

"Thanks."

"Tits ain't bad either."

"You're a charmer." She made sure to blow some smoke in his direction. "Lemme guess. Prom king?"

"I didn't go to the prom."

"Me neither. Hell, I didn't even go to high school."

"Me neither," he echoed. He could have said it with amusement. He didn't. "You grow up on the streets?"

"Pretty much. How'd you know?"

"You got that vibe."

She nodded. "You too."

"Yeah, neither of us is Ivy League material."

Wow, they were almost bonding. Sadly, this Hallmark movie moment was interrupted when a clerk from the checkin desk showed up, looking flustered. "I'm sorry, miss. No smoking."

"Yeah, yeah. This used to be a free country."

Bonnie stabbed out the cig. The clerk squared his shoulders and returned to his post.

"When'd you lose your cherry?" Frank asked.

Her eyebrows lifted. "Like I'm gonna answer that. What are you, a perv?"

"I don't mean sex. I mean, when was the first time you

put somebody on ice?"

"Oh. I was fourteen."

"Do it for money?"

"For revenge."

"Revenge for what?"

"They killed my parents."

"Sounds like a reason." Frank folded his arms over his generous stomach. "Me, I was sixteen. It wasn't so noble in my case. I got paid."

"You do it with a gun?"

"With a pipe."

"That'll work."

Frank half shut his eyes, remembering. "I pretty much took his fucking head off."

"How'd you feel about it?"

The eyes opened. "I could lie and say I felt great."

"But ...?"

"I was sick for a couple days. Couldn't keep food down. I got over it."

"How?"

"Decided to stop being such a goddamn pussy. It wasn't like Salvatore Torino was the first man ever to die." He appraised her with a critical stare. "I'll bet you didn't lose your appetite."

"I went out afterwards and had two cheeseburgers and a milkshake."

"You're one cold slice, Parker."

"So they tell me."

"And you're tough to read. I know you're a gunslinger, but for the life of me, I can't make out if you're a good guy or a bad guy."

She wasn't entirely sure of that, herself. "Depends on your perspective. I'm guessing your nephew thought I was a bad guy. You know, right before I plugged him."

"And my guys at the cottage?"

"Yeah, real shame about them. Wrong place at the

wrong time. You know how it is."

"You killed my blood relation and two of my most trusted associates. You've got to know what happens next."

"We're going to Disney World?"

"I am going to kill you."

He said it without anger, without emphasis, a simple statement of fact.

Bonnie smiled. "Seems a shame, seeing how we have so much in common."

"Yeah, I think we understand each other pretty good. You took care of somebody for killing your folks. Now I got a dead nephew, not to mention two made men who'll be tough to replace. So I gotta do what's right."

"You putting out a contract on me, Frank?"

"I don't want no third parties involved."

"I thought a man in your position would delegate this kind of job."

"Ordinarily, I'd have my people handle it for me. But you know what they say. This time it's personal."

She fixed him with her trademark blue stare. "Keeping myself alive is personal for me."

He met the stare without flinching. Second time today someone had done that. Damn, it was like she'd lost her mojo.

"That's your tough luck, Parker. You fucked up, and now you pay the price. Those are the rules."

"I'm not big on following rules."

"I know your name, your place of business, your home address. Bottom line, you're not gonna get much older. I can hit you any time."

"Unless I hit you first."

"Not a chance, baby girl."

"Baby girl? You might wanna pull back your attitude a little. What happened to Aaron Walling?"

"He's deceased, with extreme prejudice."

She'd figured as much, but it was still disappointing to hear. For one thing, it meant she wasn't going to get her balloon payment. She was not proud of this thought, but there it was.

"Where's the body?" she asked.

"In the bathroom of his condo, where his loving wife will find it when she comes home."

"You going after the wife too?"

"Should I?"

"She doesn't know anything about me. It was all Aaron's show. He wanted justice." She noticed Frank didn't ask why justice was necessary. She told him anyway. "Your nephew raped Rachel Walling."

Frank let his eyelids slide shot in the equivalent of a nod. "So I heard."

"He also killed a kid named Joey Huang, of the Long Fong Boyz. As I guess you know."

"So?"

"So he was a train wreck, Frank. If I hadn't put him down, someone else would have. You, maybe. You might've had to."

He considered this. "It's possible."

"Then what's your beef with me?"

"What was your beef with the guy that killed your folks?"

Well. There it was. He really was taking this thing personally. There was no reasoning him out of it.

"It was three guys," she said. "Not one. A crew my dad hooked up with in Pennsylvania. They thought he'd stiffed them on a job. He hadn't."

"They killed your mom and dad."

"Shot them in a motel room."

"But not you? Sloppy."

"I was hiding."

"How long did it take you to settle the score?"

"Six months. They went on the run, all the way to

Ohio. I had to track them down."

"How'd you manage it? Fourteen-year-old orphan tracking a bunch of killers. Not easy."

"Not easy," she agreed. "Especially since I didn't eyeball the perps. At first I had no idea who I was after."

"How'd you find out?"

"I followed the news. One of the shooters was identified. Fingerprints on a shell casing."

"Sloppy," Frank said again.

"His name and photo made the papers. By then, him and his pals had cleared out; the papers said so. But I recognized him from his photo. I remembered my dad hooked up with him and two other guys a couple years earlier, in Ohio. Town called Buckington. I was in the car when we dropped off my dad at a farmhouse. I knew I could find that farmhouse again. And since they'd used it before, I figured there was a good chance they'd go there this time to hole up."

"So you got hold of a piece ..."

"Thumbed my way across state lines and made my move."

"You telling me you just waltzed into this farmhouse and took out three guys? Bang, bang, bang?"

"That's what I'm telling you."

"And then you had two burgers."

"And a milkshake. Don't forget the milkshake."

"You're a piece of work."

"Thanks."

"Also, a nice piece of ass."

"Aw, you hadda go and ruin it. Please don't tell me you're getting turned on."

"Nah, I'm not hot for you. Believe it or not, I'm faithful to my wife."

"You believe in the old-fashioned virtues," she said dubiously.

"I believe in family. I respect what you did for your

parents. It was the right thing to do. Now I gotta do right by Alec."

She didn't get it. Alec Dante was a putz. A man like Frank had to know it.

"Did you even like the kid?" she asked.

His reaction took her by surprise. He lunged forward, and one meaty fist banged an armrest.

"He was my *blood*." The word echoed. People stared. "No one spills my family's blood and walks away. No one."

She met his eyes. "All right, Frankie. Let's dance."

He glared at her, and she glared at him, and there was silence.

"Excuse me." It was the clerk from the counter, the one who liked to play Surgeon General. "Is there a problem?"

Bonnie didn't break eye contact with Frank. "Don't worry about it. We got a whole thing going on here."

Reluctantly the clerk returned to the counter.

Bonnie was still watching the big man seated across from her. She could see the intensity in his eyes, the craziness. She remembered what his wife had said about evil spirits, possession. It seemed more plausible now.

"You could shoot me right this minute," she said quietly. "I can tell you want to. But doing a hit in front of a hundred witnesses—I doubt even your lawyer could get you off."

His voice came slowly, as if dragged from his very depths. "Not gonna shoot you. Gonna do a whole lot worse than that. You been living on borrowed time ever since Alec hit the water. Soon you pay the hangman."

"If you don't pay him first."

"Give it up, Parker." His face changed color, and he came alive in a whole new way, a way that wasn't good. "You're no match for me. You're just a smart-mouthed little girl."

187

"Rocca and Belletiere might have other ideas."

"Rocca and Belletiere ain't *me*. You're playing in a whole 'nother league. Look at me, Parker. I am somebody who *makes corpses*. It's what I do, and I been doing it longer than you been alive." His breath whistled in his nostrils. His eyes were dark and strange. "Take it to the bank, little girl. You are *done*. I will *end* you."

Bonnie could let him mess with her, or she could let him know she wasn't playing that game. The decision wasn't too tough.

She leaned forward. "I told you not to waste my time with that alpha dog crap. You want me dead? Whoop-de-friggin'-do. I've heard that song before. When this is over, you'll be the one in the ground."

His big fists were itching, and the pistol snugged at the small of his back had slipped a few inches sideways, making it just visible under his jacket. He could gun her down right here and now. He really could.

And she didn't give a shit.

"Gonna cut you up with a bone saw—" he began.

"Suck it, buddy boy. All your stupid threats are worth precisely dick. You're old and slow, and I am going to kick your fat ass all the way from here to Asskickistan."

His hand jerked towards his jacket, then stopped with a last spasm of self-control. "Fuck you, Parker. *Fuck* you and the pig you rode in on."

Her eyes burned into him, playing out a small contest of wills. "You think you're a big fucking man? You might've had the juice once, but you're all dried up now. You might be good enough to take down an orthodontist or some random schmuck at the grocery store, but you won't go three rounds against me. Because I am the real deal, chum. Ask your peeps on Devil's Hook. You wanna go it alone? Your funeral."

His fists clenched and unclenched, and his chest heaved. "There's a steel drum in a warehouse with your name on it, you batshit crazy little whore. And a landfill crawling with rats."

She stood, wanting to end the encounter. "You'd know about rats. That's your nickname, isn't it—the Ratcatcher? I'm guessing it's not because you got a mind like a steel trap."

She thought that was a pretty good shot, but it didn't land. Inexplicably, he became calm.

"No," he said, a sudden smile riding his lips. "That's not the reason."

"Yeah? Then what is it?"

"Wait and see."

She knew it was time to go, but she really hated leaving him with that beatific smile on his puss. "Don't try to follow me. You've lost the element of surprise."

She started to walk away. Behind her, he got in the last word.

"I wouldn't be too sure about that, Parker. There could be one or two surprises left."

29

"YOU SURE THAT'S Lazzaro?" Eng asked.

He pressed the binoculars to his eyes, watching the lobby, where Bonnie Parker sat in conference with a fat old man.

Patrick Chiu nodded. "I've seen him around." He had no need for the binoculars. His eyes were owl-sharp.

"Bitch is fuckin' *meeting* with him," Lam said in astonished outrage.

Chiu and his two right-hand men had located Parker's Jeep less than three minutes ago, and now their Cadillac Escalade was serving as a front row seat to her lies and betrayal. It was everything he could have hoped for.

Now they just had to make the snatch. A tough job in daylight on strange turf, but he was confident his guys could handle it. He believed in the men he'd recruited. To outsiders, they might look like scrawny teenage boys, but every one of them was a straight nightmare, worthy of the great days of the tong wars and the salaried soldiers.

Chiu had made a study of that era. He'd read rare books and musty old newspaper articles, and he'd spoken with those few elders who still remembered the old days. It had been a romantic age. The term "hatchet man" had been coined for the boo how doy, a tribute to their skill with the short-handled hatchet. They'd also used long and short guns, hand grenades, homemade bombs, and any other available method of mayhem and murder. Heroes like Mock Duck and Little Pete had played the role of ceremonial warriors, even while profiting from the female slave trade and opium parlors and gambling dens.

Patrick Chiu sighed. Had he been born a hundred years earlier, he could have been one of them. Then he really could have made something of himself.

"You really think that fat fuck hired the PI to chill Tommy?" Lam asked. "Why would he?"

Chiu shrugged. "Why do those crazy linguine shitters do anything? We've been pushing into Lazzaro's territory. Maybe he decided to push back. Maybe he used Parker so he'd have deniability. Maybe he's planning to knock her off so she keeps quiet. Who knows?"

"So she takes Lazzaro's cash to whack Cricket. Then lays the hit on his nephew." Eng's voice was pitched an octave higher than normal. "She a dog. She a low-down lying dog."

Unlike his men, Chiu was neither indignant nor surprised. He'd assumed all along that Parker was lying. He hadn't expected her to lead them to Lazzaro this soon, but he'd never been one to question his own good fortune. All that remained was to see that both she and the Italians paid the price.

"What d'we do, dai lo?" Eng asked, chewing his lower lip.

"We wait for her to bounce, and we take her." A snatch in broad daylight. Not easy, but worth the risk.

"Alive?" Eng was disappointed.

"Alive. She'll tell us all about Cricket and Fish Face, and what the Italians are up to."

"What about Lazzaro?" Lam asked, sounding nervous.

"That's for later."

To start a war with the Italians was not a small undertaking. It wasn't something to be done on the fly, in a crowded parking lot in daytime.

Parker, on the other hand, was no big deal. To the Italians, she would be expendable. That must be why they'd hired her in the first place.

"She's getting up." That was Eng, still glassing the window.

Chiu leaned forward. "All right. Get us back to the Jeep. Kicker, you're on point. You wait for her to show and take her by surprise like I did last night. Then we'll hustle her into the Caddy and go for a drive."

Lam was already steering the black SUV through the parking lot. A few hotel guests were visible here and there, making their way through the drizzle.

"If there are witnesses when we grab her?" he asked.

"Make them dead," Chiu said. It was the answer Mock Duck would have given, and he felt good about that.

30

BONNIE LEFT THE HOTEL via a different door than the one she'd used when entering. Always do the unexpected. This was a good rule of thumb in almost any situation, and especially when dealing with a homicidal psychopath like Frank Lazzaro.

Her little diatribe in the lobby had been unplanned, and poking the bear wasn't smart. Then again, when the bear in question was already dead set on sticking you in a steel drum, it probably didn't make much difference.

The meeting had proved productive in one respect. She'd decided Victoria Lazzaro was right. Frank was too dangerous to be allowed to make the first move. He had to be dealt with proactively.

It was his uncanny smile at the end of their little interview that convinced her. She didn't know what that smile was all about, and she had a feeling she didn't want to know.

So it's on, girlfriend, she told the absent Mrs. Lazzaro. It's on like Donkey Kong.

Frank was going down tonight. He would die in his

bed—but not peacefully. All she had to do was work out the details.

She was twenty yards from the Jeep, walking fast through a peppery drizzle, when she glimpsed a blur of jet black cruising behind a row of cars like a shark's fin breaking the water.

A Cadillac Escalade. Moving away from the spot where the Jeep was parked.

Last night the Long Fong Boyz had ambushed her in her Jeep. And bad guys had a way of repeating themselves.

She hooked left, cutting between parked cars, staying clear of the Jeep.

It could have been a coincidence. There were a lot of Escalades in the world. But she hadn't lived this long by being an optimist.

"AW, SHIT." LAM peered through the windshield. "I think she made us, dai lo."

"Park this thing," Chiu said.

"There's no spaces."

"Ditch it anywhere."

Lam pulled to a stop, blocking in three vehicles. "What now?"

"We go after her on foot. Chase her down and take her fast. She's carrying, so don't fool around. As soon as we flank her, it's guns out, guns in her face."

"How about Kicker?"

"Let him stay by the Jeep in case she doubles back."

BONNIE WAS ON the move, keeping her head down and using the parked cars as cover.

She became aware of someone looking at her. A guy unloading suitcases from his Lexus.

"Everything all right?" he asked dubiously.

"Just looking for a quarter. I know I dropped it around

here someplace."

She duckwalked on, leaving him to construct whatever psychological diagnosis he saw fit.

One row of cars ended, and another began. Navigating the lot without being seen meant cutting from aisle to aisle, taking unpredictable zigs and zags, like a lab rat in a maze.

She was weaving between a parked Honda Civic and an ancient Mustang when she caught sight of a reflection in the Honda's side view mirror. A skinny young guy with jet-black moussed hair was following her. And yeah, he was one of her friends from last night.

If one of them was around, there would be more. Gangs were like roaches that way.

She kept walking. Her pulse had quickened, but not by much. Getting all panicky was the worst thing you could do in a predicament like this.

Without turning her head, she used her peripheral vision to check for movement. There, on her left. From the guy's languid stride she identified him as Patrick Chiu. He'd let her walk away on the beach, but apparently the truce was off.

Gangbanger behind her, gangbanger on her left, probably one or two others closing in. She had a gun, but she wasn't keen on starting a shootout in a parking lot, and she didn't think she could take out the whole bunch of them anyway. All in all, it seemed like a good time to make herself scarce.

She slipped between another pair of vehicles, one of which was a van with airbrushed side panels that displayed a DayGlo pink tropical sunset. As she came even with the rear bumper, she ducked behind the van, dropped to the ground, and rolled underneath.

With any luck, no one had seen her disappearing act. But since the underside of the van was the first place anyone would look, she needed to relocate.

And fast. She heard a clatter of running footsteps. Chiu and his henchman were on their way.

On elbows and knees she wriggled under an adjacent pickup truck. The next vehicle in line was a sports car, low to the ground, a tight fit, but by belly-crawling in a decent imitation of an inchworm, she made it. She was about to try for the car that came next when she heard the footsteps come up short, yards away.

She lay still, looking over her shoulder. Two pairs of legs were visible by the rear of the van.

Her pursuers kept their voices low, and she couldn't make out what they were saying. But she could guess. Their quarry had vanished, and they couldn't figure out where she'd gone.

Predictably, Chiu's right-hand man bent down and peered cautiously under the van.

Moving as little as possible, Bonnie reached into her purse and closed her hand over the .22. If the bastard spotted her, she would open up on him and his boss. She could bust up their ankles, anyway. Not that a broken ankle would stop them from shooting her dead.

After a moment that went on much too long, the guy straightened up. He hadn't seen her.

More unintelligible conversation. The four legs shifted restlessly. She had the sense that Chiu and his pal were getting antsy, ready to move on.

Then Sammy started to sing.

At first she didn't understand what was happening. She heard a muffled melody, which she recognized as a Beatles tune, "A Hard Day's Night." Her ringtone.

Her fucking *phone*.

She crammed her hand into her purse, fumbling for the cell phone and the volume control on the side. She muted the damn thing.

Then she lay motionless, waiting.

The bad guys had stopped shifting around. They

were rigid, listening.

"You hear that?" a voice asked, just loud enough for the words to come through. Chiu's voice.

The answer was indistinct but affirmative.

No more talk. No movement.

If they looked under the van again, they might see her this time.

She tightened her grip on the gun and waited to find out if she would need it.

"I THINK IT came from over there," Lam said, pointing down the line of cars that ran north of the airbrushed van.

Chiu wasn't sure. The sound had been faint. It might have originated anywhere. It might have been someone else's phone—not Parker's at all.

"All right," he said slowly. "Here's the plan. We split up, check out the cars in both directions. Look under each one. She's armed, so—"

"Oh, man," Lam said, staring past him with an expression of disgust.

Chiu turned and saw Eng jogging their way, his face flushed, the MAC machine pistol barely concealed under the loose folds of his rain poncho.

"She's on to us, dai lo," he said. "She never showed."

Chiu rarely got angry, but at this moment he felt an urge to strike Kicker across the face. He suppressed the impulse with effort.

"You were instructed to stay by the Jeep," he said, raising his voice in his only concession to emotion.

"I told you, she figured it out—"

"Like we don't already know that?"

"I just thought—"

"Don't think. Don't *ever* think. If she knows the Jeep is unguarded, she'll make a run for it."

Lam pointed. "She already is."

- — -

BONNIE HAD CAUGHT enough of the conversation to know one of the guys had left his post. That was enough for her. She scrambled out from under the sports car and broke into a sprint.

The Jeep was dead ahead, easily identifiable by its vomit green coloring. There were advantages to driving a vehicle that was ugly as shit.

She cut across a long open stretch of asphalt, closing on her ride. When she looked back through, she saw three figures in black coming after her.

Fuckity-fuck fuck.

The movies knew how to make the most of a situation like this. The victim was always fumbling with her keys, dropping them, then having trouble starting the car, and meanwhile the bad guys were inexorably closing in.

Bonnie didn't have time for that Hollywood bullshit. She got the door open and the engine running inside of two seconds, and then she was reversing out of the space, throwing the Jeep into forward gear, tearing away with a shriek of tires. She kept her head down, expecting gunfire, but the Long Fong Boyz apparently weren't any more eager than she was to open up with their firearms in a public place.

She skidded out of the lot and onto the first on-ramp she could find.

CHIU AND HIS men said nothing until they were back in the Escalade. Then Eng hung his head and muttered, "My fuckup, dai lo. It's all on me."

Chiu had calmed himself by now. He patted Kicker gently on the shoulder. "Today wasn't the day to take her. Wrong place, wrong time."

"Little shit has nine lives," Lam said bitterly.

Eng was eager to make amends. "We can chase her down right now. Catch up to her, no problem."

"No." Chiu had already allowed impatience to master his better judgment. He would not repeat the mistake. "We wait for nightfall. Let her have the sunlight. In the dark she'll be ours."

"She shouldn't live that long," Lam said.

"Don't sweat it. There's a kill clock ticking. And we can find her again any time."

Lam pursed his lips, pouting. "I wanna dome her. Just lemme take the shot."

"First we rip her with the machine gun," Eng said, patting the MAC-11.

"Yeah, okay," Lam said, "but before she bleeds out, I want the head shot. Wanna put a Hydroshock in her brainpan. I wanna look into her bright blue eyes and kiss her dead."

Chiu smiled indulgently. "You're a crazy little motherfucker, ain't you, Monkey? Shit, you can take the shot. It's yours."

Lam grinned, mollified, and Chiu shook his head in amusement. It took very little to make his guys happy.

Really, they were so much like children sometimes.

31

BONNIE DROVE TWENTY miles at high speed before deciding the Long Fong Boyz weren't still on her ass. At that point she slowed down a little, lit a cig, and checked Sammy to see who'd been rude enough to call at the most inconvenient time.

Des. Of course.

She wasn't sure she wanted to talk to him, but she returned his call anyway. "What's buzzin', cousin?"

"Just checking in. Where are you?"

"In motion. As usual."

"Things settle down yet?"

"Oh, sure. Everything's hunky-dory. I got a mob wiseguy on my ass, plus the Asian gang I told you about. And my latest client just got snuffed."

"What?" He sounded as if he hadn't heard, or just couldn't take it in.

"The guy who hired me for the job I did yesterday. Kaput."

The startled silence on his end lasted five long seconds. Bonnie counted.

"But," he said finally, "but how ... how could that happen?"

"People get killed in this game, Des. That's something you oughta know by now."

"Yes ... sure ..."

"Don't let it throw you. I got a master plan to make it all copacetic. Just let me do my thing, and you'll hear from me when you hear from me."

"You're still not sleeping over?"

"Nuh-uh. I'm kind of a bullet magnet right now. Anything else you wanted to talk about?"

There was a beat of silence on the line. "That new cop, Bradley Walsh, came by the gallery a little while ago."

"Yeah?"

"I'm pretty sure it wasn't a purely official visit. The vibe I got is that he knows about us. And he's interested in you."

"Everybody's interested in me. I'm friggin' irresistible."

"I'm serious. I had the impression he was checking me out, sizing up the competition."

"He's a kid, Des."

"I don't know. He seems like a decent enough guy. And he clearly cares about you."

She thought of the Xeroxed file. More than you know, she thought. "You trying to set me up with him or something?"

"No, I'm just saying ..."

"What?"

"That you might be better off, that's all. A young, healthy guy like him ..."

"An action figure whose moving parts are still moving? That it?"

"I suppose so."

"Jeez, Des. I never took you for a guy with a critical

shortage of self-esteem."

"It's not that, exactly. It's ... Never mind."

She had an idea of what he wanted to say, but this wasn't a talk they could have on the phone. "Look, I gotta get off. My connection's breaking up."

That was a lie, and she figured he knew it.

"Okay, Parker. Take care."

"Always do."

Another lie. That made two in a row.

She clicked off and fired up another cig.

As SHE APPROACHED the parkway's Maritime exit, she placed a call to Mama Blessing. "Yo, Mama. Doing business today?"

"Always open," Mama said cheerfully. "I never close."

"I'll be there in fifteen."

In Maritime, she guided the Jeep into a low-income neighborhood near the hospital. The area consisted mostly of housing projects, but these projects were nothing like Crossgate Gardens. Here, people lived in neat little bungalows with postage-stamp yards and cars up on blocks in driveways.

She parked on the street. Before going inside, she circled the Jeep, poking around the chassis. It took her less than a minute to find a matte-black case, the size and weight of a cigarette pack, magnetically affixed to the Jeep's right front wheel well.

It was a GPS homing beacon. The Long Fong Boyz must have planted it last night, after leaving her on the beach. It explained how they'd found her at the hotel. They hadn't shadowed her; she was sure she would have spotted a tail. Instead they'd tracked her on a computer or cell phone, using a web interface that drew her location in real-time on a map. When they saw that the Jeep was stationary in the vicinity of the hotel, they'd driven down from Jersey City to see what was up.

Of course she could disable the tracker or just chuck it into the nearest garbage bin. But she didn't want to do that. Now that she knew about it, the homing device could work to her advantage.

She left it in place and jogged through a mist of rain to the front stoop of Mama Blessing's bungalow. She waited at the screen door, neither knocking nor ringing the bell. Mama would know she'd arrived. Mama was always watching.

In a few seconds a matronly woman ambled into view, her hair coiffed in a high-rise updo bound in an African head wrap. A Malcolm X sweatshirt bulged over her considerable frontage. Turquoise rings glittered on every finger. Her feet, Bonnie noticed as the door swung open, were shod in pink bunny slippers.

"Hey," Bonnie said, stepping into the parlor. Gray daylight filtered through the windows, providing the only illumination. "I see you survived Sandy."

Mama clucked her tongue. "That bitch didn't scare me. I sat in the dark and ate potato chips and listened to Miles Davis on my iPod all night long."

Bonnie found herself wanting another cigarette, but she resisted the urge to light up. She knew Mama didn't approve of smoking. Ordinarily she wouldn't have cared, but she respected Mama. More to the point, she needed her.

"Got cleaned out last night," she said briskly. "I'm looking to rearm with some heavy steel."

"How heavy?"

"You got an assault rifle? I mean a real assault rifle, not the bogus ones they show on the news. Full automatic, banana clip, major stopping power."

"Sister, you sound like you're in trouble."

"No. I sound like I'm planning to make trouble."

Mama nodded, unruffled. Bonnie had never been able to determine her exact age—it had to be somewhere between fifty and seventy—but she knew Mama had been in the business long enough to be unsurprised by any request. She'd been dealing guns in the neighborhood since forever, and paying off the cops to look the other way. She didn't make much of a secret of it; hell, even her sweatshirt showed Malcolm toting a gun. When she wasn't hawking small arms, she baked macadamia nut cookies for the local kids. Bonnie had tried a cookie once. It was delicious.

"I do have an item that would suit your needs," Mama said, setting herself down on a lumpy overstuffed couch. "TEC-9 conversion job. Built in eighty-nine; it's old but well maintained. Takes a fifty-round extended magazine. Fires a thousand rounds a minute. You can shoot your whole wad in a three-second burst."

"That's what I'm looking for."

"Never known you to buy a full automatic before. Aren't you the one who told me it's cheaper to buy a semi and convert it yourself?"

"Yeah. But right now I don't have the time."

"This is urgent, huh?"

"I need it yesterday."

"You can have it here and now. But it'll cost."

"How much?"

"A grand."

"That's pretty steep."

"You're pretty desperate."

Bonnie couldn't deny it, but she went through the process of haggling anyway. Five minutes later she'd talked the price down to $700 for the gun alone, with ammo to be purchased separately.

"Deal," she said, peeling off bills from a roll she'd taken from her office safe this morning. With the ATMs out of service, she'd figured she would need cash. "Now let's talk about those fifty-round mags."

"I've only got one."

"I'll take it."

They settled on a price, and Bonnie peeled off another hundred bucks. Mama Blessing spent some time folding and refolding the currency, which then disappeared into the deep valley of her cleavage. She left the parlor without a word. Bonnie stood around looking at porcelain figurines and photos of Mama's grandchildren until the woman returned, the gun in her hand, the long magazine already inserted.

"You want it gift-wrapped?" She always asked that. Bonnie was never sure if it was a joke.

"Brown paper bag will be fine." It was how she always answered.

The merchandise went into a Shop-Rite bag. Bonnie tucked it under her arm.

"Nice doing business," she told Mama with a smile.

The woman was watching her. "This isn't a hit kit, young lady. Just what are you up to?"

"I'm in a war. This bad boy ought to neutralize the enemy's advantage."

"You can do a lot of damage with a piece like that."

"I intend to."

She headed back out into the rain. Mama Blessing stayed behind the screen door. "Stay safe," she said.

Good advice. But at this point it was no longer possible.

BACK IN THE CAR, Bonnie jumped on the phone again, tracking down Walt Churchland's home number and giving him a call.

"Sparky? It's your new best friend, Bonnie Parker. You know that video camera you were bragging about? I need to borrow it."

"I don't really lend it out."

"You do now. Or your boss finds out who his fish swam off with."

"Shit. You're blackmailing me?"

"I'm calling in a favor. I did you a solid. What goes around comes around."

Churchland lived in a ground floor apartment in Algonquin, not far from the fish store. Bonnie parked outside and met him at his door. He did not appear happy to see her.

"That it?" She nodded at a squarish, toaster-size camera in his hand.

"Um, yeah. I don't feel too good about this."

"Really? I feel great. Tell me about the camcorder."

"It's a Panasonic AG-DVC30. I bought it on eBay. It's an expensive piece of equipment."

"Right, right."

"You won't be subjecting it to harsh treatment, will you? I really don't want it damaged."

"Do I strike you as the kind of person who takes foolish risks?"

"Very much so."

"No worries. I'll bring your AC-DC back in one piece."

"AG-DVC."

"Whatever."

He spent some time teaching her which buttons to push, how to set the tape speed, and how to import video from the digital videotape cassette to a computer via a four-pin FireWire input.

"I got FireWire on my laptop," she said. "Never use it, though."

"All you need is an EEE 1394 cable."

"Don't have one. But I'm betting you do."

"Well ... yeah."

"Fork it over, Dr. Venkman." She thought this was pretty good, but he didn't even crack a smile. "You know, Peter Venkman? In *Ghostbusters*?" Still nothing. "Oh, come *on*."

He regarded her with a cool stare. "I don't joke about the paranormal."

"Fair enough. So where's my EEE thingy?"

He got the cable for her but didn't hand it over. "You can shoot video with your cell phone, you know."

"Not in the dark. This toy of yours can do that, right?"

"Yeah, in infrared mode."

"Good." She held out her open palm. "Gimme, gimme."

He surrendered the cable. "You're a real pain in the ass."

"Don't I know it." She hefted the camera. It was heavier than it looked, maybe six pounds, but it fit snugly in her hand.

"What do you want it for, anyway? I can't believe you'd go ghost hunting."

"Oh, I'm hunting, Sparky," Bonnie said as she headed out the door. "But not for ghosts."

32

FRANK WAS HEADING up north, thinking he'd check in on things in Jersey City, when his phone chimed. It was Victoria, calling to say there were two police detectives at the house. "I think it's about Alec," she said in a low voice.

"What are their names?"

"Murphy and Cruz."

"Have 'em wait. I'll be there. Meantime, just take care of the kids and keep your mouth shut."

He took a detour to Saddle River. The drive home was quick enough, not that he was in a hurry. Let the two bulls rest their cans.

Murphy and Cruz. A mick and a spic. He didn't know them, but all cops were the same. Half of them were on the take, and the other half wanted to be. They were all secretly fascinated by criminals—jealous of the gangster life. Scratch a cop and you'd find a frustrated mobster underneath. Most of these guys would've been made men if they'd had the nerve. Frank despised them.

He wasn't worried about the cops, but he was a trifle concerned about what had happened in the lobby. He'd nearly made a fatal mistake. It had required all his will-power to resist pulling the gun and blasting that bitch to hell. Only the thought of doing her a different way, a much better way, had stopped him.

She'd been baiting him, sure, but he should have been able to take it. A loss of control like that—it wasn't like him. Or maybe it was, these days. The guy at the A&P ... When he was younger, even a few years younger, he wouldn't have taken that kind of chance over something so small.

He remembered how he'd come down on Alec for being headstrong and reckless, not enough in control to be part of the team. Now he was one the taking crazy risks. It bothered him.

The thought crossed his mind that Santa Muerte might have had something to do with it. In praying to her, giving himself to her, maybe he was giving the black beast free rein. Opening up the channel to his animal self a little too wide. Letting it take over more and more, so that while he might think he was still in control, he was only a puppet moved by unseen forces.

He was not an introspective man. He couldn't hold on to the thought. It brushed up against him and drifted on, and by the time he parked in his driveway, it was forgotten.

He got out of his car, noting the Ford Taurus on the street, obviously the detectives' ride. In the living room he found the two cops seated on the sofa, sipping coffee. Upstairs, the twins were crying, while Victoria did her best to soothe them with a lullaby.

"Gentlemen," Frank said in greeting.

"Hello, Mr. Lazzaro." That was the Irish-looking one, who had to be Murphy. "Can I call you Frank?"

"Sure. Can I call you dipshit?"

"There's that Old World charm. Sorry to take you away from your business, whatever that might be."

Frank appraised them as he took a seat in his favorite armchair. They were typical plainclothes humps, all dressed up in suits and ties, but with faces that belonged on a loading dock. Dumb apes carrying badges. If Howie Springer had been here, he would have advised Frank not to talk. But Frank knew he could more than hold his own against a couple of lightweights like these two. He wouldn't even have to break a sweat.

"It's import-export," he said smoothly. "And Sandy's playing hell with my inventory, so if we could skip the foreplay and get right to the point ..."

Murphy smiled. "Of course, Frank. We don't want to waste your time. When was the last time you saw your nephew, Alec Dante?"

Frank had already decided how to play it. Total ignorance. Like Sergeant Schultz, he knew nothing.

"Alec?" he said, shifting his features into a quizzical expression. "He in trouble?"

"Yeah, I'd say so."

"What kind of trouble?"

Cruz spoke up, scowling. "Just answer the question."

Good cop, bad cop. What a load of fugazy bullshit.

Frank furrowed his brow. "Last time ...? Shit, I don't know. Maybe two, three weeks ago. He's called me a couple times since then."

"About what?" Cruz wanted to know.

"He wanted to get together, have a beer."

"But you blew him off?"

"I been busy. Now what's the deal with Alec? Why are you interested in him?"

Cruz ignored the question. "How about James Rocca and Paul Belletiere? When was the last time you saw them?"

"I don't know anybody by that name."

"They're two of your known associates."

"You got bad intel. I don't know any Rocca or Belletiere."

Cruz scowled harder. "Sure you don't."

Frank braced his hands on the armrests, preparing to rise. "So, we done here?"

Murphy raised an eyebrow. "Don't you want to know why we're asking about Alec?"

He realized he'd made a mistake. He tried to recover. "I didn't figure you were going to share."

"Oh, we'll share." Murphy was still smiling, always smiling. A real friendly guy, was Murphy. "Your nephew's in some trouble, Frank. It looks like he's been a bad little boy."

"What the hell's that supposed to mean?"

"You haven't seen it on the news?"

"I don't watch the news. Too depressing."

"None of your friends or, um, business associates have called to tell you what's up?"

"Nobody's said nothing. You gonna bring me up to speed or what?"

"Sure, Frank. We just came from Alec's condo building. There was a break-in, sort of a home invasion, in the unit directly below his. You should've seen it. It's a fucking slaughterhouse in there. Two victims—the doorman and the unit owner, a dentist named Walling. Both fatalities."

"What's that got to do with Alec?"

"Some of the other residents reported there'd been trouble between Alec and this Walling guy. Sounds like it got ugly. Your nephew was partying hard, making Walling's unit unlivable. Walling wanted to sell, but the noise issue made it impossible for him to unload the place."

"Yeah, well, things are tough all over."

Cruz leaned forward. "People say Walling was scared of your nephew. They had the impression Alec might have threatened him."

"This neighbor sounds like a weak link. A loud stereo makes him want to sell out? Jesus. How about he buys some earplugs and a pair of balls?"

Murphy shook his head. "The noise wasn't the only reason he wanted to move. He needed to get out of the neighborhood. It seems his wife had a situation."

"What situation?"

"She was raped on a PATH train late one night. After that, she wanted out of Jersey City. But the upstairs neighbor problem meant they couldn't move the property or even rent it out."

"You're telling me the wife's a rape victim? Well, shit, Sherlock, there's your perp. Whoever jumped her on the PATH train probably tracked down her address and came looking for more. Find that asshole, and case closed."

"No such luck," Murphy said. "We already found him."

"You what?"

"We picked up the rapist two days ago. Undercover officer caught him in the act of another sexual assault. He's been in lockup the whole time."

"Maybe the guy you nabbed didn't do the Walling rape."

Cruz waved this off. "He did it. He already confessed."

Frank couldn't make any sense out of that. Walling had said Alec did the rape. That was his whole motive for hiring Parker in the first place. Wasn't it?

"So it wasn't the perv who killed Walling and the doorman," Cruz went on. "And there's something else."

"Yeah? What's that?"

"We went to your nephew's building because we were looking for him. He's a person of interest to the authorities on Devil's Hook Island."

"You know that cottage he keeps there?" Murphy said. "It's a crime scene. This morning the local cops were doing a sweep of the island, and they found two dead bodies there."

"You're shitting me."

"Rocca and Belletiere. Both shot to death. And Alec's car was there. But no Alec."

"That's fucking crazy."

Cruz took a long pull on his coffee cup. "It's been all over the news. But you haven't heard a thing, right?"

"What can I say? I only follow sports."

"So you didn't send Rocca and Belletiere to the cottage? Maybe to check on Alec for some reason?"

"I told you, I don't know shit about any of this."

Cruz stared at him over the rim of the mug. "Then why were your boys on the island, Frank?"

"They're not my boys. I don't know them."

"Oh, right. I forgot. You been to Alec's condo today?"

"Nope."

"So you were never in Dr. Walling's unit?"

"What, you're trying to put that on me? Gimme a break."

Murphy shrugged amiably. "Just asking. Actually we're more interested in having a talk with your nephew. You wouldn't happen to know where to find him?"

"No clue. You think Alec killed all these people? You think he's on some kind of murder spree?"

"The thought did cross our minds. But there's another possibility. The Devil's Hook cops found a parking garage ticket in Alec's car. It places him in the vicinity of Crossgate Gardens on the night of October 22. You know what happened then?"

"Nothing good, I'm guessing."

"You guessed right," Cruz said. "An Asian banger named Joey Huang got capped. So what we're thinking, Frank, is maybe your nephew did the hit, and Joey's homeboys came after him."

Frank wasn't happy to hear this. He hadn't wanted the cops to make any connection between Alec and Joey Huang. Once word got back to the gang, they might drop their interest in Parker and focus on Frank's organization instead. It would mean a gang war for sure.

"Alec wasn't into anything like that," Frank said lamely.

"Sure," Cruz said, "he was clean as a whistle. Just like you, right?"

Frank was getting pissed off all of a sudden. It was this taco bender, Cruz. The guy had an attitude. He didn't show respect.

He leaned forward in the armchair. "Let's stop the fucking dance. You know what I am. But I made Alec keep his distance from all that. I never got him hooked up. I didn't want that life for him."

"Maybe he wanted it for himself," Murphy said. "Maybe he did the hit on his own."

"Bullshit. You get all that from a ticket stub?"

"It's an interesting coincidence, don't you think?"

"Why would the Long Fong Boyz go after this Walling guy? It doesn't add up."

Cruz narrowed his eyes. "We never mentioned the Long Fong Boyz specifically."

"Don't try that shit on me." Frank was getting hot. Distantly he warned himself to calm down. "You said Joey Huang, Crossgate Gardens. I know the streets. That neighborhood's run by Chiu's bunch."

"We hear another member of that crew has gone missing," Cruz said. "Some tweaker named Tommy Chang."

"You fingering Alec for that one, too?"

Murphy shook his head. "Not yet. But we need to talk to him, Frank. Right now he's in the wind."

"With all this crazy weather, half the population of Jersey's in the wind. Alec'll turn up, and he'll straighten all this out."

"Unless he's dead," Cruz said. "Maybe Chiu's gang got him."

Fucking wetback said it with a smile. His first smile

since Frank had walked in. Goddamn bastard. Frank would've liked to punch his lights out.

"You're blowing smoke," he said, fighting to hold his voice steady. "It's all supposition, based on nothing. And you're really wasting my fucking time now, so we're done. We're fucking *done*."

"For now," Murphy said, a little less affably than before.

The two detectives rose from the sofa. Frank got up too. Halfway to the front door, Murphy made a show of remembering something, then turned back. The old Columbo routine.

"Say, Frank—you gone grocery shopping lately?"

This caught him up short, but he tried not to show it. "What the fuck does that mean?"

Cruz stepped up, too close, getting in his face. "Funny thing happened yesterday at an A&P not far from here. A citizen got a knife shoved into him."

"That so?"

"We thought you might've heard."

"If it ain't on ESPN, I don't know about it."

"Sure, because you don't watch the news." Cruz said it with just enough politeness to convey deep sarcasm.

"Yeah, that's right." Frank drew himself up, squaring his shoulders. "So what's the big deal? It's the last days of fucking Rome out there. A lot of random shit going down all over."

"Yeah," Murphy said. "Random. But the way that knife went in—pushed down vertically between the vic's neck and shoulder, deep enough to puncture an artery ..."

"It's damn similar to how Leo Rambaldi died," Cruz finished. "Remember Leo?"

"Never met the man."

Cruz watched him closely. "You were a suspect."

"I'm always a suspect. You lazy assholes try to pin every goddamn thing on me, but you can never make it stick."

"Yeah, I guess we've just got it in for you, don't we, Frank?"

It was the guy's tone that got to him. That condescending, smirking tone. From a goddamn bean-picker, for Christ's sake.

"So," Cruz went on, "if we show your picture to people who work at the A&P, none of them would remember seeing you yesterday?"

"I don't see how."

"You definitely weren't there?"

"I'm never anywhere."

"Right. I keep forgetting that. You know, for a man who just found out his nephew's on the run or maybe dead, you don't seem too broken up."

"I'm crying inside."

"Sure you are, Frank."

Frank took a step closer. "I never gave you permission to call me Frank. I'm Mr. fucking Lazzaro to you."

"Okay, Mr. fucking Lazzaro."

Cruz didn't laugh, but his eyes did. Frank felt rage beating in his skull, clawing at his insides, struggling to get out.

"Are you looking for trouble," he breathed, "you border-hopping piece of shit?"

"Okay, now—" Murphy began, but Frank wasn't listening.

"Tell you what, *muchacho*," Frank said. "Maybe you should worry less about me and more about your poor old *mamasita*. Last I heard, she was pole-dancing for pesos at a Mexicali strip joint, and sucking off a donkey in the late show. *Comprende*?"

Cruz's eyes weren't laughing anymore. They were hard and flat as nail heads. "Yeah, I *comprende*, Mr. Fucking Lazzaro. I *comprende* real good."

"Glad to hear it, *chico*. Now haul your punk ass outta here before I get your fucking green card revoked and you end up back to Mexico picking fruit the way nature intended."

Cruz gave him a long stare and turned away without a word. Murphy followed him into the drizzle, turning briefly to say, "Thank your wife for the coffee."

Frank slammed the door.

He wished he'd smashed Cruz in the face. No, he didn't. He would've been arrested for that. Would've faced serious time. Assaulting a police officer. That would've been stupid. Would've been crazy. And yet ...

It would almost have been worth it. To sock that self-righteous son of a bitch unconscious—to feel the satisfying crunch of his fist against the bastard's face—to hear the hard crack of bone—

Frank lashed out with both hands and swept a flowerpot off a table. It crashed on the slate floor of the foyer in a spray of porcelain shards and water and geraniums.

Fuck Cruz. God damn it, he ought to go after those two suits right now. Drag the spic out of his shitty department-issue Taurus and beat him to death on the fucking sidewalk.

"Motherfucker," Frank said, speech coming hard because he was suddenly short of breath. "Motherfucker. Motherfucker!"

Upstairs, the twins, who'd been quiet for a while, started crying again.

33

BONNIE'S DUPLEX WAS no messier than it had been last night, after the Long Fong Boyz ransacked the place. She locked and bolted the door, not that it would prove much of a deterrent if they came back. But she didn't think they would—not this soon. The attack in the parking lot had obviously been improvised. Now that it had failed, she would expect them to wait until dark. Predators were nocturnal. She ought to know.

She spent some time on the phone with Victoria Lazzaro, working out a few details. After that, she switched on a tablet with a cellular connection and used Google Earth to perform a thorough aerial reconnaissance of Frank's property in Saddle River. Then she searched the web for any local hardware store that was still open. She found one in McKendree Park and made a mental note to stop there on her way north.

Her plan for tonight was simple. First she would take care of Frank Lazzaro at home. The Long Fong Boyz would be monitoring her movements, but the GPS tracker wouldn't be accurate enough to pinpoint the Jeep if she hid it in the woods behind Frank's place. And they probably wouldn't come after her in Frank's neighborhood, anyway. They would wait for a better opportunity.

She intended to give them one. After leaving Frank's house, she would lead Chiu's gang into an ambush. With the Jeep parked in some deserted location, she would wait for their arrival, then open up with the TEC-9. With any luck she could blip them all in one three-second burst.

Sparky's camcorder would come in handy after that—if she made it that far.

She had two advantages over the gang. Number one, she knew about the GPS and they didn't know she knew. Number two, she had a machine gun. They didn't know about that, either.

Even so, the odds weren't exactly on her side. But hell, when were they ever?

Someone knocked on her door. The noise startled her. She thought maybe she'd been wrong about Chiu's posse waiting till nightfall. No, that couldn't be it. The Long Fong Boyz wouldn't knock.

The face in the peephole belonged to Bradley Walsh. Bonnie opened the door and saw his squad car parked at the curb a few doors down. Apparently he didn't want to advertise his visit to her house.

"Hey, Bonnie. Saw your Jeep parked outside."

"Just passing by?"

"I've been swinging past pretty regularly. You know, just to keep an eye on the place."

"Thanks. You wanna come in?"

"Just for a sec."

He entered the living room and stood there shifting his feet like a man walking in place.

"I've gotta thank you again," she said. "For what you did. It was super helpful."

"Don't worry about it." He looked down at his shoes.

"Bonnie ... I read the file."

"Did you?"

"Yeah. While I was running off the copy last night."

"Then you know what Maguire suspects me of."

"I know. And if you did it—not that I want to know, one way or the other—but if you did, I wouldn't blame you."

"That's kind of a strange attitude for a law enforcement officer to take."

"Maybe I'm not a very good law enforcement officer."

"Or maybe you're wise beyond your years."

He smiled at that. A bashful smile. But his face turned serious when he said, "I overheard the chief on the phone a couple hours ago. He's talked the state police in Ohio into deposing the gun shop owner."

"When?"

"Tomorrow, it sounds like."

"Okay. Thanks for the heads-up. You don't have to keep sticking your neck out for me."

"Maybe I like it."

"Yeah, it's all fun and games until somebody gets hurt."

"You're the one I'm worried about getting hurt."

"I can take care of myself, Bradley."

"Brad."

"Huh?"

"Only my mom calls me Bradley."

"Right. Okay, Brad. I appreciate your help, but I'll take it from here."

"You going to get a lawyer?"

"I may not need one."

"I don't know. Once the gun guy talks ..."

"Maybe he won't."

"He talked to the chief."

"That wasn't official. Maguire has no jurisdiction in Ohio."

"Tomorrow it'll be official."

"Tomorrow is still a long way off. And Maguire's had some real bad luck dealing with me. It could be he's about to have some more."

"You're a cool customer, Bonnie Parker."

"In these veins—ice water."

"I believe it. Hey, I don't know if I should say this. I mean, I don't exactly know what your situation is."

"My situation?"

"Desmond Harris. You know."

"Oh."

"Maybe I'm out of line, but—well, I guess you know I'm interested."

"I might've picked up on that."

"Yeah. So if your deal with Harris isn't too serious, or if anything changes—"

"Sorry, Brad. It's not gonna happen."

"Because of Harris?"

He was offering her a way out, but she wouldn't take it. "Because of me," she said firmly. "You don't want to get involved with me. I'm not a good person."

"I think you are."

"You don't know me the way I do. Maguire is probably right. I probably should be locked up. I do bad things, and I don't even feel bad about it. I ... hurt people. I hurt them in all kinds of ways. I would hurt you too, if you ever gave me the chance."

"You can't talk me out of the way I feel."

"That's your hard luck."

She liked him. She was grateful to him. But she would never hook up with him. For once in her life she would be kind. And though he didn't know it, the greatest kindness she could show him was to keep him at the distance.

It wouldn't be hard. She kept everyone at a distance. Everyone except Des.

"I'm not giving up on you," Bradley said.

"You should. Because it's never gonna happen, kiddo. You can take that to the bank."

He flashed that smile again. "We'll see."

"I appreciate everything you've done. Even if it was a little crazy of you to take this kind of chance."

"I like to go a little crazy every once in a while. See you, Bonnie." He tipped his cap to her as he walked out the door.

She watched him go. Then she shut the door, re-locked it and re-bolted it, and released a long-held breath. Nobility didn't come easy to her. It kind of cut against the grain of her basic asshole-ishness.

She could have led him on, kept him on the line. He meant well, he was willing to overlook a whole lot of things about her, and—okay—he was young and studly and fuckable. But none of that mattered. Let him find some normal girl to romance. Someone whose life wasn't a hedge maze strewn with land mines. Someone who didn't kill people for money—and get people killed, people like Aaron Walling.

No one was safe around her. Not her enemies, not her friends. It had been that way since the farmhouse. It would always be that way.

The farmhouse. She'd been so young then, a kid. Young enough to believe she was ending something. Young enough to believe she could kill three people and just walk away and go back to her life.

IT HAPPENED IN the winter. She remembered snow on tree branches. Early dusk. She'd arrived in Buckington and holed up in an abandoned barn. She'd learned to find such places. This one was inhabited by squirrels and spiders. She stole food from a neighborhood market, stuffing loose items into her pockets as she warily watched the counterman. In the barn on the evening before the killing, she gulped candy bars, chewing hard, sucking down sugary energy to power her resolve.

She was scared. She had never killed anyone. Had never pointed a gun at anyone until the gun shop owner followed her into the parking lot. She was only fourteen, and she'd lived on the street, fending for herself, since her parents had been murdered in the motel. She'd learned to steal and hide. Twice she'd sold her body for cash. She'd given a nervous guy a blow job in a toilet, and allowed another guy to put his dick between her legs. Afterward she'd worried about herpes, AIDS, getting pregnant. She hadn't done it again.

She'd met other kids, runaways, but never bonded with them. They were into booze and drugs; they just drifted, with no purpose. She had a purpose. She would find the ones who killed her parents.

Why? She couldn't say that she'd loved her parents or that they'd loved her. It wasn't about vengeance, much less justice. It was because—because the men in the motel had scared her. She couldn't shake free of the memory of huddling in a bathtub behind a shower curtain, terrified of discovery. They had reduced her to helplessness and fear, and she couldn't forgive them for that. And the only way to lose the fear was to face them and put them down.

They were older than she was, nearly as old as her dad had been. They were experienced at killing. She could tell that much from their casual brutality in the motel room. And she knew they wouldn't hesitate to kill her if they caught her in the house. But first they would rape her. A gang rape, ritual humiliation. Running a train on her—that was what it was called. She wouldn't let it happen. If things went that way, she would use the gun on herself.

But she didn't intend to die that night. She intended to make the three of them dead. It would be dangerous and rough, but she'd been steeling her nerves for six months, and she was ready.

The farmhouse ranged lazily on a spread of fallow land hemmed in by yards of chicken wire strung between stubby, paint-flecked posts. She had no trouble crawling under the wire and onto the property. Lights in the windows were on, and from inside came the babble of the TV and drunken laughter. She hoped they really were drunk or high. Anything that slowed their reactions would give her an edge.

A quarter moon played tag with scudding clouds. She waited for an interval of darkness, when the moon was hidden. In that temporary blackout, she darted across the field to the back door, where she crouched, hugging the wall, expelling feathery clouds of breath. Her heart was beating fast and hard, fairly knocking at her ears, and she was cold and lonely. Part of her wanted to turn back. But it was only a small part, easily ignored.

She tested the door. Locked. She had neither the tools nor the skills to pick a lock. But the nearest window, though shut against the cold, was unlatched, or maybe the ancient latch was broken. Whatever the explanation, she shoved it up, straining with both hands, worried by the low squeal of protest as the sash grated against the frame.

When it was up, she waited, afraid someone had heard and would come. But no one came, so she gathered her strength and climbed through, alighting on a threadbare carpet in a storage room.

What happened after that seemed to take forever, yet it was all over in less than a minute. A single minute, hardly any time at all, but long enough to end three lives.

She emerged from the storeroom just as one of the three ambled out of the kitchen, a beer bottle in his hand. He was making conversation with his friends in the other room, shouting something about how they had to make a beer run tomorrow because their stash was running low. She was grateful to him for speaking, because she recognized his voice. He was one of the three who had been at the motel—not Lucas Hatch, the triggerman identified by the police, but one of his friends. Her last doubt was erased, and it was actually easy for her to point the gun and shoot.

The distance wasn't great, but she missed on her first attempt, the bullet plowing into a plasterboard wall. He turned, dropping the bottle, which shattered in a foaming geyser on the floor, and from his waistband he plucked a sleek semiauto pistol, a weapon much nicer than hers.

If she missed him a second time, he would kill her. This thought was absolutely clear in her mind as she took aim and squeezed the trigger once.

The second shot caught him high in the chest, just below the collarbone. He went down in a tangle of jerking limbs. From the other room came a stampede of footsteps. His two friends, charging this way.

Bonnie closed the distance between herself and the dying man in two long strides. She plucked his gun from the floor where he'd dropped it. She'd never fired a semiautomatic before. Luckily for her, he'd already released the safety. She wouldn't have known how. She only knew it was a better gun than the antique revolver she'd brought to this show.

The other two appeared at the end of the hall, weapons drawn. Beer and rage had made them invincible, or so they thought. And their adversary was only a little girl.

They rushed her, howling, and she snapped off four shots and brought the lead man down.

The one at the rear sobered up in a hurry. He spun, retreating. She steadied the gun and shot him squarely in the back.

Blood everywhere, and low moans, and her ears ringing. She remembered being surprised that gunshots were so much louder indoors.

The first man in the hallway was Lucas Hatch, the one whose picture had been in the paper, the one whose prints were on the cartridge cases, the one who'd murdered her folks. He was gutshot and stunned, but still alive until she calmly aimed the gun at him at point-blank range and drilled the coup de grâce through his forehead.

The other man had died instantly, the bullet stopping his heart. Sheer luck, but she would take it.

She knew there was no chance the shots would bring the police—not in a location this remote, in a rural area where people fired off guns at foxes and deer. She took her time cleaning herself up—there was blood on her, but not her own—and making sure to wipe down any surfaces she'd touched. It had never occurred to her to wear gloves.

When she was done, she searched the house and found some money, which she took, and more cash in her first victim's pocket. She took that also.

Before leaving, she spent a minute looking at the three corpses she had made. Her first victim had taken the longest to die—a slow, rasping, gurgling death as he lay flat on his back, eyelids fluttering like moth wings. Now he lay still, as did the others. Three lives wiped out in less time than it took to tell it. She wondered how she felt about that. She gave the question serious thought, rejecting several possible answers. The word she settled on was: satisfied.

Yes. It was satisfaction she felt, the sense of a job done. A dirty, miserable job, maybe, a demeaning and ugly job, but a necessary one. Nobody else would have done it for her. The police had scarcely looked for these three, had scarcely cared. The authorities talked a good game, but you couldn't count on them. Couldn't count on anyone except yourself. On this night she'd proved she could take care of business even if no one else would or could. She could take a life, and another and another, and calmly wash up afterward, and wipe down the walls and fixtures, and walk away.

She left the farmhouse and hiked back into town, where she found a diner. She downed two cheeseburgers and a milkshake. It was the best meal she'd ever tasted, and she paid for it with a dead man's cash.

So that was what had gone down in Buckington, Ohio, fourteen years ago.

Nothing ever changed. Tonight she would break into the farmhouse again.

34

THE BEDROOM CURTAINS were shut, lights off. A white noise machine hissed on the nightstand, camouflage for the caterwauling of the twins down the hall.

Frank Lazzaro knelt on the hardwood floor, naked, his bare knees resting on polished mahogany. Around him flickered a semicircle of votive candles. They were black, the color of protection and vengeance, and they were planted in tall glass jars inscribed *Muerte Contra Mas Enemigos*. Death to My Enemies. Their flames cast a dim wavering glow over the shrine to Santa Muerte.

It was a low altar bedecked with flowers, bearing an effigy of the saint in miniature, carved out of ironwood by a sculptor in a Newark barrio, the wood painted white as bone. Vestments of velvet robed the figure; a silken shawl hooded the skull. In the chancy firelight, the crevices and hollows of the face seemed to twitch with stirrings of life. A gilt-edged oval mirror, propped behind the statue, caught Frank's own face and threw it back at him, and somehow the two faces blended, merged, like images in a fever dream.

"Holiest Death," Frank whispered, "deliver my enemy into my hands. Give me the one who seeks my life. Let me teach her pain. All this I ask, as your faithful servant."

On the floor beside him was the knife from the car, the blade already purified in a thread of candle flame. He lifted the knife and drew the blade across his the palm of his left hand, opening a thin seam, then held the hand over the shrine and let dark red drops patter into a bowl.

"A blood offering," he said solemnly. "My blood for hers."

He knew his appeal would not go unheard. His dark angel had never failed him. Throughout his life, some power greater than himself had been looking out for him, directing his steps, keeping him whole. And preserving within his heart of hearts his greatest asset, the uncomplicated will to hate.

People talked all the time about the power of love. They hardly ever acknowledged the power of hate. Yet for Frank's money, hate could be one hell of a motivator. Hate founded empires, crushed enemies, built riches. Hate made sheep into wolves and meadows into battlefields. Frank loved hate. He nurtured it. He drew strength from it.

Hate would give him the edge. It was why he would destroy Bonnie Parker. The girl didn't have enough hate in her. She thought she was tough. But she didn't know what real toughness was, the toughness that would make a man with a broken back crawl over needles with a knife clenched in his teeth, for the pure pleasure of revenge.

For all her street smarts, she was an innocent compared to him. She had no idea what she was up against, or what lay in store for her. If she knew, she would put her gun into her pretty mouth and squeeze the trigger right now.

"Holiest Death," Frank intoned again, "deliver my enemy ..."

He repeated the prayer. There was a shit storm coming at him from all directions, and he needed more than mortal resources to see it through.

Parker was only one of his problems. There was the coming war with the Long Fong Boyz. And the A&P thing. It was possible that witnesses would place him at the store after he'd denied being there. But maybe no wits would come forward. And if any did, he could use his police contacts to learn their names, and then he would find a way to make them change their story or, failing that, to disappear.

It could all be handled. Nothing could bring him down.

He wished the supermarket thing hadn't blown back on him, though. It had never occurred to him that the killing might be connected with the hit on Leo Rambaldi, a twenty-year-old job that should have been long forgotten. He'd assumed the police would regard the murder as entirely random.

Random ...

A voice penetrated his thoughts. Bonnie Parker's voice.

You might be good enough to take down an orthodontist or some random schmuck at the grocery store ...

The words had flown right past him in the lobby of the Sheraton, but he zeroed in on them now. How the hell could she have known anything about a grocery store?

She sure as shit hadn't made the connection with Rambaldi, a hit that took place when she was still in elementary school. Hell, she couldn't have known he was even at the A&P. No one knew. No one but him ... and his wife.

He raised his head. Deep within him, the black beast stirred.

Down the hall, the babies had quit yowling. Victoria must have finally soothed the damn kids to sleep.

He thought about her. She'd been increasingly distant and difficult. She'd even dared to suggest divorce.

But she couldn't be working against him. No way. Even if she'd somehow found out about Parker, she would never hook up with an assassin. Would never try to take out her own husband, the father of her children.

Would she?

The beast was prowling now. Slinking out of its cave, sniffing the air. Restless. Hungry.

Frank stood. He turned on the lights but left the curtains shut, the candles burning. He applied a Band-Aid to his hand, then dressed himself, taking the time to fasten his French cuffs and knot his tie. He wound his belt slowly through all eight belt loops, enjoying the feel of the soft leather and the hard stainless steel buckle.

Leaving the bedroom, he descended to ground level. He found Victoria in the kitchen, stirring a pot of marinara sauce. The housekeeper, Gabrielle, had left early, and Frank and his wife were the only adults in the place.

"I heard you went out today," Frank said. "Gabby mentioned it."

This was a lie. She had said no such thing.

"Oh," Victoria said. "Yes. I was out for a while."

Frank leaned against the counter, watching the ladle as it made slow spirals in the sauce. "Where'd you go?"

"Lydia's." There was a pause. She seemed to feel the need to say more. "They don't have power. She asked for help cleaning out the fridge."

"What'd you do with the food?"

"Had to throw it out."

"You could've brought it here. We have room."

"I guess so. I didn't think of that. It wasn't very much anyway."

"If it wasn't much, why'd she need your help?"

"I think the storm had her kind of shook up. She wanted someone to talk to."

"You were out for a long time, Gabby said. Hours."

"Was I?"

"Wouldn't have thought you'd spend that much time with Lydia."

"I guess I didn't notice the time."

He watched her hands. One hand on the ladle, the other holding the long handle of the pot.

People thought liars gave themselves away with their eyes. Frank knew better. It was the hands. It was always the hands.

"Go anywhere else?" he asked.

"No. Just drove around a little."

"Drove around? In this mess?"

"Looking at the damage."

"Along the shore?"

"In that direction."

The ladle stirring, stirring, its actions jerkier than before. The other hand gripping the pot too tightly. Knuckles going pale with pressure.

"You didn't go south?"

"South?"

"To Brighton Cove?"

"No. Why would I go there?"

Her hands were trembling, palsied. A liar's hands.

That low warning rumble only he could hear—it was the black beast's growl.

"Frank?"

He didn't answer.

Slowly he unbuckled his belt and began to slide it free.

35

BONNIE TOOK A LAST look at herself in the Jeep's rearview mirror, steadying her nerves.

Stripes of eye-black scored her cheeks like war paint. A navy blue watch cap helmeted her hair. A zippered warm-up suit, navy also, concealed the rest of her. She wore black sneakers and black leather gloves.

A shadow among shadows. That was the idea. She might not cut quite the same stylish figure as Anne Hathaway in her Catwoman getup, but she was going for the same general effect.

The Jeep was hidden in the dense pine woods behind the Lazzaro house. She'd gone off-road and stashed it among the evergreens as the sun was setting. Now the sky was turning purple, the stars and moon blotted out by a carpet of heavy cumulus. Forecast: cloudy with a chance of bullets.

She slid out of the driver's seat and opened the Jeep's rear compartment, where all her goodies were stored under a blanket. For now, she didn't need the TEC-9 machine pistol or the infrared camcorder. She took Alec's gun, the

Walther .22, and stuck it in her waistband. The rest of her gear was already stowed in a blue-black backpack. Dark blue, as any good burglar knew, made better nighttime camouflage than pure black.

A yard from the Jeep, a footpath snaked through the woods. Google Earth's satellite photo had clearly shown the path's circuitous route, a route that terminated at the rear gate of the Lazzaro residence.

Using her keychain flashlight, she hiked the path until Frank's property came into view. By Saddle River standards, it was a modest home, not one of the monster mansions put up by Wall Street bad boys to prove they had the biggest dicks on the planet. The house occupied a large parcel of land protected by a high wrought-iron fence. Lights burned in windows on the ground floor and the second story; Victoria had said the place was running on a generator hooked up to a natural gas line. The backyard was checkered with strategically placed ground lighting that showed off a kidney-shaped pool, presently covered by a winter tarpaulin, and a gazebo draped in ivy. Blown debris lay everywhere, a gift from the storm.

There was the requisite three-car garage, the rooftop satellite dish, the landscaped beds of fall flowers. The whole setup was a visual lesson to the younger set: Yes, kids, crime really does pay.

In the breezy night, amid the softly stirring pines, Chez Lazzaro actually seemed like a pretty nice place to live.

Except for the screams.

Bonnie didn't hear them at first. They were faint, muffled by distance and double-pane windows. Then the wind shifted, and they reached her—a woman's cries, part shriek, part sob.

Victoria's cries. They had to be.

Bonnie's intention had been to wait until the windows were dark, the house asleep. It looked like her plans had changed. Frank was doing something awful to his wife, and it had to stop.

At the hardware store in McKendree Park, she bought a bolt cutter, which she'd stashed in the pack. She applied it to the padlocked chain, severing one of the links, then opened the gate wide enough to slip through.

Quickly she crossed the dangerous open ground of the backyard and caught her breath, huddling against the rear wall of the garage, just as she'd huddled against the farmhouse in Ohio fourteen years ago.

At this distance, she could hear the screams more clearly, along with some garbled, plaintive words. It sounded like Victoria was begging her husband to stop. He wasn't listening, of course. The words were interrupted by an ugly percussive noise, the sound of impact. He was beating her.

From her phone conversation with Victoria, Bonnie knew that the way into the house was through the garage. She placed duct tape on a side window, shattered the glass with her elbow, and peeled away the shards along with the tape. She climbed through, finding herself in an unlit space occupied by a Mercedes and a BMW. His-and-hers luxury autos. Sweet.

The door at the other side of the garage would lead her into the house. The only obstacle was the alarm system. The garage wasn't on the system, but all access points to the house itself were always armed.

Victoria had described the setup in detail. The door was on a thirty-second delay. The keypad was just inside. Bonnie didn't care about the keypad. Entering the passcode would make it obvious that the hit was an inside job, which was the very thing she wanted to avoid. What she was after was the main control box, which would set off the alarm siren and send a telephone signal to the police via landline thirty seconds after the door opened.

It was standard procedure to separate the keypad from the system control panel. In her duplex Bonnie had hidden the alarm system's control box at the back of her bedroom closet, behind a sheet of plywood that created the false wall. Frank had been less clever—or less paranoid. The control box for his system was mounted in a hall closet just ten feet past the door to the garage.

Easy peasy, except for one little hitch. The ten-foot stretch of hallway was covered by a motion detector—and it had no built-in delay.

The alarm system operated on different zones, and according to Victoria, her husband typically activated the ground floor level when the two of them had gone upstairs for the evening. Which meant the hallway sensor might be working right now.

Happily there was a workaround. From Victoria, Bonnie had learned the make and model of the alarm system, as well as the helpful fact that all the motion sensors were wireless. After that, she'd spent time searching the web to track down the proprietary radio frequency used by the system's manufacturer for their wireless connections.

Now here was the beauty part. Two years ago, when working a particularly challenging surveillance job that had required a little B&E, she'd purchased a signal jammer—a box the size of a cigarette pack that could be adjusted to interfere with a range of frequencies. At present it was set to 319.5 MHz. If her research panned out, it would render the motion sensor incapable of communicating with the master control. She could stroll right past the sensor without fear.

All she had to do was get the door open, sprint down the hall to the closet, and tear the master control out of the wall. With the wires disconnected, the system would be completely disabled.

That was the theory, anyhow. If she was wrong and

the signal wasn't jammed—or if she didn't reach the control box in time to beat the countdown—then a very loud siren would start blaring. The police would be called too, but she didn't care about them. It was Frank who worried her. The siren would spoil any chance of taking him by surprise.

She produced the pick set from her pack and went to work on the door. She could have done the job more quickly by bumping the lock, but that method was noisy.

As it was, she needed less than a minute to drop the pins into the right configuration to unlock the door. She entered the house, moving fast because she now had less than thirty seconds to kill the alarm.

On tiptoe she advanced down the hallway to the closet, mentally counting the seconds.

One hippopotamus ... two hippopotamus ...

She reached the closet. Tugged at the door. It didn't budge. She pulled harder. Nothing.

Locked.

Shit.

Victoria hadn't said anything about that. Maybe she forgot. Maybe the closet usually wasn't locked. Maybe something else, but it didn't matter now. What mattered was getting the damn door open before she ran out of time.

Six hippopotamus ...

She dug into her burglar's kit again. Couldn't worry about making noise now. It was lock bumping time.

From the kit she pulled out a bump key she'd filed herself, using a downloaded template. She pushed it into the keyhole and struck it with the bolt cutter, the closest thing she had to a blunt instrument.

The rap of metal on metal sounded painfully loud to her, but she didn't think it would be heard upstairs.

The first bump didn't work. She hadn't struck hard enough, probably.

Thirteen hippopotamus ...

She gave it a harder whack. This time the knob turned under her hand.

She was in.

Stepping into the closet, she looked for a metal box mounted on the wall.

Another unwelcome surprise.

There were three boxes.

Okay, keep it together, you've got plenty of time.

Nineteen hippopotamus ...

She snapped on the closet light and checked the first box. It carried a *Danger High Voltage* sticker, which meant it was probably some kind of junction box. Not what she wanted.

The second box was full of circuit breakers. A fuse board.

Which left number three, a featureless gray rectangle. That had to be the one.

She grabbed hold of the thing with both hands and gave a hard yank, ripping it free in a powdery shower of drywall plaster.

The wires were still attached, though. They extended from the back of the box into a hole in the wall.

Twenty-six hippopotamus ...

She closed her fist over the wires and tore them loose.

Twenty-eight hippopotamus.

She'd beaten the clock with two hippopotami to spare.

For a long moment she remained in the closet, letting her pulse return to normal and listening to the voices in the house. They were coming from upstairs, and though they'd been audible the whole time, she hadn't had the luxury of paying attention to them until now.

"We can go at this all night." That was Frank.

"I'm telling you the truth." Victoria, exhausted, hopeless. "I don't know anything about this—this Bonnie Parker."

"Quit fucking *lying* to me!"

A meaty smack, a groan from Victoria, and the babies started crying.

Bonnie took out the Walther. She didn't have a silencer for it; she'd planned to use a pillow or something to muffle the shot. Now silence wasn't an issue.

She could make all the noise she wanted when she killed Frank Lazzaro.

Moving fast, she climbed the staircase and started down the upstairs hall. The voices were coming from the far end, the last door on the left. The door hung open, the door frame limned by a strange flickering light.

She checked the gun as she proceeded along the corridor. The safety was off, a round already chambered. This had to be a quick kill, nothing fancy, a double tap in the chest and one in the forehead. She couldn't allow Frank time to think or react. Though she'd taunted him in the hotel by calling him old and slow, in truth he was a stone killer, and she could give him no quarter.

She was alongside the doorway now. From inside the room came the sound of another blow. She didn't think it was a fist. More like a whip. A strap.

It was a bad idea to peek around corners, but in this case she risked a glance. She needed to know what she was walking into.

Her glimpse lasted a half second, and she didn't process it until she'd ducked back out of sight. Then she focused on the image that was frozen like a screen capture in her mind.

Victoria on the hardwood floor, topless except for a blood-smeared bra, her back scored with thick red welts and bleeding gashes. Frank looming over her, his back to the doorway, in a suit jacket, his necktie loose and flapping around his neck, a long leather belt in his hands.

Behind them both, a semicircle of candles on the floor, lighting up a skeleton idol.

It was a picture of raw insanity, something out of a medieval dungeon or a Black Mass. She'd known Frank was a bad man, but what she'd just seen was beyond ordinary evil. This was nightmare fuel, torture porn.

And it ended now.

She pivoted into the room, the gun in both hands, ready to open fire and send Frank Lazzaro to hell.

But she couldn't.

In the space of a few seconds, everything had changed. Frank no longer stood with his back to the hallway. His belt lay on the floor like a discarded snakeskin. He had pulled his wife to her feet, using her as a human shield. In his hand was a hunting knife, the blade laid across her throat.

"Hello, Parker," he said, his face half hidden behind the tangled mess of Victoria's hair.

Bonnie trained the gun on him. She didn't know how he could have known she was there. Maybe he really did have supernatural powers, as his wife had said.

She almost believed it, until she saw the oval mirror that backed the shrine. It must have picked up her reflection when she'd looked in.

God damn it. It was always the little things that tripped you up.

"Shoot me," Frank said, "and I'll rip open her throat like a paper bag. Unless you think you can drop me so cold I won't have time to twitch. Is that what you think, Parker? Are you that good?"

"Do it, Bonnie," Victoria whispered. "It doesn't matter. Just do it."

"Sure." Frank was smiling fiercely, his eyes as dark and crazy as they'd been in the hotel lobby. "Go ahead, Parker. Save the fucking day."

Bonnie steadied the gun. She almost had the angle

she needed. If she could direct the bullet just past Victoria's left ear and ding Frank in the temple ...

Down the hall, the babies were still crying. Babies who would be orphaned if she messed this up. Losing a dad like Frank would be no tragedy. But they'd be left without a mom also.

"What are you waiting for?" Frank said. "Prove how good you are."

"Go ahead," Victoria said. "Whatever happens, it's all right."

"See how noble my wife is? She's a fucking saint, Parker. You can help send her to heaven."

The babies were what decided things. It was stupid, probably, but she couldn't risk the shot while they cried for their mother.

Bonnie let the Walther drop from her fingers, then kicked it across the polished floor.

An inarticulate noise was dragged out of Victoria, a cross between a sigh and a groan. It was a sound that belonged at a funeral. It seemed to fit the moment.

"Well, what d'you know." Frank's mouth was a mirthless smirk. "Looks like my prayers have been answered."

36

FRANK WAS FEELING very damn good about things. He didn't know how he could ever have worried about giving himself to the animal within him. There was no danger. Even now, though the black beast was loose, he remained in control. He had not surrendered his identity or self-mastery. He had surrendered nothing. He and the beast were one.

He released his hold on Victoria and stooped to retrieve Bonnie Parker's gun from the floor.

He'd been right about the girl. She didn't have enough hate in her, or enough ruthlessness. At the crucial decision point, when it counted most, she'd proved herself soft, weak. She'd traded her life for another's.

Frank intended to make her regret that trade.

"Okay," he said smoothly, the pistol riding light and easy in his hand. "Here's how we play this. You and me, Parker—we're taking a trip."

"I'm guessing it's not to the Bahamas."

"Funny girl." He slid the knife into the sheath on his arm. "Turn around. Face the wall."

"If you wanted a look at my ass, all you had to do was ask."

"Just turn."

She obeyed. Frank pulled off his necktie and tossed it to his wife.

"Tie her hands with that."

Victoria stared at the coil of fabric as if she'd never seen a necktie in her life. "Frank ..."

"Just do it. Parker—hands behind your back."

The PI put her wrists together. She wore black leather gloves, Frank noted. They went with the rest of her outfit. Ninja clothes.

"Nice outfit," he said. "You're dressed to kill. Which I guess was the plan."

"You got it all wrong, Frank. This is my Halloween costume. I'm a day early."

He grunted. "Yeah, you're a comedian. You're right about one thing, though. Halloween's coming early for you."

He watched closely as Victoria wound the blue-striped tie around Parker's wrists.

"Tighter," he ordered.

"I'll cut off her circulation."

"Her circulation won't be an issue for long. Tighter. Now tie a knot."

His wife's hands were shaking. Parker's, he noted, were steady. Cool customer. Cooler than some made men he'd known. Leo Rambaldi, for one. That sad little pussy had been weeping and begging at this stage of the dance. The PI, at least, was facing the end with dignity. For now.

He'd see how dignified she was when Virgil went to work on her.

"Knot it again," he instructed Victoria. "Even tighter."

"I'm sorry, Bonnie." His wife's voice was a whisper, blurry with tears. "I'm so sorry."

"Not your fault," Bonnie said evenly. "Shit happens, Murphy's Law, you know the score."

Victoria finished knotting the tie. Parker's hands twisted uselessly, the necktie binding her wrists like rope. Victoria had used only half of its length; the other half hung down like a lolling tongue.

"Good enough," Frank said. "Now where's your ride?"

Parker turned. "The woods." Her face was calm and blank, but he thought he saw a glitter of moisture at the edges of her eyes.

"Where in the woods?"

"Just off the footpath, not far from the rear gate."

"She give you the combo of the lock?" His gun nodded in Victoria's direction.

"No. I cut the chain."

"Alarm system?"

"Crash 'n' smash."

"Motion sensor?"

"Jammed."

"Impressive. You're fuckin' James Bond, you know that? Except 007 never loses."

"I haven't lost yet, Frank."

"Optimism. That's good. I like it when people have hope." He gestured toward the door. "Start walking. We'll take your wheels. I don't need your fucking DNA in my car."

Victoria stepped in front of him. "Where are you taking her, Frank?"

"You don't need to know."

She stretched out her hands. In her tattered bra, with her bloodied arms and haggard face, she looked like a victim in a war zone. A lost soul.

"Frank. Please."

With his free hand he slapped her smartly across the face, hard enough to send her stumbling backward. She fell on the floor and didn't get up. Her hair hung over her face in a shapeless snarl.

"Stupid bitch," Frank said.

He pushed Parker through the doorway, into the hall. A few doors down, the twins were squalling as usual.

"Your kids don't seem to like it here, Frank," she said as they went down the stairs. "Can't say I blame them."

"Yeah? What's the matter with my house?"

"It's the atmosphere. Let's just say you and your wife aren't exactly a match made in heaven."

He shrugged. "No marriage is perfect, but we make it work."

They reached the ground level. He steered her toward the back door, thinking about the Jeep in the woods, the short drive to the warehouse, and Virgil in his cage.

"You shouldn't have gone off on me in the hotel, little girl," he said. "I was gonna kill you quick, until you made me mad. All that stupid shit you said—it gave me other ideas."

"Care to share?"

"You'll find out soon enough."

"Can't wait."

"Oh, I think you can. One of Chiu's boys got the treatment just last night. He didn't like it. And he got off easy. With him, I was just playing around."

As they reached the back door, he tugged her by the hair, whipping her head back so he could look into her eyes.

"And Parker … I'm not playing anymore."

37

BONNIE SPENT THE RIDE into Jersey City twisting her wrists behind her back, trying to loosen the damn necktie. She made no progress. Under Frank's watchful eye, Victoria had been obliged to do too good a job.

"Scared, Parker?"

That was Frank, at the wheel of the Jeep. He was studying her as she squirmed in the passenger seat, where he'd strapped her in with lap and shoulder belts so she couldn't leap from the vehicle.

"Just pissed off," she said. "I don't like other people driving my car."

"I wouldn't worry about it. When the ports reopen, this piece of shit goes on a cargo ship. It'll end up in Jordan, with a new VIN and phony paperwork. Completely untraceable. Just like you."

"I'm going to Jordan?"

"You're going into a Jersey City landfill, where you'll be as untraceable as your ride."

"Right, right. You got a drum of cement with my name on it."

"No one'll ever know what happened to you. You'll just disappear."

Her hands were slick with sweat inside the gloves. She could feel her heart jumping in her chest.

"How about your wife, Frank? Does she come out of this alive?"

"She's the mother of my children."

"Is that a yes?"

"I won't kill her. I'll just make her wish she was dead."

"You've been doing a good job of that already."

"I can do better. My wife will be taught a serious lesson. That comes later. First I'll put you in hell."

"Looks like I'm the one who's been putting you through hell lately."

"Yeah, you made things rough on me. But now you're all done, little girl. When the sun comes up, I'll still be here, and you won't."

She didn't know what to say to that.

HE GUIDED THE JEEP into an industrial district, all the streetlights dead. An eerie darkness surrounded the vehicle. Bonnie had never realized how accustomed she was to the reassuring glow of electric light.

The Jeep pulled past a windowless two-story brick warehouse, a place so nondescript there was no name displayed above the front door, and turned into an alley at the side of the building. Frank parked by a loading dock, then unlocked the huge freight door. With the power off, he had to raise it by hand. The door moved on tracks with counterbalancing springs, but it still must have weighed a ton; he handled it like it was a sheet of tissue paper.

Strong as a goddamn ox. Psychopathic, sadistic, happy to beat his own wife half to death in front of a voodoo altar while his babies cried. Oh yes, she was in the very best of hands.

She corkscrewed her wrists, fighting to work free of the knots. This might be her last chance. And she couldn't do it.

Then Frank was back behind the wheel, shifting the Jeep into gear and rolling up the concrete ramp into the warehouse.

The place was lit only by the twin cones of the headlights. He cranked the wheel to slant-park the Jeep, and the beams blurred across tall shelves rising to a distant ceiling, and behind them, a wall with a door that must lead to the front of the building. She glimpsed a steel drum standing upright, its sides streaked with dry concrete, and wondered if Chiu's guy, the one Frank mentioned, was inside.

Frank killed the engine and lights. Darkness thumped down, solid as a casket lid.

She felt his hands on her, unbuckling the lap and shoulder belts, then pushing open the passenger door. The dome light should have come on when that happened, but she'd unscrewed it a couple years ago to customize her ride for surveillance work.

"Out," Frank said.

"I don't know about you, bright eyes, but I can't see for shit."

A flashlight snapped on, held in his left hand, balancing the gun in his right.

She swung her legs off the seat and found the floor. The urge to take off and run was almost overpowering. The freight door stood open, yards away. If she could get outside ...

She couldn't. He would gun her down before she reached the door. Wouldn't kill her, though. He'd take out her knees so she couldn't run, then drag her across the smooth concrete floor—she could picture the long snail trail of blood—and finish her off at his leisure.

The gun prodded her between the shoulder blades.

He had come around behind her.

"Move."

One part of the warehouse looked the same as any other, but if he wanted her to move, she would move. As long as she was in motion, she wasn't being tortured to death. Hell, she would walk all night if he wanted her to.

"That's far enough," he said as she reached the middle of the room.

Something was there, an item she hadn't seen in the gloom. A straightback chair, old and battered, with peeling strips of duct tape on the arm rests and a spatter pattern of dried blood on the floor.

"You know that Monty Python routine about the comfy chair?" Bonnie asked.

"What about it?"

"I'm pretty sure this ain't it."

He snorted, a sound that might have been laughter, and she made her move.

Pivoting, she snapped a sideways kick at his midsection. She connected. She heard a grunt of surprise as he dropped the flashlight. She closed with him, ramming his chin with the top of her head. His jaws clacked. She felt a fierce exhilaration—she'd hurt him, *hurt him*—but it didn't last.

He grabbed her and threw her into the chair. As the flashlight rolled, spinning spirals of light across the shelves, he yanked her wrists up against the vertical slat that provided back support.

"Fucking whore," he muttered. "You don't know when to quit."

"That's right, Frank. I don't."

He wound the remainder of the necktie, the lolling tongue, around the slat, knotting it in place. Tying her to the chair.

"I don't get to use the armrests?" she asked.

"No."

"Other people've used them." She could see peeling strips of duct tape that must have held their arms in place.

"Other people didn't get what you're getting."

"Gee, Frank, you sure do know how to make a girl feel special."

"I like how you're trying not to be scared. Because that'll make what happens next just that much better."

He gave the knot a final tug, cinching it tight.

"You think I'm gonna beg, Frank? Like your wife did?"

"You'll beg."

"No way."

He leaned in close, studying her face.

"You'll beg," he said once more, not arguing, not threatening, merely stating a fact.

He picked up the flashlight and returned to the freight door, lowering it by hand. The big door came down with a series of rattles and clanks before hitting the floor with a cymbal crash. She heard Frank turn a key in the lock, sealing them in.

Just the two of them, together in a pitch-black space without windows, without air. A place where she could scream, and no one but Frank would hear. A place where she could die, and no one but Frank would know.

It was a lousy way to go out. She was beginning to regret not taking the shot in the bedroom. Maybe she could have nailed Frank cleanly in the forehead and prevented him from slashing Victoria's throat. And even if Victoria had bought it—well, so what? That was the life she'd chosen, right?

But everybody made choices. Bonnie herself had followed a path that was always likely to end this way. She'd taken the first step down that road in a farmhouse in Buckington, and fourteen years later she'd come to the end of the line.

Frank crossed the floor, his shoes slapping concrete. He went past her and continued to the far end of the room, the flashlight showing him the way. He disappeared through the door that led to the front of the building. Must be an office in there or a supply room or something.

She twisted, but the knots wouldn't weaken. It would take hours to work herself free. She didn't have hours. Frank was already coming back, and in his hand he held a small steel cage.

A cage was bad. Nothing good lived in a cage.

He brought it closer. The flashlight, hooked to his waistband, splashed an oval of light on his shoes.

In the bouncing glow, Bonnie made out a dim, restless creature chained inside the cage. Hairy and long-tailed and ... squeaking.

So that was why they called him the Ratcatcher.

"Meet Virgil," Frank said cheerfully. "He's a good pal of mine."

"Hey, Virge." Bonnie found it suddenly difficult to speak, maybe because there wasn't a speck of moisture in her mouth. "How's it hangin'?"

"You'll like Virgil." Frank pulled a crate alongside the chair, setting the cage on top. "He'll give you a French kiss you won't believe."

The rat scrabbled at the bars, its small pink hands scratching.

"I'm not feeling the romance," Bonnie said, her voice thick.

"You will. I'm gonna tie you to his cage with your own hair." He plucked off her watch cap and tossed it aside, letting her hair unfurl. "Then I'll open the cage door and let him go at it."

"Sounds like a plan." Her eyes were fixed on the rat's wrinkly nose, its small yellow teeth.

She couldn't quite make it real. Things like this just

didn't happen. Not outside of horror movies.

"Usually I let him work on the hands," Frank said. "Sometimes on a guy's junk. Never done the face before. I think it'll be a hoot."

"You're sick, Frank." She pulled in a ragged breath. "You're a sick, crazy fuck."

"I'm guessing your eyes will be first to go. He'll suck 'em right out of the sockets and slurp 'em down like grapes. Then he'll start snacking on your skin. He'll chew off your lips, your nose—"

"Stop it." She heard a querulous note in her voice. It surprised her. She'd never heard that particular note before.

"I'm just telling you how it'll be. Once he gets going, he'll strip your pretty face right down to the bone—"

"Stop it."

She felt puke rising in her throat. She forced it down. She would be all right if she didn't have to look at the goddamned thing. But she couldn't stop looking. The rat couldn't be more than a foot long, but it appeared much larger. Gigantic, a monster.

"What's the problem, Parker?" Frank grinned. "You don't like this kind of talk? All I'm saying is"—he plucked the cage off the crate—*"you are federally fucked."*

He thrust the cage at her face.

She recoiled in the chair, shoulders hunched, head averted. Frank eased the cage closer. The rat pawed at the bars and squeaked and bristled.

"Get it away," she whispered.

"Say please."

"Go to hell."

"That doesn't sound like please."

"Get it away from me, you crazy motherfucker!"

"Not till you take a good look." He wrapped a hand around the back of her skull and turned her face toward the cage. "Open your eyes."

She didn't want to. Really didn't want to. But she did.

The rat was inches away, wild with blood fever. Clawing at the cage, gnashing its teeth, forcing its narrow, bullet-shaped head between the bars. She could smell its breath on her face, a smell like the inside of a garbage disposal.

She squeezed her lips shut against the threat of a scream. She wouldn't break down. It wasn't about pride or dignity. She didn't give a shit about that. She just wouldn't give Frank Lazzaro the satisfaction.

"Like what you see?" Frank asked.

"Fuck off, asshole."

"Just say please. I want to hear it. After we get started, it may be too late. It's tough to talk without a mouth."

"Fuck yourself and die."

He drew the cage closer, the rat almost near enough to inflict bite wounds. She struggled to pull back, but Frank held her securely, his hand clamped on her head.

"One simple word," Frank said.

She could swear she felt the thing's claws on her eyelashes, the hairs of its snout bristling against her nose.

"Please," she breathed.

"Please what?"

"Take it away. Please."

"That's what I wanted to hear."

He withdrew the cage, planting it on the crate again.

"I knew you'd beg," he said with satisfaction.

She couldn't answer. She was shaking all over, her world wet with tears. She heard the explosive chuffs of her own breath, the triphammer pounding of her heart.

"You can't do this," she whispered. "Give me a bullet. That's fair. This ... isn't."

Frank squinted at her, leering. "You asking for mercy?"

She shut her eyes. "Yes."

"No luck, Parker. You spilled my family's blood. Now

253

you pay. You pay in the worst way possible, and you pay long and hard. It's not my say-so. It's not on me. *You* fucked up. *You* did it. Now you go out screaming. Because that's the fucking *rule*."

It was useless to talk to him. She saw what Victoria must have seen, the raw craziness in him, the animal hunger, and she knew she was not speaking to anything human.

"Hey," he added with a sound that might have been laughter, "don't sweat it too much. If you're still alive after an hour or two, I'll put you out of your misery."

He shoved the crate directly in front of the chair, then grabbed a clump of her hair and pulled her head forward. He would tie her to the bars, and then she would be wearing the damn cage like a mask, and even before the cage door opened, the rat would be chewing and tearing.

She whipped her head back and forth, but she couldn't pull free of his grip. Already he was threading her hair through the bars, even as she threw her weight from side to side, making the chair wobble, trying to knock it over and buy herself more time.

But she was all out of time. She knew it.

Panic climbed up her throat, impossible to suppress. She opened her mouth to scream—

At the front of the building, there was gunfire.

38

PATRICK CHIU HAD been doing the eye-in-the-sky thing on the GPS signal from Parker's Jeep throughout the night, keeping his crew on standby. He'd balked at going after her as long as she was in Saddle River, Lazzaro's home turf, but once she was stationary in the warehouse district, he and his people had moved in.

For tonight's action he'd brought along some new talent—three more soldiers, newbies who needed to see combat. They were Mouse and Fire Ant and Bucket Head. They'd all been friends of Joey Huang, and the only hard part would be keeping them from killing Parker too soon.

Of course, Kicker and Monkey were there too. No way they would miss this show.

"What the fuck's she doing in there?" Eng asked as they studied the warehouse's impregnable front door.

"Running an errand for her boss," Chiu said, "after she dropped by his house to suck him off."

"Yeah, okay," Lam said, "but why's it taking so long?"

Chiu could think of a reason, but it was not a good one. "She might have made us."

"For real?"

"Why else would she be holed up in there this long? A drop-off or pick-up takes only a couple of minutes."

Eng glanced around self-consciously. "You really think she knows were out here?"

"It's possible. The warehouse could have security cameras running on battery power, or a window some-place we can't see."

"If she knows—"

"She's already called Lazzaro. Yes. I realize that."

Eng hefted his MAC. "We can handle anybody he sends."

Chiu frowned. "Maybe. But I don't want to start that fight this soon."

"So we book? Let that bitch have another twenty-four?"

The thought was galling. She should have been dead already. Every new breath she took was an insult to the memory of Joey Huang.

"No," Chiu decided. "We go in. We snatch her before the fucking cavalry arrives. That way we can get her and as much of Lazzaro's merch as we can carry."

"Go in how?" Lam asked.

"Through the front door."

Lam regarded it dubiously. "Even if we get it open, she can lay low and bust caps at us."

"Not if we go in heavy. That tote bag of hers—it's still in the Caddy, right? And she was carrying grenades."

"Only flashbangs."

"Bring them. And the tire iron."

Lam tilted his head quizzically. "What's the plan, dai lo?"

"Shock and awe, little brother. Shock and mother-fucking awe."

Chiu knew something about security doors. They were built to withstand gunfire, but no door was actually bulletproof. Bullet resistance was the best it could offer. If you hit it enough times with enough firepower in the right places, it would fail.

The bolts and hinges were the vulnerable spots. Blow them to pieces, and the door could be levered out of the frame.

Of course, all that noise would provide Parker with plenty of warning. She would be waiting for them to come in. But he had an idea about that too. Old Sing Dock had tossed firecrackers into a dark theater and made history. Patrick Chiu intended to make some history of his own.

Lam returned with the grenades and the tire iron. Chiu crammed the two stun grenades into his pockets and instructed Eng on what to do and where to aim. Ordinarily you couldn't do much aiming with a machine pistol, but Eng was fucking surgical with that bitch.

"Got it?" Chiu asked.

Eng nodded, grinning hugely. He loved shooting off that gun. The chance to empty a full mag into a stationary target was like candy to him.

Chiu gave the tire iron to Bucket Head, a strapping youngster whose real name was Benny Kee. "When the door's been shot up enough, you pry it open."

Kee nodded. He and the other four formed a tight circle around their dai lo. Chiu turned slowly, surveying the troops.

"Man up, all of you," he intoned. "We are going to put a big hurt on a little lady tonight."

He nodded to Kicker, who broke from the circle and took aim at the armored door.

"Hinges and bolts," Chiu reminded him, just before the MAC went to work.

39

FRANK KNEW AUTOMATIC weapons fire when he heard it. Somebody was unloading on the front door with a machine gun, trying to blow it off its hinges.

It would work too. No door could stand up to that kind of punishment for long.

Virgil and Parker's romantic rendezvous would have to wait. It didn't matter. Parker wasn't going anywhere. There would be plenty of time for him to watch her die.

First he had to take care of the fools who'd dared to come knocking at his door.

Under other circumstances he might have tried a tactical retreat—take the Jeep and escape through the freight door—but here and now, running was not an option. He was alive with the power of the beast. He would stand and fight.

He found the side door to the office and slipped inside. The office's main door looked out on the foyer, with the street door beyond.

The machine gun coughed again. The door groaned, weakening. By now it must have been fatally compromised, but it was still upright, wedged in the frame. Then the gunfire fell silent, replaced by frantic scraping noises. Someone outside was working to pry open the door.

Wouldn't take long. In a few seconds it would give way, and then the intruders would enter.

And he would gun them down.

A .22 wasn't much good against people toting a machine gun, but he was unconcerned about that. Nothing could hurt him, not tonight. In the past few hours he had become something greater than a mortal man, a thing of raw fury that could not be stopped. He could take on the world and win. Let them drop a nuclear bomb on him; he would walk away.

These dumb bastards thought they had the edge, but they didn't know what they were going up against.

He would kill them all, and drink their spurting blood.

IT TOOK BONNIE a few seconds to process the fact that the cage wasn't in her face and Frank Lazzaro had gone away. Though she'd heard the noise from the front of the building, somehow its significance hadn't registered.

Then her head cleared, and she got it. The Long Fong Boyz had come calling.

They might kill Frank, or he might kill them. One thing was certain. Whoever survived would be more than happy to kill her.

"Never knew I was so friggin' unpopular," she murmured.

The little joke cheered her, made her feel more like herself. She might have lost it for a minute, but she was still alive—and, for the moment, alone.

Except for Virgil. In the deep darkness she could hear the rat's soft squeaks and the clinking of his chain.

A LAST SCREECH of metal on metal, and the outside door leaned in and toppled with a crash.

Frank tensed, ready to fire.

Nothing happened.

Nobody entered through the doorway. Nobody was there.

He heard a sound, a faint metallic rolling sound, like a tin can kicked down the road. Something round or cylindrical, tossed through the doorway, traveling across the floor ...

Grenade.

The thought reached him a split second before the thing went off in a shockwave of glare and noise. He spun, staggering, his world lost in a whiteout, his ears ringing. He felt drunk, his mind clouded, the floor strangely spongy under his feet.

A concussion grenade. Distraction and disorientation. It would provide the enemy with a few seconds when they could enter unopposed.

Fuck that. He didn't need eyes or ears. He needed only the gun in his hand and the black beast at the heart of his soul.

He groped his way back to the office doorway and fired into the foyer, aiming at nothing, seeing nothing, but knowing the bastards were there. The gun bucked in his hand.

They thought they could take him out with a glorified sparkler. Idiots. He would empty the magazine and kill them all.

Already his vision was clearing. There were four of them, five, half a dozen. But one was already horizontal, and when he squeezed the trigger again, another one went down in a flop of limbs.

Two out of commission so far, and he could take out the rest. The blood he'd fed to Santa Muerte's altar would guarantee his protection, now and forever.

He was taking aim at the asshole with the machine gun when the automatic opened up, a new burst stitching a seam in the drywall and showering him with plaster, and abruptly his hand was empty.

His gun was gone.

He didn't understand it at first. The gun simply wasn't there anymore. It had vanished. Magic.

In the next moment a wave of electric pain reached him, setting his arm on fire, and he realized the gun had been shot out of his hand, taking some of his fingers with it.

The room swam back into focus, and just like that, the animal was gone. The beast had retreated into some distant darkness, deserting him, and he was only Frank Lazzaro again. A man, nothing more. A beaten man.

Frank retreated in a daze, half blind, half deaf. A high hum rose in his ears, competing with the chiming of bells. He fumbled for the knife sheathed to his arm. He wasn't sure what he could do with the knife, but he needed a weapon, any kind of weapon, and the knife was all he had.

A desk occupied a corner of the office. He found it more by chance than intention, stumbled behind it, and fell heavily into a swivel chair.

The knife was in his hand now—his left hand, because the right was a bloody mangle. He remembered an old-time hood nicknamed Johnny Three Fingers. If Frank lived, he might acquire that moniker for himself.

But he wasn't going to live. He knew that.

Bodies crowded into the office. Someone switched on a flashlight, blinding him once more as it found his face.

"Jesus," the one with the flashlight said in obvious surprise. "It's fucking Lazzaro."

So they hadn't even known who they were shooting at. That was rich. Over the years, plenty of made men had gone out of their way to try to get rid of him, and they'd all failed. Now some bunch of nobodies had pulled it off without even trying.

The flashlight shifted, allowing Frank to see their faces. Chinks. Ridiculously young. Fucking kids, for Chrissakes.

He recognized the leader, holding the flashlight. Patrick Chiu of the Long Fong Boyz.

It looked like the war had started early.

"Where's Parker?" Chiu asked

Frank liked that question. He liked it because he knew the Boyz would make Parker just as dead as he wanted her to be.

"Main room." Each word came with grinding effort. "Tied to a chair."

Chiu nodded. "She your gal Friday or some shit?"

Frank debated how to answer. If he told the truth, they might realize Parker hadn't taken out Joey Huang, and maybe even let her live. That outcome was unacceptable.

"Yeah," he said. "She hit your guy."

"On your orders?"

"Sure." What the hell, they'd never believe him if he denied it.

"If Supergirl's your bitch, what'd you tie her up for?"

"She's a loose cannon. A liability. I always planned to take her out."

"You were worried about her, but not about throwing down with us?"

Frank raised himself a few inches, summoning his dignity and his remaining strength. "That's right, Mr. Moto. I never lost no sleep over you pissant chop suey eaters. My organization ain't gonna be taken down by some crew of fucking wannabe punks with more tats than brains."

Chiu smiled slowly. "Don't be so sure, Don Corleone. It's a new world. Our world."

"Tell that to your good pal Fuck Face."

"Fish Face was his name. Where is he?"

"In a drum back there"—Frank nodded toward the main room—"swimming in concrete."

"Did you kill him yourself?"

"You know it, slope. One bullet right between his slanty eyes."

Chiu's face, lit from below in the backsplash of the flashlight, showed no reaction. "And Parker? Is she dead too?"

"Not yet."

"Good."

Chiu raised his gun and shot Frank twice. The impact knocked him off the chair. He fell on the floor and put his hand on his waist, where he felt a quick pulse of blood.

Gutshot, and bleeding out. A crappy way to die.

But Parker would go with him. He drew comfort from that.

40

CHIU COULDN'T REGRET dispatching Lazzaro, not after what he'd done to Cricket and Fish Face. Still, it was too soon. Retribution should have come later, when it could be co-ordinated with other tactical moves.

That was a problem for later. Right now they had to move fast. The grenade and the gunfire were sure to draw attention even in a mostly deserted industrial neighborhood.

Lam had gone to check on the two who'd fallen by the door. He came back, breathing hard. "Mouse and Fire Ant," he whispered. "Both cold."

"We'll give them a good send-off. Parker's the deal now." Chiu's glance moved from Lam to Eng to Kee. "Last night this girl played me for a fool, and I let her walk. She doesn't walk this time."

His men nodded tensely, their blood up.

"Remember, we take her alive. We limo her some-place, and make her bleed. We use harsh fucking measures. What the hell, maybe we break out the hatch-ets, like the *boo how doy*. Slice and dice. Come on."

He led his men forward, through the side door.

Parker was in the main room, Lazzaro had said. Tied in place like a staked goat. And he and his men were the tigers moving in for the kill.

He came around the high wall of shelves, his flashlight sweeping the cavernous room. It alighted on a solitary chair in the middle of the floor.

The chair was empty.

He slowed his steps, aware that the situation had abruptly turned dangerous.

"Watch it," he whispered to his guys. "The bitch is loose."

She couldn't have gotten far. The freight door was still closed. She must be hiding somewhere among the rows of shelves, or in her Jeep, parked yards away.

Time slowed, as it always did when there was danger in the air. Flanked by his men, Chiu approached the spot where Parker had been secured. His flashlight lit up a crate positioned directly behind the chair. On the crate was a small steel cage, and in the cage was a rat.

The flashlight dipped, revealing streaks in the dusty floor where Parker had pivoted the chair. She'd spun it around so the cage butted up against the rear slat. Around the slat lay a coil of tattered cloth. It looked like a necktie. It must have been used to bind her to the chair.

Chiu understood then. He knew exactly what Parker had done. With Lazzaro out of the room, she'd maneuvered the chair so the rat could get at the necktie. The animal had shredded the tie with its teeth and claws, setting her free.

And it had bitten her. There was blood on the tie.

Blood on the floor too. Teardrop-shaped splotches measled the concrete.

He raised the flashlight, letting the beam follow the trail. It led to the Jeep. The front passenger door hung open. A disarranged blanket hung halfway out.

Something had been stowed under that blanket. Something Parker had wanted.

Chiu pondered that blanket and what it might have concealed. Last night Parker had been carrying a whole bag of goodies.

What the hell was she carrying tonight?

"Go back," Chiu said, his voice smaller than it should have been.

"What's that, dai lo?" Eng asked.

"Go back!"

UNDER THE JEEP, prone on her belly, Bonnie dragged the TEC-9 into position, lining up the shot.

The Long Fong Boyz were fifteen feet away, their position marked by the flashlight in their leader's hand.

And sometimes the figures before her were Patrick Chiu and his gangsta crew, and sometimes they were two men in a farmhouse at the end of a dark corridor.

It made no difference either way. The outcome was always the same.

CHIU WAS TURNING to run when the shooting started.

Automatic fire. It came from the Jeep—from behind it—no, from underneath. Short, deadly bursts fired from cover at Chiu and his men, who stood exposed in the middle of the room.

To his left, Chiu saw Eng fall in a mist of blood. To his right, Lam went down.

Chiu's flashlight made him an easy target. He threw it away, retreating as the machine gun stuttered again, taking out Benny Kee.

Nowhere to run. No place to hide. But he had a second flashbang. If he could toss it under the Jeep, it would take Parker out of action long enough for him to finish her off.

He fumbled the grenade out of his pocket and pulled

the pin, and then his legs buckled as hot rounds plowed through his knees.

He hit the floor screaming. The grenade slipped from his grasp and rolled away. He groped for it in the stroboscopic light of the machine gun's muzzle flashes. Got his hand on it.

And it went off—blinding explosion of light, deafening concussive roar, slap of searing heat on his face. The world tilted, the floor sliding away, everything canted at a crazy angle as his sense of balance went haywire, and his face was burning, his eyes—something was wrong with his eyes ...

Another burp of machine gun fire. Concrete vaporizing around him. Sudden pain in his back, in his side, in his neck.

Got me, he thought with surreal clarity. Severed the jugular. That's a lethal hit.

But if it was lethal, why was he still alive? He didn't understand. It was a riddle.

He was still pondering the problem when a last spate of fire took off the top of his skull.

BONNIE STAYED UNDER the Jeep for what seemed like a long time after the TEC-9's magazine was empty. Her ears were clanging. Her vision swam with the afterimages of muzzle flashes and the retinal imprint of the stun grenade's flash. She smelled dust and cordite, smoke and blood.

Not her own blood, though. None of the shots had hit her. Virgil had nicked her arm while gnawing through the necktie, but her leather gloves had protected her from most of his bites and scratches.

Somehow, despite everything, her plan had worked. She'd left the GPS beacon on her Jeep in order to lure the Long Fong Boyz into a trap, and though she hadn't expected it to play out quite this way, she couldn't argue with the results.

There was still the question of Frank Lazzaro. He was probably dead, but with a man like Frank, probably just wasn't good enough.

Slowly she emerged from underneath the Jeep. The TEC-9, out of ammo, was useless; she let it slip from her hand.

The flashlight had broken when Chiu tossed it away, leaving the warehouse utterly dark. She groped for the Jeep's storage compartment and took out the camcorder, already set to infrared mode. With the power on, the viewfinder gave her a decent view of the area in black and white. She pressed the record button and moved forward.

Three bodies lay before her. She approached them without emotion. A strange stillness had come over the warehouse, and with it the weird sense that maybe she was dead too and didn't know it—a ghost haunting this place.

She had felt this way before. In the farmhouse. No fear, no rage, nothing but the deadly calm at the center of a storm.

As she passed the fallen, she checked to see if they were dead. One wasn't—the guy with the MAC-11. He moved feebly, his right hand clenching and unclenching. The hand was decorated in elaborate tats. He must have felt like a big man when he got that ink. He wasn't so big now.

She picked up one of the scattered handguns and capped him, one shot through the temple. A simple gesture, thoughtless, routine. Like stepping on a roach.

Kill or be killed. That was her life.

She took a closer look at the gun. It was a Glock nine, and it was one of hers. And the grenades—those must have been from her kit, too. The Long Fong Boyz had been trying to off her with gear they'd stolen out of her own stash. Ironic, or something.

She checked the pistol's magazine. Six rounds left.

Chiu lay a few yards from the other two. The flash-bang had burned him badly. His face was a scorched mask. His brains had spilled out of his skull in a wet pile.

The chair had been shot to pieces. The crate was scored with bullet holes. The cage had been knocked to the floor. Virgil, remarkably enough, appeared unhurt. Bonnie wedged the gun in her armpit and retrieved the cage.

Silently she crossed the room, stepping past the last row of shelves and through the side door into the office, where Frank Lazzaro lay in a corner, armed with only a knife.

One of his hands was mostly gone, and a bloody puddle was pooling in his lap, but he was still breathing.

She put down the cage and took a step forward.

"Gotta hand it to you, Frank," she said. "You really know how to throw a party."

He turned his head, his face swimming into focus in the viewfinder. He stared at her, and something died in his eyes.

"So you made it," he whispered, his voice dragging. "You came through."

"Looks that way."

"The machine gun I heard ..."

"Mine. From the Jeep."

"Well." He lowered his head. "You're just full of surprises, aren't you?"

"I have my moments."

He squinted at her, frowning. "What is that, a camera? You making a snuff movie or something?"

"Or something."

"You some kind of fucking ghoul?"

"You're one to talk."

He coughed up a chuckle. "Fair enough. I told you Halloween was coming early."

"That you did."

"And I made you beg, Parker. You cried like a little bitch. You were scared."

She couldn't deny it. "I was scared."

"You're not as tough as you like to pretend."

"Nobody's as tough as they pretend." She watched him, her gaze ticking from the video monitor to the ragged shape bleeding in the dark. "You know, sometimes I feel bad about what I do. Guilty, I guess. I forget there are people like you around, and without someone like me, there's nobody to put you down. Without me, you'll just go on fucking up everything and everybody that gets in your way. 'Cause that's just who you are, Frankie."

"Don't call me that," he muttered sullenly. "I'm not Frankie. Haven't been for a long time."

"You know what you're like? A hurricane. You're big and brainless, and you rip up everything, and afterward there's only darkness. Because darkness is what you are. It's all you are. And now you're gonna die here in the dark."

"Bite me."

"Yeah. That's the general idea."

Bonnie picked up the cage and let him hear the rattling of the chain. She saw his face go through changes as he understood.

"Get ready for your close-up," she whispered, "you son of a bitch.

41

LOOKING BACK, SHE realized she must have hurried to leave the warehouse as the police sirens closed in. But at the time she had no sense of urgency. She'd gathered up the remaining weaponry, including Mama Blessing's TEC-9, and her watch cap, which contained hair samples of possible value to the CSI techs. She'd raised the freight door by hand, struggling with the weight, working hard, and steered the Jeep into the alley, proceeding toward the back of the building and exiting via a rear street just as the first cop cars arrived at the front. She'd left them with a big mystery—both the Lazzaro and Chiu gangs decapitated in one night.

A close run thing, all around. There were plenty of ways it could have gone south. But apparently it hadn't been her day to die. Tomorrow, maybe. But not today.

She sorted things out as she drove. Frank had kept his vendetta personal. There was no reason anyone in his organization would be aware of her connection with him.

That left the Long Fong Boyz. There must be a few of them left; the whole crew hadn't been at the warehouse.

But with their leader dead, the remaining soldiers would probably scatter. They'd be running from the police and worried about retaliation by Frank's people. They would have neither the time nor the inclination to deal with her.

No physical evidence or witnesses could link her to the warehouse. She'd worn gloves and hadn't left any prints. No one alive had seen her enter or leave.

It looked like she would be okay.

She didn't get on the phone until she was safely out of Jersey City. Then she used a burner from her glove box to call Victoria Lazzaro.

"Oh my God, is it really you?" Victoria sounded like she'd been crying for a long time.

"Big as life. I'm still in the picture. And your husband ... isn't."

"He's dead?"

Bonnie flashed on her last sight of Frank Lazzaro. "By now he is."

"Thank you, oh, thank you ..."

"No need. I don't get any karma points. I was just saving my own ass."

"Well, you saved me too. And my babies. You're a miracle worker. You're a saint."

Bonnie almost choked on the cig she was smoking. "Yeah, well, I don't expect to be fitted with a halo anytime soon. Look, the police are gonna have a lot of questions for you."

"I won't tell them anything."

"Lady, you don't have to sell me. I saw how you held up to Frank's style of interrogation. If you can handle that, you can handle anything the cops throw at you. Just be prepared to act all shocked and grief-stricken when they give you the news."

"Of course."

"That voodoo altar in the bedroom—it raises too many questions. You might wanna get rid of it."

"With pleasure. I'll use a hammer on the goddamned thing and burn the pieces in the fireplace. Then I'll move out of this house forever. My babies—they cried all the time in this house. They knew it was an evil place. They've been crying all night."

"Well," Bonnie said, "it sounds like they've stopped now."

Victoria paused. "That's true," she said. "They're asleep. It must have been about five minutes ago when they calmed down. Was that when Frank ...? When he ...?"

"I don't go in for that *Twilight Zone* stuff," Bonnie said with a shade more assurance than she felt. "Just enjoy the silence."

"Thank you, Bonnie. Thank you so much. I'm so glad it ended the way it did."

"You're not the only one."

But it wasn't over yet. There was still a gun shop owner in Ohio to deal with.

And there was Des. Yeah.

Him too.

42

BONNIE MADE IT home at dawn, breezing through the Brighton Cove checkpoint because Maguire was nowhere in evidence. The power was still out, and according to the radio it would probably stay out for a week. Which was a giant pain, but still not as bad as having a rat give her a facial peel. All in all, she wasn't complaining.

It was time to deal with the Ohio problem and put the kibosh on Danny boy's little witch hunt. Funny thing. She remembered thinking, just a couple days ago, that maybe she would let Maguire go ahead with it, let him put her away. But she couldn't remember why she'd ever felt like that. Right now it was the furthest thing from her mind.

In her duplex, she booted up her laptop, which still had some juice in the battery, then connected it to Sparky's camcorder via the cable he'd so thoughtfully, albeit grudgingly, supplied. As promised, it was easy enough to transfer the forty seconds of video she'd shot to the laptop's hard drive. After that, uploading it to her phone was a cinch.

Having stopped off at her office to retrieve the boot-
leg copy of Maguire's file, she could easily look up the
contact details for Mr. Samuelson, gun store proprietor in
Buckington, Ohio, the witness who was scheduled to be
deposed today about the little blond girl he'd encoun-
tered in his parking lot thirteen years ago.

What she wanted was his cell number. Happily, one
was provided. She called, using one of the untraceable
throwaway phones that still remained in the floor trap.

After six rings a grumpy voice answered. "Yeah?"

"Mr. Samuelson?"

"Who the hell is this? Why are you calling me so
fucking early?"

"I'm sending you a video, Mr. Samuelson. It'll show
up on your phone in a second. You need to look at it."

"What's this all about?"

"It's about what happens to people who make trouble for little blond girls."

She forwarded the video, ended the call, and destroyed the phone.

He would watch. Anybody would. What he would see
was forty seconds of black-and-white infrared footage,
handheld but not too unsteady. It began as the camera
tracked from one gunshot victim to another, three in all,
scattered on bloody concrete. Two of the men were dead,
and the third died on camera with a bullet fired into his
brain.

The camera blurred across yards of empty flooring,
through a doorway, into a confined space that might have
been an office or store room. There was a break in the
video, and when it started up again, something was happening in that room, something bad. It took the camera a
moment to zero in on the action and hold focus. Then all
was clear.

A man lay sprawled in the corner with a steel cage
jammed over his face, wedged in place like a catcher's

mask. He writhed and thrashed, and with one hand he stabbed furiously at the cage with a knife, slashing at the thing inside, sometimes cutting his own face when his aim was off. His other hand was a ruined thing, no more useful than a club; he batted it blindly against the bars, fighting to dislodge the cage from his head. He was screaming.

And inside the cage, a rat was squeaking and clawing and biting, driven to frenzy by the smell of blood and the bite of the knife.

No one could identify the man from the video alone. What could be seen of his face was a horror show of torn flesh and eyeless sockets and a tongueless mouth gargling blood. To those whose minds ran in such a direction, he might have appeared reminiscent of Santa Muerte, the skeleton saint with the face of a leering skull.

The camera held this image in close-up for several long seconds as the screams went on and on. Then the video ended.

Bonnie hoped Mr. Samuelson would enjoy the show.

It was possible, of course, that sending him the video would backfire. Instead of being properly intimidated, he could choose defiance. He could turn it over to the authorities, implicating her in the warehouse action, which the newsreaders on the radio were already calling the Jersey City Massacre.

But he wouldn't do that. She knew people. She remembered the fear on his face when she'd pointed the gun at him. He had been afraid of her then, and he would be afraid of her now.

Next came cleanup. She dumped the photocopied file into a metal wastebasket and ignited it with her cigarette lighter, then watched the papers curl and crinkle and burn. She erased the video from her phone, her hard drive, and the camera's digital tape. Finally, she shed her clothes and took a long shower. The hot water gave out after the first two minutes, but she didn't care. She stood under the icy spray and let the dust and blood of the warehouse wash away.

After that, there was just one more job she had to do, but it might be the hardest one of all.

She toweled off, dressed, and went to visit Des.

43

DAN MAGUIRE SLAMMED down the phone and stared moodily at the litter of papers on his desk.

He'd arrived at his office just ten minutes ago, getting an early start because everyone was pulling twelve-hour shifts during the emergency. He'd been in high spirits. Today was a big day for him—the day he would forge the first link in the chain that he would eventually wrap around Bonnie Parker's neck.

When his desk phone rang, he assumed it was yet another resident call complaining about the power outage or the flooded streets—as if he could do a damn thing about any of that.

But it wasn't a resident. It was Hector Samuelson, and he had bad news.

"I'm not talking to the police," he said with an odd hitch in his voice. "The whole thing's off. Just forget it."

Dan's jaw snapped shut with an audible clack. "What you mean, forget it?"

"I was wrong about what I said. I don't remember the girl. I don't know what she looked like. It was a long time ago."

"You picked her photo out of a six-pack."

"I don't recall doing that. I was ailing that day. I was all hopped up on cold medicine. The stuff made me loopy. I didn't know what I was saying."

Red heat rose in Dan's face, and his head started to pound. "That's bullshit."

"I'm sorry, Chief. There's nothing I can do."

"She got to you, didn't she? What did she say?"

"I gotta go."

"What did she say?"

A dial tone hummed in reply.

So that was that. Somehow Parker had wriggled out of the trap.

Maguire stood up slowly. He looked around like a man in a daze. On impulse he grabbed the nearest object he could find, a plastic wastebasket, and flung it against the wall. It bounced off and lay on the floor, dented, trash dribbling out.

He kicked his chair. He kicked it again.

"Son of a bitch," he muttered. "Son of a motherless goddamn bitch."

But none of it helped. There was a level of anger and frustration so deep you couldn't kick or scream or beat your way clear of it. You could only ride it down into darkness.

The darkness took him, and he found himself once again seated at his desk, his head cradled in his hands, his mind a giant bruise slowly turning black and blue.

He didn't see how it was possible. How could she have known about Samuelson? Sure, he might have mentioned something about her parents the other night, but could she have used that tiny, meaningless hint to guess the details of his investigation?

He didn't believe it. She would have to be one of those TV psychics, the ones who were always solving

MICHAEL PRESCOTT

crimes for the police.

All right, so maybe she *was* psychic. A goddamn witch or something. A sorceress practicing black magic. At this point he wouldn't put anything past her.

"Chief?"

He lifted his head from his hands and saw Bradley Walsh in the doorway.

"You okay?" Walsh asked.

Maguire studied him. He felt a cold finger of suspicion poke him in the gut.

"My investigation into Parker just hit a brick wall," he said carefully.

"Oh. Sorry to hear that."

Was he? Was he really?

"You wouldn't know anything about this, would you?" Maguire asked.

"Me?"

"You know Parker. You're friendly with her."

"I wouldn't say friendly."

"Right."

Maguire kept staring at him. The kid gazed back, his eyes unblinking and ingenuous.

In his mind he heard Bernice say, *Oh, pish posh, Dan. You're just being paranoid.*

She could be right. His wife was a smart gal.

More to the point, Bradley Walsh wasn't so smart. He was a naïve kid barely out of diapers. No way he could put one over on Dan Maguire.

There had to be some other explanation.

Dan shifted in his seat, breaking eye contact. "Okay, Walsh. Sorry if I got on your case. I know it wasn't you. I'm a little overworked, is all."

"Understood, Chief. We're all pretty worn out."

Walsh moved on, leaving Dan alone. And just like that, it was back, pressing down on him—the full weight of his failure. He'd been hours away from getting Samuelson on the record, and now he was back to square one.

And somewhere Parker was laughing at him.

Laughing as she walked away scot-free.

Again.

44

ON HER WAY to 113 Chestnut Avenue, Bonnie took a detour to the beach. In the rising sun she surveyed the line of support beams and concrete trestles where the boardwalk had been, and the eroded dunes, and the battered hulk of the pavilion where she'd shot it out with Pascal only a few weeks earlier.

A lot of damage, but it could all be repaired. The damage she was about to deal with was a different story.

When the sun was a thumb's width over the horizon, she decided she couldn't put it off any longer. She got back in her Jeep and navigated the maze of drivable streets. One house was hung with the blasted remnants of ghosts and ghouls, reminding her that today was Halloween. It seemed appropriate—a day for wearing masks.

Des was not a morning person. She rapped on his front door until he opened up, a terrycloth robe hastily thrown on.

"Jeez, you're up early," he said as he wheeled himself backward to let her in. "Or didn't you even get to bed?"

He said it with a smile, but then he saw her face and his smile faded.

"We need to talk," Bonnie told him.

She stepped into the living room, where they'd sat by the fire eating steak on plastic plates on the night of the hurricane. He rolled his chair after her.

"Sounds serious." He gestured to the couch. "Sit."

She didn't. "Yesterday I was in Alec Dante's cottage on Devil's Hook. He's the man I shot on Monday. I killed him in his basement. Two bullets to the heart."

Des watched her, his expression unreadable. "Why are you telling me this?"

"In the cottage there's a painting over his bed. A painting of a wolf. Wolves, actually—there's a bunch more in the background. I recognized the style right off. Didn't even need to check the signature. It's one of yours."

"You killed a fan? Shame on you. I don't have that many."

She slammed her palm down on the coffee table. "*Don't* fucking joke about it."

"Christ, why are you so worked up?"

"It's a small world, Des. But it ain't *that* small. When I saw the painting, I knew. I figured it out, right then and there."

"Figured what out?"

"That you had some kind of relationship with Alec Dante. And after that, a lot of things started to make sense. Like how you were so sure the guy deserved it, even before I gave you the details. And why you were in the mood to celebrate—you said so yourself, remember? Maybe it even explains why you were so hot to trot that night. It's kind of a rush, isn't it? Getting somebody killed?"

"Whoa, whoa. You're way off base, Parker. I may have sold Dante a painting, but that doesn't mean I had anything to do with Aaron Walling—"

He stopped. Too late.

"And how'd you know that name?" Bonnie asked quietly.

"You told me."

"I never identify my clients, Des. I'm real fucking discreet that way." She leaned on the back of the sofa, her arms crossed. "Still wanna play innocent?"

He looked away. "I never meant ..." His voice trailed off.

"Oh, you *meant*, buddy. You meant it all. The only thing I don't know is why. What'd Alec Dante ever do to you?"

His fingers drummed the wheelchair's armrests. His mouth was a bloodless line.

"He put me in this chair," Des answered.

"How?"

"You know how I always used to drive too fast? Yeah, well, Alec—he was the same way. You told me he had reckless driving convictions on his record."

"So?"

"Sometimes he would come by the gallery in the summer. He liked my stuff. One night we met up, I had too much to drink, we started bragging about who was better behind the wheel. To find out, we ended up racing out on Nighthorse Road. I took a bad curve too fast. That's when I flipped my car and plowed into a power pole."

"You never told me there was anyone else involved."

"I never told anybody. Dante booked. I kept quiet about it. There was no percentage in admitting to street racing on top of everything else."

"Okay. So you did something stupid, and you paid for it big-time. It wasn't Dante's fault."

"I think it was. Because when I sobered up, I realized I'd done nearly all the drinking. He'd barely touched his glass. He got me liquored up and then talked me into racing. He played with my head, did a number on me. For kicks. As a joke."

"You don't know that for sure."

"I know he didn't hang around after I crashed. He fled the scene and left me there. Never came to the hospital, never called."

"That still doesn't prove—"

"Yeah, you're right. It doesn't. But then there's this. Last year I ran into him in the lobby of his condo building in Jersey City. He looks at me in my chair, and he says, 'Man, you seen better days.' And he laughs." Des lowered his head. His hands had tightened into fists. "He goddamn *laughed*. And when I got angry, he said, 'What are you gonna do about it, gimp?'"

Bonnie took a breath. It would be easy for a story like that to get to her. But she wouldn't let it. She was on a fact-finding mission, and she would not be deterred.

"Let me guess," she said. "You were at the condo building because you were visiting the Wallings."

"Yes."

"They're your friends."

"Aaron is. I know him from way back."

"Rachel Walling really was assaulted on a PATH train, wasn't she? The story she and Aaron told the police was true."

"Yes. It was true."

"Dante never had anything to do with it."

"No."

"How'd you find out about it?"

"When it happened, Aaron was so freaked—he needed someone to talk to. He called me. That was last month."

"So for a whole year there'd been nothing you could do about Dante except stew in your own juice. Then I leveled with you about what I do. That planted the seed. And not long after, your pal's wife—Dante's neighbor—gets raped on a train. You just put two and two together."

"I guess I did." He was almost sullen.

"Just like that, the master plan. I suppose you were springing for it, too?"

"Aaron and I were going to split the cost. I, uh, I guess I owe you half."

"Keep your money. What I want to know is, how'd you get Walling to go along? Friendship has its limits, and I'd think becoming an accessory to homicide is a bit much."

"Aaron wanted something done about Dante anyway. He wasn't exactly the perfect neighbor."

"Oh, terrific. What'd he do, play his stereo too loud?"

"As a matter of fact, yes. Dante didn't have much of a social life. He would sit home and get high and crank up the volume all night long. Sometimes he'd have call girls come over and they'd party till dawn. When the Wallings complained to the condo board, Dante went ballistic. He wasn't exactly accustomed to being told what to do. He didn't take it well. He started hassling Aaron and Rachel. Cursing them out in the elevator, making faces at them in the lobby."

"Faces. Well, that changes everything. If he was making faces, obviously he deserved to be shot in the fucking heart."

"You don't understand. This was a bad situation. He was crazy, and they couldn't touch him. He threatened them. Once, he showed up at their door, high on something, and told them if they ever made trouble again, his relatives would see they paid the price."

"So they were scared."

"Terrified. Aaron even talked about getting a gun. He didn't go through with it, but you have to understand, this is a guy who'd never even fired a gun or held one in his hand. A total pacifist. That's how worked up he was— he and his wife, the two of them."

"They could've moved."

"They wanted to. Really wanted to. After Rachel was attacked on the train, they were desperate to get out of Jersey City. But they couldn't find a buyer for the unit. Couldn't even rent it out, what with the noise situation. They were trapped. It all came down to Dante. He was making their lives hell, and there was no way out."

"Except my way." Bonnie spread her hands. "Look, Des, Alec Dante was a piece of garbage. No one's disputing that. But he didn't rape Rachel Walling and he didn't need to be killed just so the Wallings could get a good price on their condo."

"If we had told you the truth—the whole truth, including the part about me and the crash—would you have done the job?"

"No, Des. I wouldn't."

"Because you have standards."

"That's right."

"Well, that's why Aaron had to say what he said."

"What you coached him to say. You, the mastermind."

"Yeah, that's right. Me, the mastermind, with the master plan. I came up with it, and I talked Aaron into it—"

"And now Aaron's dead."

"Don't go laying that on me."

"Chum, I'm laying it *all* on you."

"It never should have gone sideways like that."

"These things can always go sideways. That's why it's a last resort, just like it says on my office door."

"You know what Dante did to me, and what was going on with the Wallings, and you're still not sure he needed to be put down?"

She flashed on Alec Dante's face in a moment before he fell. His eyes wide, mouth agape. Killed for some reason he didn't even understand. "You got it, Des."

"Then I don't know what more I can say. It was pretty

clear to me. Aaron wanted to get rid of Dante. So did I. I saw a way to do it. So I set him up."

"No—you set *me* up." She stepped away from the couch, closing on the wheelchair. "You used me. That's what really hurts. I trusted you, and *you used me.*" She stared down at him for a long moment, then turned away. "I don't like to be used. And that's something I can't forgive."

Neither of them said anything more for a moment. She was tired of talking, tired of being here. The little bit of trust she'd learned had been unlearned. The little bit of closeness she'd risked had set off a chain reaction that killed Alec Dante and Aaron Walling and Frank Lazzaro and Patrick Chiu and all the others. And her, too, very nearly.

What was that thing about the butterfly that flaps its wings and starts a hurricane halfway around the world? Des was the butterfly. And the storm he'd unleashed had ended up with one hell of a death toll.

Outside, a distant siren whooped—cops or first aid on the way to another emergency. It faded, and there was only the tense silence between them.

"So what does this mean?" Des asked quietly. "We're done, just like that? We're over?"

When she spoke, her voice was steady. "Yes. That's what it means."

He swung the chair around with a sudden violent lurch of his shoulders. "Then go back to being alone. Don't reach out. Keep your distance from everybody. It's what you do best."

She nodded. He was right. She only wished she hadn't needed him to show her.

"Goodbye, Des," she said, walking out of the living room, to the front door.

He came after her, his face ablaze.

"I'm not sorry for what I did, Parker. That son of a

bitch deserved it."

"Maybe he did. But I didn't."

The door closed behind her, pushed shut by the wind.

Bonnie returned to the Jeep. The sun was higher now, and patches of sky were clear. She drove away, going nowhere, needing simply to be in motion, constant motion. Sharks were like that. They had to move or die. And she was one of them. She always had been, and she wouldn't fight it anymore.

She was a shark, and she swam alone, and where she swam, there was always blood in the water.

AUTHOR'S NOTE

First, I invite readers to visit me at michaelpres-cott.net, where you'll find links to all my books, news about upcoming projects, contact info, and other good stuff.

Blood in the Water is a sequel to *Cold Around the Heart*, which introduced Bonnie Parker. This book grew out of my own experience of Hurricane Sandy, which made landfall on October 29, 2012. Writers are always told to write what they know, and though I've seldom followed this injunction, I did so in this case.

The lines of poetry at the front of the book were written by the historical Bonnie Parker, partner of Clyde Barrow, as part of a long poem titled "The Trail's End." I've taken the liberty of changing plural pronouns to singular.

Many thanks to my friend and fellow author J. Carson Black for helpful feedback on the cover design, and to Diana Cox of www.novelproofreading.com for her usual fine job of proofreading the manuscript—and for catching one major inconsistency in the plot.

—MP

ABOUT THE AUTHOR

After twenty years in traditional publishing, Michael Prescott found himself unable to sell another book. On a whim, he began releasing his novels in digital form. Sales took off, and by 2011 he was one of the world's best-selling e-book writers. *Blood in the Water* is his most recent thriller.

CPSIA information can be obtained
at www.ICGtesting.com
Printed in the USA
LVHW090010200420
654088LV00001B/33

9 781501 061370